Walls and Doors

Walls and Doors

Austen Shepherd

Walls and Doors

First Edition

Printed in the United States

ISBN 978-0-578-80100-1

For all my sisters in the faith.

Part One: Spring

Chapter One

"It is not good for the man to be alone. God created everything, and He saw that it was good, except it wasn't good for the man to be alone. So, He made a suitable helpmate for the man," Pastor Derek said, introducing the new sermon series on marriage. He thought it was exactly what the congregation needed to hear. Many of the husbands and wives smiled at one another, reaching to hold each other's hands. How happy was the man not to be alone, and the woman to have been found!

And, all the unmarried people? Well, they had an array of responses. Some discreetly rolled their eyes, having never been married but already tired of talking about it. Others looked down at their Bibles, pretending to read the scriptures, ignoring any glances or elbow nudges thrown their way. Still others, the very-anxious-to-be-married—but weren't they *all* eager to be married?—leaned forward, piped up and opened their notebooks, prepared to jot down any line of wisdom, which would hopefully be useful to them in the near future. Silently they prayed, "Please, Lord."

Among these unmarried people were many young women and only a few young men. It is not good for the man to be alone, but the woman often is. In this church, in churches around the world, there are always more single women than men. One of these single women, trying her best to pay attention to the sermon, was Dahlia.

"Now, you singles don't zone out," Pastor Derek said. "This applies to you also. Statistically, the majority of you will get married. We even have some weddings coming up this spring!"

He sounded very enthusiastic, so Dahlia wanted to be also, willing and desiring to be happy for the happy couples. *But the church consists of 60% women and 40% men,* she thought, concluding that every wedding further reduced the number of available men. She wasn't bitter or envious—at least she tried not to be—but she was logical. She didn't want to belong with the group of singles who sighed or rolled their eyes, but also refused to join those so anxious to be married that they could think of little else.

So, when the sermon ended and she stood, she was somewhat uneasy as her eyes met Erica's from across the sanctuary. They were good friends, but Erica often found some way, without meaning to, of making Dahlia feel inadequate. From the huge smile spread across Erica's face and the excitement in her raised eyebrows, it was clear she had something very important to share. Dahlia chose not to avoid it and headed in her direction.

"Why weren't you in first service?" Erica asked immediately. "You're always in first service."

Dahlia shrugged. "I stayed up late helping my mom with some floral arrangements, so I slept in today."

"Hmm…well, guess what you missed?" she asked, her grin making it obvious.

Dahlia squinted her eyes as if she was thinking of the answer. "I'm going to assume it has something to do with a guy?" she asked with a slight smile.

Erica instantly frowned. "Why would you assume that? Do you think that's all I care about?" She seemed genuinely hurt, which was not Dahlia's intention.

"No, no, I don't think that," she assured her younger friend. Now truly interested, she said, "Please, tell me what I missed in first service."

"Well…it *is* about a guy," Erica confessed, looking sheepish. "Well, two guys to be exact. Two *new* guys!"

"Oh." Dahlia tried not to sound disappointed that her assumption had been correct. Knowing it wouldn't take much to coax Erica into an hour-long description of both men, she asked, "So, did you talk to them?"

"Of course not! Why would I do that? Don't you know you can't just go up to a guy and introduce yourself the first time he comes to church?" She playfully rolled her eyes, but was really bothered by Dahlia's ignorance. But Dahlia wasn't ignorant; she did know that. She never introduced herself to men at church. She just didn't realize Erica knew that.

She faltered on where to go next. Erica hadn't taken the bait. "Okay, so…you just wanted to let me know there were two new guys?" she asked.

"Of course that's not all." Erica was beginning to regret trying to share with Dahlia. "Don't you want to know anything about them? What they look like? How old they are? Whether they came alone, ya know, without girlfriends or fiancées?" Erica desperately wanted her to show some excitement and interest, like the other girls did. But she just didn't understand Dahlia's disposition. The fact that Dahlia was entertaining the conversation meant she was interested; she just didn't get giddy about it.

"I'm guessing you wouldn't be telling me about them if they had girlfriends. Besides, how could you know much about them if you didn't talk to them?" Dahlia asked, partially teasing her friend, knowing Erica had probably spent every last minute researching as much about them as possible.

"Oh, you're infuriating! I mean, really, you are going to be thirty in a few months. You'll be joining the old, unmarried women, and you don't make an effort to fix it."

"Thirty isn't old," Dahlia said firmly. "And my marital status doesn't need *fixing*."

"You know what, I'm not going to tell you anything about them. You can find out for yourself," Erica said with a smirk and then turned and walked away. It wasn't that Erica wanted to make Dahlia feel inadequate. She didn't intend to be rude. She truly believed what she said to Dahlia was meant in kindness, and that Dahlia needed someone to encourage her to take her love life more seriously. The previous day, Erica's abuelo had told her *again* that women are useless after the age of twenty-three, and while she knew it wasn't true, and she didn't think he really believed that statement either, the concept had been embedded into her mind since she was a little girl. She was feeling the pressure—she would soon be twenty-four—and that pressure projected itself onto every single woman she knew.

Dahlia was aware of all this—she had met Erica's abuelo—so she did not take the words too much to heart, and even if they faintly echoed how she felt deep down, she would never admit it. But her friend had piqued her curiosity about the two new men, and she actually *was* disappointed that Erica hadn't shared the details. She would have to wait and see for herself—if the men came back. They would often show up for one Sunday, never to be seen again.

During the service, Dahlia had been briefly distracted by a text message from her best friend Jina. *I'll be waiting outside,* she had said. Jina and Dahlia had graduated from the same Christian school and known each other since the third grade. Jina was not a member of Dahlia's church, even though she wanted to be, but she had secretly visited on several occasions—only after going with her mother to the local Korean church. Dahlia found her in the lobby having a chat with Erica who quickly said her farewells when she saw Dahlia coming toward them.

"She was just about to tell me about some new guys she met," Jina said, watching Erica walk out the door.

Dahlia laughed softy and rolled her eyes. "She didn't meet them. She *saw* them." Jina appeared confused. "I'll explain at lunch."

But before they could exit, Ted Neal, an older, established church member who sometimes taught Sunday school, stopped them. "Dahlia, who is your new friend?" he asked, always excited for potential new members.

"This is Jina. We've been friends for years, and we work together."

"Nice to meet you, Jina. I'm Ted. Is this your first time here?"

"No," she replied. "I've been here several times." Jina was always smiles and lightness.

"Oh, I must have missed you," he said. "So, you're a teacher like Dahlia?"

"Yes, sir. I'm the music teacher at the same school, but what I would really love to do is open a music and theater school. And possibly work with a music missions' organization."

"Oh, really? That would be pretty neat…I know it's hard waiting to be married."

Jina and Dahlia didn't even need to glance at each other to know they were both thinking: *where did that come from*? Dahlia looked at the floor, unable to think of a response. But Jina was quick-witted. "Well, I guess it can be," she said. "But I'm not waiting to be married. I'm living the life the Lord has laid out for me, and if it happens, it happens."

Ted's eyes bulged a little before he recovered. "Well, that's great." He began to back away. "It was good seeing you girls. Have a great week."

"You too," they both said, relieved the conversation was over.

Ted was one of those men who had not married until his thirties, and it had obviously been a difficult task for him to wait all those years in search of a wife. Because it had been hard for him, he presumed it was hard for everyone else also. Especially young women, who must long to be wives and mothers.

"Can you believe that guy?" Jina whispered.

"Actually, yes. Everyone who knows him could believe it."

"Does he really think that's what we do with our lives—just wait around to be married? I mean, I was sharing with him my goals and never even mentioned a husband."

"The new sermon series is on marriage. It seems that's all anyone is thinking about."

Just then as she was glancing around, Dahlia's eyes met with the resident church creeper—the one who made a point to introduce himself, in an uncomfortable manner, to any single woman who entered the building, the one who was very eager to find a wife, the one who was reminiscent of a young Ted Neal. He hadn't met Jina yet, and Dahlia was determined to spare her for as long as possible. It would happen eventually, but didn't have to be today. She grabbed Jina's arm and led her out the front entrance into the parking lot. Erica saw them walk by as she sat in her car, searching all of social media for any information about the new men at church.

—

Dahlia was perpetually early, and she liked that about herself. Her father Alan was the same way, so she knew he would arrive at the restaurant before her. She and her two sisters had been invited to a nice dinner with their father, whom they hadn't seen in months—which was not unusual. Their parents divorced when they were young, and Alan had moved an hour's distance away. Infrequent visits and surface conversation were the nature of their relationships with him. Dahlia took some deep breaths before stepping out of her vehicle, knowing her sisters would be late and the first few minutes would just be the two of them. When she was little, they would spend hours together in comfortable silence, each of them consumed with their own quiet activities, but things had changed since the divorce, and now silence between them often felt strained.

She found him in a dimly lit corner at a large, round table. He was talking on his phone, but ended the call when he spotted her. "Hi, dad," she smiled and hugged him before taking a seat.

"Hi, honey. How are you doing?"

"Good. Work and the after-school program have been keeping me busy. How are you?"

He smiled. "For once, I don't think I can complain."

She was relieved to hear that. Did that mean, for once, she wouldn't have to be a counselor? "That's great," she said. "Anything in particular you can't complain about?"

"Maybe," he teased with a grin in his eyes. He thought this might make her beg it out of him, but he didn't know her well enough to know that she enjoyed surprises and had great patience in waiting for them. So, he added, "Wait 'til your sisters get here. I'll tell you all together."

Even though they both already knew what they would order, the two of them scanned their menus to avoid the awkward silence. After a minute or two, Alan asked, "So, are you dating anyone?"

She shook her head. "No, I'm not."

"Oh, come on! I'm sure you have lots of boyfriends."

"No, really. Not even one." She could tell her answer disappointed him.

"Well, I just can't understand that," he said. "Any guy should be lucky to date you."

He meant it in kindness. She knew he did. But his words did not line up with her reality. No guy had ever deemed himself lucky to date her. She had only dated two men seriously, and both of them seemed to have grown bored with her after a while, as if they had learned all there was to know about her—even though their effort had been lacking, and they had hardly scratched the surface.

Thankfully, her sisters arrived in time to end the conversation. Violet and Lily had different shades of strawberry blond hair and green eyes like their mother; Dahlia, the middle child, took after her father with dark waves and blue eyes. Dahlia noted how beautiful and happy they each looked, laughing together, as they approached. They hugged their father, Lily giving him a peck on the cheek, and then took their seats on both sides of Dahlia.

Then it was a standstill, all of them—except Dahlia—smiling broadly, all of them—except Dahlia—appearing ready to burst at any moment, all of them—except Dahlia—had secrets to share. "What's going on?" Dahlia asked, reading the table. *Do they already know dad's news?* she wondered.

"I don't know what's going on with them," Violet pointed at Lily and her father, "but I have some great news to share."

"So do I," Lily and Alan said in unison, then looked at each other and laughed.

"Looks like you'll have to take turns," Dahlia said.

"Okay," Lily agreed, smiling and taking it as an opportunity for competition. "Rock, paper, scissors?"

"You and Violet go ahead," their father said. "I'll go last."

"Paper covers rock!" Lily exclaimed. "And while you were so distracted by my paper covering your rock, I'm sure you didn't notice the rock on this hand!" She displayed her left hand for all to see. "Brian and I are engaged!"

Violet grabbed her hand to examine the ring. Dahlia wasn't sure how she had missed it.

"Oh, honey, that's wonderful," their father said. "Brian seems like a great guy."

Dahlia wasn't sure what kind of guy Brian was, and she wasn't sure how her dad could make such an assessment of him either.

"Well, you can't like him more than Adam!" Violet teased.

"Of course not. I love all son-in-laws equally," he said with a smile.

Dahlia knew she was required to say something, so she put on her biggest smile and congratulated her sister. The congratulations were genuine—she loved to see her sister happy—but so was the apprehension. She had only met Brian two or three times, and she was almost positive her father had only been introduced to him once. She wasn't even sure how long Lily had known him before they'd moved in together.

"Thank you all," Lily gushed. "I'm so excited that you're all here to share this. Just wish mom was here also. Then it would be perfect."

No, it wouldn't, Dahlia thought with dread. *It would be a disaster.*

"Wait," Violet said, "does mom know?"

"Of course not!" Lily exclaimed. "She can't keep a secret to save her life!"

"Don't I know it!" their dad joked.

Violet and Dahlia exchanged worried and annoyed glances, knowing how upset their mother would be to find out last, knowing they would be the ones to hear about it while she pretended nothing was wrong in front of Lily.

"Okay, enough about me. What's your news, Violet?" Lily prodded.

"Well, I'm sorry Adam couldn't be here, but he gave me permission to share the news without him." She smiled. "I'm pregnant. We're having a baby!"

All of them were ecstatic over this news. No apprehensions, only joy at the prospect of a baby in the family. Their father joked about becoming a grandpa at such a young age, to which Violet reminded him that she was thirty-two, therefore he was not as young as he fancied himself to be.

After spending most of the dinner discussing Lily's wedding and Violet's baby, their father cleared his throat and said, "I hope my news will be as well-received."

They were quiet in anticipation.

"You girls know I've been doing some online dating in the past few months."

No, they didn't know, but said nothing.

"Well, I have met someone," their father continued. "Her name is Morgan. And...we have decided to get married."

Each sister had her own internal reaction to this news. They had never known either of their parents, since the divorce, to be serious about any relationship, especially not to the point of marriage. Externally, Violet was pensive, Dahlia was expressionless, and Lily looked as if she might cry.

Violet broke the silence. "How long have you known her?" She wanted to gauge how angry they should be that he had never mentioned Morgan before.

"Not long, just a couple months," he responded, hoping the backlash would be minimal.

He could tell they wanted further explanation. So, this man of few words, who wasn't used to having to explain himself, attempted the best he knew how. "I honestly didn't expect our relationship to progress so quickly. But when you know, you know, right?" He nudged Lily's arm and winked at her, trying to provoke a smile.

Comparing his situation to hers was not the right move. The tears that had welled up in her eyes began to trickle down her face. Somehow, though she had never realized it until that moment—she was the only one who had never realized it—she had always hoped her parents would either remain single or get back together.

Violet tried again to redirect the conversation in order to keep Lily from exploding, as she was prone to do—like their mother. "When can we meet her? And when is the wedding date?"

Maybe we can do a double wedding, Dahlia wanted to say sarcastically, but didn't. That would certainly send Lily over the edge.

"I was hoping we could all have brunch next Sunday at our house. After you go to church, of course, Dahlia."

"*Our* house?" Lily finally spoke. "She's already living with you?" It was a question, but sounded more like an accusation.

"Yes, honey." He wanted to calm her down. He couldn't handle her emotions. He could never handle their mother's either. "She only just moved in last weekend. You girls will really like her. She can't wait to meet all of you."

"Wish we could say the same," Lily responded with a tinge of anger.

Desiring to keep the peace, Dahlia finally spoke. "I am excited to meet her, dad. If you like her, she must be great." She attempted to mask the sarcasm in her last words. She knew the kind of women her dad had dated over the years, so she didn't get her hopes up about Morgan being great.

Violet took a cue from her sister. "Yeah, dad," Violet agreed. "We look forward to meeting her. I'll make sure Adam can come also." She wanted her husband there because he knew how to make light of any situation.

Although she was pouting, Lily conceded. "I'll see if I can fit it into my schedule." They all knew she would. Once she got over herself, the curiosity would be too much to resist.

The more pressing matter: who would tell their mother?

Chapter Two

When Dahlia arrived to school the next morning, she found one of her favorite students, Chris, sitting on the floor outside her classroom. The hallway was empty except for the two of them. "Good morning, Chris," Dahlia said with a smile as she unlocked the classroom door. "How can I help you?"

"Granny told me to come ask you for some extra help," he said, rising and grabbing his backpack. Dahlia knew and adored his granny.

"Okay, let's see what we can do in the next twenty minutes," she said. There were thirty-five minutes until the first bell, but she knew students would begin trickling in before then—she also knew Chris would be embarrassed if any of them saw him. He didn't have her class until third period. She pushed two desks together as he pulled out the math worksheets from the previous night's homework, and then she began explaining the concepts to him again as they worked through the problems.

Dahlia and Jina worked at a public middle school in the suburbs of Atlanta. It was very different from the small Christian school they had attended, and they loved it because of the diversity in their students. Dahlia wasn't sure either of her parents had more than a nominal association with the Christian faith, but they had sent her and her sisters to the school because they believed it offered a better education than the public schools in the area. Dahlia was grateful for it because it's where she met Jesus—and Jina. One of the reasons they had become such good friends was because they had both felt like outsiders—Jina had been one of the only Asian students, and Dahlia and her sisters had been the only ones with divorced parents. They often felt like they related better to their students than they had with the kids they'd grown up with.

When the first bell rang, Dahlia said, "We can work on this some more after school, if you need." She could tell he was getting the hang of it.

"I've got basketball practice."

"Well, tomorrow morning works too."

"Okay, thanks for the help." He slung his backpack over his shoulder. "Are you still coming over this Saturday?"

She smiled. "Yes, we'll be there. Please tell Ms. Anna I'm looking forward to it."

Just as he left the classroom, Jina appeared in the doorway.

"Ooh, your coffee bearer is on his way," she said with a smirk.

"Again?" Dahlia sighed.

She peeked around the corner to see the eighth-grade science teacher headed their way, even though his classroom was in the opposite direction. Robbie was a good co-worker and a great teacher. He was cute and kind and funny and loved children. But he didn't love Jesus. He'd been raised Catholic, and then became an atheist when he was in college. Dahlia could have been interested if it weren't for the lack of that one essential requirement.

He was a new teacher that year, and all the other teachers, staff, and students adored him. Dahlia did too—as a friend. *Because he can't be more than a friend,* she told herself. *In the long run, it wouldn't work,* she reminded herself often, whenever she found herself subtly flirting with him.

"It's just coffee," she said to Jina, trying to brush it off.

"He's not bringing *me* coffee," Jina said.

"Do you want him to bring you coffee?" Dahlia teased as she quickly grabbed a few dollars from her wallet, knowing he would refuse payment like every time before. "I'll ask him to bring you coffee."

Jina playfully glared at her. "No. I'll just drink yours." Dahlia wasn't much of a coffee drinker; Robbie didn't know that.

They stood outside the classroom, monitoring the hallway as it filled with students and the sound of lockers opening and slamming shut. Jina had a free period first, so she often stuck around until the final bell rang, unless she had to meet with students before school. Robbie finally reached them. Dahlia could tell he was wearing new glasses, and she liked them, but she didn't say so because she didn't want to give him the wrong idea by complimenting him.

"Good morning," he said, handing the cup of coffee to Dahlia. He always felt awkward when Jina was there and he didn't have a cup for her, but he also wanted it to be clear that Dahlia was the focus of his attentions.

"Thanks," she said, trying to hand him some cash. "You know you don't have to do this."

"It's no problem," he said with a smile, brushing the money away. "I'll see you guys at lunch."

When he was out of earshot, Dahlia said, "I should have told him the first time that I don't really drink coffee. Now it would just be uncomfortable." She took a few sips, handed the cup to Jina, and then went inside to welcome her students.

—

The lunchroom was loud with the chatter of hundreds of students. Down the center of the room were round tables reserved for teachers, giving them the best view to monitor their classes. Jina and Dahlia always sat at the same table with Mrs. Herd, and Robbie always joined them about halfway through their lunch period. Mrs. Herd had been teaching for thirty-five years, longer than they'd been alive, and they respected her as a mentor and felt comfortable with her like an aunt.

"Robbie, you want to know what happened last night?" Mrs. Herd asked.

"What happened?" He was expecting to hear a funny story about one of her grandchildren.

"My youngest daughter was visiting, and she was on one of those dating apps, and *your* picture popped up. She said, 'Mama, isn't this the teacher from your school?'" She chuckled.

Robbie's face froze in embarrassment, and then he let out a nervous laugh.

"Ooooh," Jina said with a mischievous grin. "Did she swipe right or left?" Jina had easily fallen into the habit of making fun of him like a brother.

Mrs. Herd cut her eyes away and said, "I couldn't say, but I think I'd accept him as a son-in-law."

"Listen, I haven't been on that app in a long time," Robbie said in his defense. "I don't even remember what my profile says."

Jina laughed. "It's okay. It's always cringy to come across people you know on those apps. Dahlia, remember when we tried it for a day and came across *David's* profile?"

Dahlia grimaced. "I just hope he never saw *our* profiles."

"I really haven't looked at the app in a long time," Robbie repeated.

"It doesn't matter if you have. You're allowed to be on a dating app," Dahlia added, hoping her words might inspire him to place his attentions elsewhere.

"Yeah, I know," he said. "But I'm really not on there anymore." He was adamant.

"Did you have any success with it when you were?" Jina asked, curious.

He hesitated. "I met a few people."

"But no long-term relationships?" she asked.

"No…I mean, that's not what most people use those apps for anyway."

Mrs. Herd leaned forward, serious. "Then what do they use them for?"

She already knew the answer, but wanted to see Robbie squirm a little as he realized he'd backed himself into a tricky corner. *Hook ups*, Dahlia and Jina both thought at the same time as they looked at each other, trying to think of an appropriate way to answer her.

Dahlia noticed the clock. "Time to go, y'all."

She stood, began gathering her things, and signaled to her class to begin dumping their trays. Jina and Mrs. Herd did the same. She whispered, "You're welcome," to Robbie as she walked away. He smiled as he watched her go.

—

Dahlia pulled into the driveway of her mother's little cottage house. Elaine had sold the large family home several years earlier as soon as Lily had left for college, choosing a smaller place with some acreage for all her gardening needs. She was a florist who spent her days designing arrangements for lavish events and spent her early mornings and evenings in her greenhouse. She was excellent at her job because she loved what she did, and she endeared herself to her clients. The relationships with her daughters were where she floundered.

Dahlia dreaded going inside because she didn't want to be the bearer of what her mother would consider bad news. In the years since the divorce, her mother would make remarks under her breath about how her father had been unfaithful, and that being the reason for the divorce. Dahlia had never asked if it was true, but she suspected her father's only mistress had been his work. More than twenty years later, the divorce was still a hard and bitter subject for Elaine, so Dahlia could only imagine how she would respond to the announcement of her ex-husband's engagement.

After knocking with no response, Dahlia used her key to enter the house and found her mother lounging on the sofa in the sunroom, wearing a brightly-colored caftan, the television tuned into reruns of *Say Yes to the Dress!* and a box of cookies open on the table beside her.

Dahlia had become a professional at assessing her mother's mood quickly. Elaine already knew. But which of Dahlia's sisters had told her? If it was Violet, then the news would have been delivered in a matter-of-fact manner intended to minimize Elaine's negative response. But if it was Lily, it would have been expressed in the most dramatic display intended to create an equally volatile reaction, so that they could commiserate together. Dahlia hoped it was the former.

"Hey, mom, how are you doing?" she asked as she leaned over to hug her.

"I'm just wonderful," Elaine replied sarcastically.

Dahlia's natural response would have been to sigh loudly at her mother's attitude. Their natures were so completely different that they'd always had a hard time understanding each other. But she didn't sigh, knowing it wouldn't help the situation, nor would it be very loving. "So, you spoke with Violet? Or Lily?" she asked, hesitant and hopeful.

"Lily came by last night, immediately after your secret dinner," she said, looking pointedly at her middle child. "I don't know why you and Violet did not join her."

"Well, Violet was really tired."

"Right. She's pregnant." She said it in a way as though she'd forgotten that bit of good news in the wake of their father's announcement. "So, what's *your* excuse?"

"I guess I don't have one." Admitting fault would be the best way to placate her mother. *A gentle answer turns away wrath, but a harsh word stirs up anger*, she recited to herself. "I had some things to prepare for class today. But that's no excuse. I apologize."

"Oh, what does it matter…" Ready to move on to the real problem, she cried, "Can you believe your father is getting married?"

"No, I can't. But, aren't you excited that Lily is also getting married?" Dahlia wanted to point her toward positive thoughts.

"Of course. But we all expected that to happen! We didn't expect your father to find a new wife, especially after all this time. It's not like he's gotten better with age. What do you think about it?"

"I'm not really sure what I think yet. I guess it will depend on meeting her."

"Really, Dahlia, why do you have to meet her in order to have feelings about it? It's like you have no thoughts in your head sometimes."

Dahlia's eyes narrowed in anger and she failed to give a gentle answer this time. Firmly, she said, "I have thoughts, mother, just not premature opinions."

"It doesn't matter what this woman is like! She could be Mother Theresa! It's about the fact that your father is getting remarried, and he sprung this news on all of you, giving you no time to prepare your hearts or minds!"

Giving you *no time to prepare* your *heart and mind,* Dahlia thought.

Elaine always had a difficult time understanding why Dahlia was, in *her* opinion, so passive. "Why aren't you angry at how inconsiderate he is?"

She'd grown accustomed to her father being inconsiderate. It wasn't a surprise. Dahlia wasn't sure how to answer, but gave it a shot. "I guess Jesus just gives me peace about these things. *Who of you by worrying can add a single hour to your life?*"

That wasn't the right answer.

Elaine narrowed her light green eyes at her daughter. "Do not quote scripture to me, Dahlia. If

God didn't give me so many things to worry about, maybe I would have peace too."

Dahlia paused to think of a way to rephrase her thoughts, to say it in a way that would be better received. "I just meant, you and dad have been divorced for more than twenty years. Did you expect he would always be single?"

"I expected I would find someone before him!" she somehow managed to yell and whine at the same time. And there was the truth: it was a competition.

"I'm sorry it worked out this way, mom." Dahlia was genuinely sorry that her parents had divorced instead of working through their problems. After so many years, it was hard to imagine they had ever been together. "There is still time. Your life isn't over yet."

After a moment of silence, Elaine said, "You're right. You're absolutely right! I'm going to find a man, and I'm going to have a date for Lily's wedding." She rose from the sofa and twirled around, the colorful caftan floating through the air. "Your father's going to kick himself when he sees me!"

"That's not exactly what I meant," Dahlia mumbled, but her mother ignored her.

"And while we're at it," Elaine continued, "you need to hurry up and find a man too! Your younger sister is getting married before you! How does that make you feel?"

How did that make Dahlia feel? Dahlia didn't share her feelings except with a trusted few. And she'd been trying to ignore any personal feelings about Lily's engagement, about her younger sister getting married before her, but her mother always wanted to bring feelings to the surface, and then never paused long enough to hear about them. Without missing a beat, and suddenly very inspired, Elaine said, "We should try online dating! That's what your father did, isn't it?" She didn't wait for a reply. "Thank you, my dear daughter."

She grabbed Dahlia's shoulders and kissed her cheek. "I'm off to fix myself up and take pictures for my dating profile! Thanks for stopping by. Love you." She practically danced out of the room and up the stairs, leaving Dahlia dumbfounded and irritated. She stared at the old family portrait on the wall, one that included her father, one from before their divorce, and wondered why it even still hung there.

Chapter Three

A few nights later, Jina decided she would go to Bible study with Dahlia. Although it was a college, career, and twenty-somethings ministry group, most of its members were university students, and only a handful were older like Dahlia and Jina. The church had tried more than once to move Dahlia to the singles' ministry, and she had dodged it for as long as she possibly could. But with thirty looming in front of her, she was sure this group would soon no longer be a welcome place for her. Besides Dahlia and the church creeper—whose name was David—all of the other members were in dating relationships, engaged, married, or single females.

Jina's church held its Bible study on Wednesday nights, so her mother would never know she was going with Dahlia on Thursday evening. It's not that Jina enjoyed keeping things from her mother, but having been her daughter for twenty-nine years, she knew what her mother could and could not handle. She had very specific ideas for how Jina should live her life; one of those ideas, the most important one, was that she attend the Korean church with great dedication and find a good, successful Korean man to marry.

Dahlia, who lived in the same apartment complex as Jina, walked down two flights of stairs and knocked on her friend's door. It was Jina's mother, Ms. Yoon, who opened it. "Dahlia, what are you doing here? You two don't see each other enough at work?" she asked. Her tone was serious even though she was making a joke.

"No, Ms. Yoon, I guess we don't." Dahlia smiled. "Do you and Jina have plans?" She couldn't see Jina inside, so she was attempting to figure out whether or not she would still be going to church with her.

"I was visiting a friend who lives nearby. She has been ill, so I brought her some stew," Ms. Yoon explained. "And, when we were talking, she said her nephew is coming to visit from Seattle. He is to be a doctor soon." She flashed a huge smile, and Dahlia knew exactly what that meant. "We are going to set up a dinner."

"That will be nice," Dahlia said while internally cringing. She and Jina usually ate popcorn and laughed after her blind dates, discussing every detail, but she knew Ms. Yoon was disappointed every time they didn't work out. Dahlia had been strategic enough to avoid the few blind date attempts her own mother had made.

Just then Jina emerged from her bedroom. "Sorry about that. I had a parent-teacher conference call." She noticed Dahlia standing in the doorway and, from the look on her face, she could tell Ms. Yoon had shared the *wonderful* dinner plans.

"Jina," her mother began, "I looked at your calendar and marked down the days when Steve will be here. It is not until the middle of next month, so you have plenty of notice. Do not make any plans. Okay?"

"Yes, umma."

"Okay, I must go now. You girls be good."

They assured her they would, then shut the door behind her. Dahlia did her best impression of Ms. Yoon. "You get to marry a doctor, Jina! Don't mess it up this time."

"Oh, believe me, I will do my best," Jina said with a laugh. And she meant it, sort of.

—

When they arrived at church, Erica, who had been waiting anxiously, rushed up to them. "They're here!" she exclaimed in a loud whisper.

"Who's here?" Jina asked.

"The two new guys."

"Really? You mean the ones you didn't get to tell me about on Sunday?" Jina said with sarcastic enthusiasm. Erica either ignored it or thought she was serious. Dahlia chuckled silently. She was in a generally playful mood and was by then officially curious about the two strangers.

Once inside, Erica directed them to the snack table where they would have a good scope of the entire room. The group was divided into its usual cliques, so new faces were easy to spot. Dahlia saw the famous new guys standing nearby, cornered by both Ted and David. Ted was a mentor to some of the guys in the group, and he would occasionally drop in on their gatherings. Dahlia instantly felt bad for the new guys, and from the expression on Jina's face, it was obvious she did too.

Dahlia was surprised she found the young men attractive because she usually didn't agree with Erica on such matters, and it was clear she wasn't the only one who thought so. Almost every conversation in the room was focused on the newcomers—and the fact that there were no rings on their left hands or wives on their arms.

Ted's voice was loud and deep, therefore it carried—or he made sure it carried—and Dahlia overheard him say to the two men, "It's really great to see you young bucks here!" Because she knew Ted, she was acutely aware of his main reason for being glad to welcome them; she only hoped they were not conscious of the reality that they were currently being imagined as the future husbands of more than one young woman in the room. Where there is an unmarried, attractive man of God, there will be no shortage of single Christian women with their eyes on him. Scarcity of potential husbands, increased competition; it was open season.

Dahlia had recently read an article about the single church-going male population in England, and how much pressure to marry they experienced when they attended a new church. And while she thought it was probably different in America, where most single Christian men she knew were marriage-minded at a younger age, she still wondered if the newcomers felt uncomfortable.

"Have you met them yet?" Jina asked Erica.

"Yes! Ted introduced me earlier," she said proudly. "Their names are Andrew and Daniel. And while Andrew may be the better-looking one, Daniel is much nicer."

"They are both good-looking," Jina admitted quietly.

These words made Erica uneasy. She already had enough competition without adding Jina to the long list. "But they're not Korean," Erica reminded her in a smiling, yet serious, way. "So, they're no good for you."

Jina didn't need the reminder, neither did she appreciate Erica's jealous undertones. Dahlia heard them also, but before she could reply in her friend's defense—for she believed Jina had the option to marry whomever she wanted, Korean or not—the group leader, Chuck, called them all to their seats.

Erica strategically held both of their arms, to keep them from walking too quickly, so that Andrew and Daniel would sit first. Then they could choose seats near them. It almost didn't work because all the ladies in the room had the same idea, but Erica fought for what she was passionate about, and they ended up in the row behind her future husband and his friend.

Erica heard none of the lesson, Jina most of it, and Dahlia all of it. She loved Chuck as a Bible teacher. His teaching was the main reason she continued to attend the group, and she really hated the church wanting her switch to the singles group. She despised being categorized by her marital status.

After the lesson and prayer, Chuck called Dahlia up to share with the group about an opportunity to serve their community. She explained how one of her students—Chris—lived with his grandmother; they had no other family nearby. She and Jina wanted to get a group together to help do some house repairs and lawn work.

"We plan to do it this Saturday and the next," she said. "Jina and I would really appreciate all the help we can get. If you're interested, talk to us after, and we can give you the address." She immediately returned to her seat.

One young woman spoke up, "You know Josh and Maggie are getting married this Saturday." She paused for a moment, but when Dahlia didn't respond, she continued, "We were all invited. We could try to come in the morning, but probably won't make it."

"Okay." Dahlia tried to hide her annoyance. She didn't plan her life around weddings, and *she* had not been invited to Josh and Maggie's, so she had absolutely no concerns about the scheduling conflict. Sometime in her late twenties, Dahlia had grown weary of weddings. They never failed to remind her she was alone—a reality she was generally content with—and she was always pleased to not be invited or to develop a good excuse not to attend the weddings of people she barely knew.

Chuck stepped in. "That's fine, Sasha. If you can make it, great. If not, there is always next Saturday. It was good seeing all of you tonight. Please feel free to hang out. Get some more food and drinks. See you next week!"

When everyone began to mingle among themselves, Jina whispered to Dahlia, "Like you're supposed to remember when everyone's weddings are."

"Yeah, I know."

"But how could you forget?" Erica asked.

"Because I wasn't invited, and even if I had been, I wouldn't be going," Dahlia stated bluntly.

This was blasphemy to Erica, and she had some words of chastisement to shower upon her friend. But before they could exit her lips, Andrew and Daniel turned around and introduced themselves to Dahlia and Jina. They covered the usual introductory topics: names, occupations, how long they had attended that church, and what brought them there.

"Andrew and I are cousins," Daniel explained. "We're going to join his father's law practice once we pass the bar. But right now, we've come to stay with my sister for a while because she is pregnant, and her husband is deployed overseas."

"Oh, that's exciting" Dahlia said. "I just found out my sister Violet is pregnant."

Erica was incredulous. "You didn't tell me that!"

"Oh, yeah, sorry." Dahlia hadn't spoken to her since then. "Are you done with your social media fast?"

"No…" Erica said, remembering how she'd accidentally broken her fast on Sunday when she'd researched the guys.

"Well, then you also don't know that Lily's getting married."

This was almost too much for Erica to handle. She gasped and then squealed with delight and then flashed angry eyes at Dahlia for waiting so long to tell her. "I have to call her!" She grabbed her purse and walked off, momentarily forgetting her future husband.

"So, you just have the two sisters?" Daniel asked Dahlia.

"Yes, just the two. And that is quite enough."

"Violet, Lily, and Dahlia," Andrew said, somewhat like a statement and somewhat like a question, but either way, not sounding impressed.

"Yes," Dahlia replied, feeling his judgment. "My mother loves flowers. She's a florist and landscaper."

"At least she didn't name you Begonia or Petunia," Jina joked. "Or even Daffodil!"

"Just call me Daffy," Dahlia quipped. Their eyes went wide at the thought of it, and then they fell into laughter.

Their humor and manner of interaction, as is common between best friends, was such that it resulted in listeners being either amused or annoyed. In that moment, it appeared they were inspiring both responses in their new acquaintances. Daniel smiled, always encouraged to meet friends who obviously really loved each other and enjoyed one another's company. Andrew, who in general took himself and life too seriously, thought they were silly. He wanted to finish the conversation, so they could leave. He brought up the subject that had first made them to turn around. "We would like to help on Saturday and wanted to know the time and place."

"Oh, that would be great!" Jina said with a smile.

"Yes, we could use the help, since it seems like we'll have a small turn out," Dahlia added.

She jotted down the information for them, while Jina exchanged numbers with Daniel—in case they got lost or couldn't make it for some reason. Even though it seemed like Daniel would have stayed longer, knowing his cousin the way that he did, he decided not to make Andrew suffer any longer with the social interactions.

When Erica returned, she was disappointed to see the guys were gone, but she had new gossip to share. "Y'all will not believe what I just heard. Marie was talking to Michelle in the lobby, and she said her husband has left her. I mean, we all knew he wasn't coming to church anymore, but now he's left her."

Jina didn't really know the people Erica was talking about, but Dahlia had always admired Marie who had once been her youth leader. Dahlia, as a teenager, had been so excited to attend Marie's wedding, and her heart sunk to hear about the current state of her marriage. "You really shouldn't be sharing that information," she said, feeling protective of Marie. "She was talking to Michelle—not us."

"I just thought you'd want to know," Erica said apologetically, shrugging her shoulders. "She said she's just going to wait and pray for him to repent and come home."

"Well, then we should just support her by praying for those same things," Dahlia said. "And keeping it to ourselves."

"You're right," Erica agreed. "So…what did the guys want to talk about?"

"They're coming to the work day this Saturday," Jina said.

Erica was both thrilled and disappointed. Dahlia and Jina could see the wheels turning in her head as she tried to figure out how she could help them *and* have enough time to prepare for Josh and Maggie's wedding. She decided she would come work in the morning, then leave early to be ready for the event.

"By the way," she threw at Dahlia as they were going their separate ways, "Lily and I are coming over tomorrow night to talk about wedding stuff!"

"Looking forward to it…I think," Dahlia joked with a smirk. When Erica and Lily got together it was always an entertaining time—it could also be draining for an introvert like Dahlia. But they knew her home was always open to them.

"Don't worry," Jina whispered. "I'll come too. It will be fun."

—

When Jina entered her apartment, she was greeted by her affectionate, demanding cat. As she picked him up and switched on a lamp, her eyes fell on the wall calendar where her mother had left a yellow sticky note with the name *Steve* in bright red ink. Jina had met so many Steves. She sighed as her mind ran through all the men her mother had introduced her to during the last seven years. As soon as she had graduated from college and secured her first teaching position, her mother's quest had begun.

The first several guys had been typical blind dates, ones that were awkward, but friendly, and didn't go anywhere. But Jina had loved the seventh one, Jun. Jina's father had really liked him too. They dated for nine months before he decided to take a job in another state and had determined, without any discussion, that he didn't want a long-distance relationship. They could have gotten married; Jina could have gone with him. But he didn't ask her to, and she'd concluded that he just hadn't loved her enough for *that* kind of commitment. Her mother had concluded that there must have been someone else, and she still said so on the rare occasion his name was mentioned. Jina would never admit, not even to Dahlia, that whenever she felt viscerally lonely, she sometimes scrolled through his social media profile. Jun married only a year after their breakup—maybe there *had* been someone else—and they had two beautiful children.

Three months after their breakup, Jina's father died from a heart attack. He had always been the one to help Jina and her mother relate to one another. Without him, they struggled through their grief and their relationship. Ms. Yoon became even more determined to find her daughter a husband, and Jina became determined to never love a man again. She had pushed away, buried deep, any hopes for marriage, any daydreams of a wedding—especially if her father couldn't be there to walk her down the aisle—and had instead focused on Jesus and work and all the goals she had described to Ted Neal at

Dahlia's church. Since her father's death, any dates she had been on had simply been to appease her mother.

So, as she sat on the couch with her purring cat, it bothered Jina that she had been bothered when Erica had said the new guys were no good for her. *Why does it bother me? Why do I care?* she wondered. Why was she suddenly curious about Daniel, and why was she scrolling through *his* online profile? She hadn't been interested in a non-Korean guy since ninth grade when she and Dahlia once had a crush on the same boy. *Is it just because Erica told me he's off limits?* she asked herself, examining her feelings and motives. Before falling asleep she decided that it had nothing to do with Erica's words and everything to do with Daniel's kind, smiling blue eyes.

Chapter Four

Erica and Lily arrived to Dahlia's apartment the next evening, their arms overflowing with bridal magazines and notebooks. Dahlia didn't remember wedding planning being so complicated when Violet got married, back before Pinterest and Instagram became popular. It had been simple, and Dahlia had been full of youth and excitement to be her maid of honor—now, she felt old. Even though Lily had chosen one of her college sorority sisters to be her maid of honor, she lived out of state, so Dahlia anticipated most of the responsibilities leading up to the wedding would fall on her; it would be more extensive and time-consuming this time around. *Maybe Erica will help a lot,* Dahlia hoped.

Dahlia and Jina had staked their claims on the couch, snuggled in among the pillows, with bowls of popcorn, deciding they were mostly just there for commentary and solicited opinions. Erica and Lily sat on the floor with their laptops and magazines open, spread across the coffee table. "We have set the wedding date for October," Lily stated. "Which means, we need to go dress shopping immediately. Can any of you go tomorrow?"

"No, I'm sorry." Dahlia shook her head. "We have other obligations."

"More important than finding me a wedding dress?" her younger sister demanded.

"I want to be there for you as much as possible," Dahlia said, "but you're gonna have to schedule things in advance. We can make an appointment and go next weekend."

That seemed to appease Lily, for the moment. "Well, what are y'all doing tomorrow?" she still wanted to know.

"We're going to help fix up an old lady's house and yard," Erica explained. "But we also get to spend time with those two new guys from church. Remember the ones I told you about?"

"Ooo, the cute ones?" Lily was intrigued. She, like the rest of her family, wanted her sister—and Erica, of course—to meet someone. "I want to see what they look like."

Erica smiled. "Let me show you."

Dahlia and Jina sat quietly during this exchange, casually observing and flipping through the bridal magazines. Erica found Daniel's online profile quickly and turned her laptop around so everyone could see. Dahlia simply glanced at it, preferring to learn more about him in person. Jina pretended she was seeing it for the first time, attempting to be subtle about her interest.

"He is good-looking," Lily agreed. "Not my type though. I'm not into blondes. Don't need to date someone who looks like my brother. Have y'all noticed how so many couples look like siblings? Plus, he doesn't have enough muscle for me. What about the other one?" Dahlia rolled her eyes at Lily's criticisms, thinking that Brian drank too many protein shakes and spent too much time at the gym.

"Well, Andrew doesn't have a profile, but he's in some of Daniel's pictures," Erica said as she clicked through them, looking for the right one. "Here he is. That's him."

"Wow." Lily was impressed. She didn't need to say more than that one word. "He's got some cute dimples and nice eyes. Tall, dark and handsome, yes please."

"Yeah," Erica concurred. "But he didn't talk much or seem friendly. And he doesn't even have a Facebook profile."

"What does that matter?" Jina asked.

"It means he has something to hide," Erica said confidently.

"That's not true," Dahlia doubted. "Not everyone has Facebook. You can't blame a person for valuing their privacy. I hardly ever post anything on my profile."

"When people are *that* private, they're hiding something." Erica was very sure of this. "It's fine if a guy doesn't post a lot, but to not have any online presence is weird."

"She's right," Lily agreed, nodding her head, very serious.

Jina and Dahlia looked at each other, choosing not to argue with their logic. Dahlia wondered if it was true—did Andrew have something to hide?

"So, Dahlia, are you gonna snag one of them for a husband?" Lily could stop herself from asking. "Although Andrew is cuter, I'd go with the Daniel. Less risk of rejection."

"Or just a *kinder* rejection," Dahlia joked with a smile.

"But he's the one I chose," Erica said, staking her claim.

"Don't worry, Erica. I'm not really in the habit of snagging men," Dahlia assured her.

Lily and Erica laughed, knowing the truth in her words, knowing her limited experience with relationships. They didn't understand that it wasn't that she had trouble meeting men—available men were everywhere—but she *chose* to wait for the right kind of man, one who loved Jesus as much as she did. She could have started dating Robbie months earlier, but it wouldn't have honored the Lord. So before the girls could go down a path of giving her unwanted advice, she refocused the conversation on the wedding. They worked out a schedule, figured out a day for dress shopping, and discussed having the ceremony at their father's house since he had a large, private estate.

"Oh, I almost forgot," Lily began, "Mom is going to throw an engagement party for me and Brian in a few weeks! You're all invited, and I *require* that you all bring dates. Dancing won't be any fun otherwise." She looked pointedly in the eyes of each of them, daring them to protest. When nobody did, she was satisfied. Dahlia knew better than to argue so far in advance; she would probably just show up alone when Lily could do nothing about it.

Lily's phone beeped as they were heading out. She read the message and said, "Mom wants to help you with that lady's yard tomorrow. She got some flowers for a good price that she would like to plant. So send her the details, what time and the address."

Dahlia stared at her sister. "How does she know about it?"

"I texted to let her know we couldn't dress shop tomorrow because of your plans." Lily flashed a huge, devious smile. "I'm sure you'll have fun spending the *whole* day with her."

"I will," Dahlia stated with confidence as she shut the door. She was determined to have a great day with her mother, and at the thought of it, she began praying, *Holy Spirit, please help me to show my mom love and respect and patience and kindness. Jesus, please don't let me become easily annoyed, but help me to look on her with compassion, as you do. Let me see her as You see her, and love her as You do. In my own strength, I always fail. I can do no good thing apart from You.*

—

It was a perfect early spring morning when Dahlia and Jina arrived at Ms. Anna's house. They had planned to arrive first, but were surprised to find not only Daniel and Andrew there already, but so was Robbie. All three guys were standing by their vehicles, talking.

"What's Robbie doing here?" Dahlia asked Jina before they got out of the car. "Did you tell him about it?"

"No. Are you sure you didn't?"

Dahlia shook her head. "No, I never mentioned it." On the hood of his SUV, she could see that he had brought coffee—for everyone this time.

"Erica doesn't know about Robbie," Jina said, reading Dahlia's thoughts. "Or him liking you." She paused, then added with wide eyes, "Oh, and your mom is coming."

Dahlia closed her eyes for a second. "Please, Lord Jesus, do not let today be awkward."

"Amen," Jina said as they opened their car doors.

"Good morning," Daniel greeted them cheerfully, while Andrew fussed with yard equipment in the truck bed. "We didn't know what we might need, so we brought everything from my sister's garage."

Jina smiled. "Thank you so much. That's awesome."

"Hey, Robbie. How'd you know we were doing this?" Dahlia asked, trying to sound nonchalant.

"Chris told me at basketball practice," he said, handing Dahlia and Jina cups of coffee. She had forgotten he was the assistant coach, and Chris really looked up to him.

"Oh, right. Well, welcome," she said with a smile, while internally deciding what to do with the coffee. "I assume y'all already introduced yourselves to each other." They nodded. "Thank you for bringing equipment. We thought we were going to have to borrow a lawn mower from a neighbor. But now we don't have to." Dahlia was impressed with their thoughtfulness, but mentally questioned if it was all Daniel's doing, since Andrew had not yet said a word, and she wondered if he wanted to be there.

"Erica should be here shortly, and Dahlia's mom is coming later to plant some flowers," Jina explained, as they began unloading the necessary tools and equipment. Robbie's ears perked up at the mention of Dahlia's mother, thinking that if she liked him it might work in his favor.

"Then I'll get started mowing the lawn," Andrew said, "so it will be ready for her."

"Wait." Dahlia touched his shoulder without thinking. "Let me make sure Ms. Anna and Chris are up, so we don't wake them."

Just then Chris burst through the front door, the screen slamming shut behind him. He went to Robbie first with a fist bump, and then shook hands and introduced himself to Daniel and Andrew. Dahlia felt proud as she observed how mature he had become and how much taller he was than her. He used to run and hug her when she would visit, but he considered himself too grown for that now. Instead, he just said, "Hi, Ms. Marshall and Ms. Han. Granny is making lots of food, and there are drinks. She said not be shy about coming to get something when you're hungry or thirsty."

"Jina and I will go say hello," Dahlia said.

On their way up the sidewalk, Chris came up between them and whispered, "Are they your boyfriends?" Jina blushed; Dahlia noticed.

"No, Chris." She smiled. "They are... acquaintances, really. We only met them two days ago at church."

"Oh, so you're bringing strangers to my house now?" he joked.

Dahlia laughed. "Why don't you go help those strangers?" She saw Daniel grab his toolbox from the truck. "Go show Daniel where the fence needs to be repaired."

Chris took off in his direction. Andrew was already cranking up the lawn mower, and Robbie had hedge clippers in hand as he assessed the bushes and trees. "This might go pretty fast with all of them working," Jina said. "Maybe you could have gone to that wedding after all."

Dahlia rolled her eyes, saying a silent *no thanks,* as she knocked on the door, opening it and calling out, "Good morning, Ms. Anna!"

She appeared in the kitchen doorway, beckoning them to come inside. Ms. Anna and her late husband had bought the old house shortly after their wedding. The hardwood floors in the hall creaked, the green tile in the kitchen was chipped, and the wallpaper was ripped in some areas; it was one of Dahlia's dreams to help them refinish the home, one project at a time, so it could last for many more generations.

"Ms. Anna, you didn't have to prepare anything for us," Dahlia said, giving her a hug. "But that cornbread sure does smell good."

"You know I show my love and appreciation through cooking," Ms. Anna said with a smile, the wrinkles around her eyes and mouth giving a hint at her age. She didn't look as old as she was, but she felt older.

"We know you do," Jina said. "And it's always delicious."

"We're gonna get to work," Dahlia said. "Holler if you need us."

Ms. Anna's house was neat and well-kept, but it rarely got a good, deep clean, the get-on-your-knees or stand-on-a-chair kind of clean. So, they decided the guys could tackle the yard work, while they worked inside, dusting, cleaning ceiling fans, scrubbing baseboards and door frames, washing mirrors and windows, vacuuming, sweeping, mopping. When Erica arrived an hour later, they saw her from an upstairs window and waved, but she didn't see them, her eyes curious about the new guy in the yard.

They went down to meet her, calling her onto the porch.

"Who's the guy with no shirt on?" she asked immediately.

"That's Robbie," Dahlia said. "A teacher from our school."

"He took his shirt off?" Jina asked, curious.

Dahlia added, "It's not *that* hot out here."

"He's clearly sweating, and you obviously haven't seen him, or you wouldn't be complaining," Erica said, encouraging them to walk around the side of the porch and get a glimpse. But neither of them moved. They worked with him every day and didn't *need* to see how good his body looked, especially Dahlia who already found him attractive with his clothes on.

"Is he single?" Erica asked.

Jina hesitantly said, "Yes," glancing at Dahlia.

"Come inside and help us clean the house," Dahlia said, grabbing Erica's arm.

Erica stopped in her tracks, pulling away. "Wait, y'all have been separated, like boys and girls separated all morning? Women doing the housework, men in the yard? No, no, no. I'll stay out here, where the view is nice, and clean out the flower beds for your mom. I only have two hours. I'm not wasting them inside the house when there are three single men out here."

"Don't make yourself look desperate," Dahlia joked.

"Oh, it's not desperation," Erica said with a confident smile. "It's availability. Just letting them know I'm available for any decent advances."

They laughed, shrugged their shoulders, and went back to cleaning the house with worship music in the background, until Dahlia's mother pulled up outside. *Lord, please give me patience, and please don't let her embarrass me, or rather don't let me be embarrassed by anything she might do,* she quickly prayed as she headed outside to see Elaine.

When Elaine saw the three men in the yard, she immediately became flustered. As her daughter approached the window, with annoyance she said, "Dahlia, you didn't tell me there were going to be men here." She looked in the jeep's rearview mirror and began straightening her short blond hair.

"Mom, it's just a couple guys from church and a teacher from school. You don't need to impress them. Besides, they are young enough to be your sons."

Elaine rolled her eyes. "Thanks, Dahlia, for the age reminder."

Dahlia could see her own disheveled reflection in the side mirror, her dark wavy hair in a messy bun, and wondered if she should have put more effort into her appearance that morning. Erica had arrived looking like perfection in short shorts and a tank top, and even Jina had put on makeup. Dahlia had a suspicion it was because they both wanted to look pretty for Daniel. She quickly brushed the thoughts away—she had come to serve Ms. Anna, not compete for male attention.

Chris was shooting hoops with some neighborhood kids in the street. Daniel and Andrew were taking a water break, and Robbie was approaching the curb with a wheelbarrow full of vines and limbs—thankfully, he had put his shirt back on. Dahlia introduced Elaine to them quickly, and then ushered her away to show her the one-acre lot. She loved to see her mother become excited about a gardening project; it was always a joy to see her use her creativity in bringing her visions to fruition. She left Elaine to get started.

"Hey, Daniel, is the fence repaired so we can paint it now?" Dahlia asked.

"Oh, we're painting the fence today too?" Robbie asked.

"Well, I just thought we'd get started, and finish it next weekend," she said. "But none of you have to stay. You've already done a lot, and if you need to take off, you can."

When Robbie realized that neither Daniel nor Andrew were leaving, he decided to stay as well.

Just as Daniel said the fence was ready for paint, Jina came out and asked for his help—or rather she asked to borrow his tools, and he offered his help. They disappeared into the house to fix a leaky faucet, and Erica stared after them.

Erica helped Elaine unload the plants from her jeep, while the rest of them started painting the fence a crisp, bright white. Erica continued to check the time on her cell phone and prattled on and on about Josh and Maggie's wedding that evening—Elaine was delighted to hear all about it.

They were planting flowers around the bushes along the fence line, and Elaine couldn't be around so many people without making conversation. "Dahlia, did you make an online dating profile yet?" Elaine asked loudly, for everyone to hear.

Dahlia's face felt instantly hot. "No, mom. I never said I was going to do that."

"But, why not?" Erica said. "It sounds like a great idea."

"Yeah. Why not?" Elaine did not understand her daughter. "My profile hasn't even been up for a week, and I have met tons of men."

Dahlia kept her eyes on the fence, hoping that Andrew and Robbie had gone temporarily deaf. "It's just not really for me. I'm glad it's working out for you though." Was she though? What kind of men was her mother meeting?

"Oh yeah, it must be those sexy pictures I posted." She posed with her hand on her hip. Erica giggled at this.

"Mom…" Dahlia was now officially mortified. But her mother would not be chastised or quieted on the subject.

"What, Dahlia?" Elaine demanded. "There is nothing wrong with the word 'sexy.' You're always such a prude."

Dahlia knew better than to respond. Nothing would prevent things from escalating into an argument better than silence. Elaine took this as an opportunity to tell her more.

"I have a date tonight with one of the men. He is a rich banker, and so handsome. You never know, maybe I'll be married *before* your father. Have they set a date yet?"

"Not that I know of. I haven't met his fiancée yet. Just please be careful when you meet men from that site. Don't let them pick you up at the house," Dahlia cautioned. She hated Robbie and Andrew learning so much about her family this way; she felt exposed. She wasn't in control of how the information was presented, and she had no idea how they were receiving it; they remained silent.

Erica felt right at home in Dahlia's family because they were like her own. She started asking more questions about Elaine's online dating experience so far. Dahlia wondered why she had such a difficult time communicating with her mother, yet Erica could do it so flawlessly.

"I created a dating profile a few weeks ago," Erica eventually confessed.

"See, Dahlia? It's not that hard," Elaine said.

Dahlia wasn't sure when Jina had returned or how much she had heard, but suddenly she asked, "Erica, did you come across Robbie's profile? That's been happening lately."

Robbie stopped painting and turned to playfully glare at her.

"No," Erica said. "Sadly, I haven't. What app are you on?"

Erica missed the joke, but Dahlia knew Jina had sacrificed Robbie to spare her more comments from her mother. Robbie was flustered, like he had been at lunch earlier in the week. "I'm not on an app anymore. Just forgot to remove my profile."

Dahlia set down the paintbrush and headed to the back porch when she saw Ms. Anna come out and take a seat in her rocking chair. "I really want to thank you all for coming out today. You always take good care of us," she said to Dahlia, patting her hand. "And, it's so good for Chris to have men to spend time with."

They watched him playing basketball in the road. "Have you heard from his father?" Dahlia asked quietly.

The old woman shook her head. "He should still be working on an oil rig off the coast of Mississippi." Chris' mother had died from a drug overdose when he was young, and his father left him in his grandmother's care.

"You do a really great job with him," Dahlia praised her.

"So do you." Ms. Anna smiled softly.

Dahlia grabbed several glasses of lemonade to take to the others. She paused on the steps to observe

Jina and Daniel. He was encouraging her to sit on the bench swing he had repaired earlier, daring her to trust his handiwork. She slowly, gingerly sat down, a nervous smile on her face, but then he plopped down hard, as if he might break it again, and she let out a little scream. It was all quite picturesque, and though she had not yet discussed her suspicions about Jina's feelings, she was pretty sure something was happening there. Erica looked on in defeat, coming to the same conclusion.

"Here's some lemonade." She offered the last glass to Andrew. "Ms. Anna's setting the table for lunch shortly." Because Andrew had never appeared very conversational, and she considered herself to be very poor at small talk, she didn't intend to say more than that. But he did.

"So, your parents are divorced?" he asked. She hated that he got to know these things about her when she hadn't been the one to tell him.

"Yes, they have been since I was seven."

"Does your dad live in town?"

"No, he lives in Rome, about an hour away."

"That's where I'm from."

"Really? Is that where Daniel's from also?"

"No, he grew up in Chattanooga mainly. So, you didn't go to high school in Rome?"

She shook her head. "No, I lived here with our mom."

"Are you talking about me? I heard my name!" Elaine teased as she and Erica approached.

"No, ma'am," Andrew replied. "Just talking about high school."

"Oh, high school! What I wouldn't give to go back there! I sure would do some things differently." She nudged Dahlia's arm with her elbow and winked. Her daughter already knew what things Elaine would do differently, the most important being not dating or marrying her father.

"Ms. Anna almost has lunch ready." Dahlia changed the subject.

"Oh, Erica and I can't eat a thing!" Elaine exclaimed. "We were just talking, and we're going to leave now. We're going to help each other get ready."

"Erica's gonna help you get ready for your date?" Dahlia asked, surprised.

"Yes! And, I'm going to help her get ready for the wedding, which she tells me you aren't going to." She wagged her finger at her daughter. "You know how many single guys will probably be there and you aren't going! I don't understand it at all."

Thankfully, Ms. Anna called them all inside for lunch before Dahlia had to present her defense. Elaine and Erica said their goodbyes and promised to return the following Saturday to finish what they had started. Robbie took this opportunity to head out as well. Everyone else spent the rest of the afternoon and evening in genuine enjoyment, although Andrew did revert back to his quiet, seemingly unfriendly demeanor. He only came alive again when he played Frisbee with Chris and Daniel.

The three women sat on the porch watching them and talking until dusk.

Dahlia was still observing Jina and Daniel, while Ms. Anna was making observations of her own. She had noticed a glimmer of interest in Andrew's eye whenever she caught him looking at Dahlia. It was very subtle—Dahlia was oblivious—but the old woman was a master at studying people, and she was sure of it.

On the car ride home, Jina lamented, "I wish I could go with you to church in the morning. But I have to serve breakfast before our service."

This was Dahlia's opportunity. "Why do you want to come with me so badly?"

"What do you mean? I love your church."

"Yeah, but you don't usually get upset if you can't go. Are you sure it's not because you want to see a certain guy?" she asked with raised eyebrows.

Jina sighed. "Yes, but I know I shouldn't."

"Why not? He is a great guy, so far anyway."

"He is. He is kind and patient and funny."

"He loves Jesus, and he's easy on the eyes." Dahlia gave her a playful look.

"Yes, it was so fun listening to him and Andrew and Ms. Anna talk about scripture." She smiled and then immediately sighed again. "But have you forgotten about Steve and my matchmaker mother?"

"No, but Jina, you don't *have* to marry a Korean man."

"According to my mother…" Jina shrugged. "I feel like it's what my dad would want too."

Dahlia sighed. "I know we must respect our parents, but they're human too, and they don't *always* know best."

"I know…I still feel like I at least need to give it a shot."

"Yeah, your mom can line them up, and you can shoot them all down," Dahlia joked.

Jina gave her a half smile. "Besides," she said, "Daniel's probably not interested in me like that."

"From what I witnessed, he definitely is."

Chapter Five

Dahlia attended the first church service and snuck out a few minutes early to drive to her father's house for brunch and the official meeting of his fiancée. She was so familiar with the route, the hills, the curves, the bends of the Appalachian foothills, that her mind wandered. During service, she noticed Erica sitting beside Daniel, Andrew on his other side. Now that Dahlia knew Jina was interested in Daniel, she felt a little protective of him. What she didn't know was that after Erica had observed Daniel and Jina together, she had decided to give up any thoughts or intentions toward him—until the wedding didn't yield the results she'd hoped for; the only single males at the wedding had been teenagers.

When Dahlia entered her father's private gated estate, she found Violet and Lily parked down the street, waiting for her to arrive before approaching his house. Lily had ridden with Violet, or else she may not have come at all, and they wanted to show up together and get it over with as soon as possible. Violet's husband Adam was the only one without any feelings about the situation; his only concern was that Violet, and their baby, were free from stress.

Their father had purchased the estate about ten years earlier. It was a completely refinished Victorian-inspired home built in 1883 on almost six acres of land, surrounded by forest. It was a landscaper's dream; it was their mother's dream—the dream she thought she would achieve when she helped put their father through medical school. Dahlia had stayed in the carriage house apartment one summer when she'd taken classes at the local college; Lily had lived there all four years of college. Every time Dahlia pulled into the brick-paved driveway, it almost didn't feel real, like the house was something from a storybook.

"Why didn't y'all go ahead in?" Dahlia asked when they all stood in the driveway. "Now we're all late." She hated being late, even "right on time" wasn't good enough for her.

"Lily wouldn't let us," Violet said with annoyance. *"Not 'til Dahlia arrives,"* she mimicked

Lily's voice. Violet and Lily were six years apart. Sometimes they got along wonderfully, especially when they were ganging up to make fun of Dahlia, and other times all they did was bicker.

As they ascended the many steps, Gail, the housekeeper, opened the door before they could knock; she had been waiting for them with anticipation, and hers was the face they were most pleased to see. She had worked for their father since the divorce and had become like a second mother to them. Now that they were adults, they visited less, and she missed them more. She hugged Violet especially long, placing her hand on the very tiny baby bump.

"Your father and Ms. Morgan will be down in a few minutes," she said, leading them down the hall and through the kitchen to the sunroom where she had set a stunning, magazine-like table.

They began to make inquiries into the nature of their father's fiancée.

Lily whispered, "What's she like?"

But Gail would not offer them even one detail. Knowing the sisters the way she did, she wanted them to develop their own opinions, not simply adopt her own.

"I can't believe she already lives here," Lily said with irritation once they were seated around the table. "I just visited a month ago, and daddy made no mention of it." Lily was the only one who still called him daddy.

"She only just moved in two weekends ago, remember?" Dahlia reminded her.

Gail entered with drinks for them, knowing their preferences, not needing to ask. Orange juice, no pulp, apple juice, orange juice, extra pulp, two percent milk with ice. They all expressed their thanks.

"She sure does like to keep us waiting," again Lily complained, ignoring the fact that her father was also not yet present. "It *is* Sunday. I have other things to do."

Although the waiting was giving Dahlia and Violet more anxiety, it was nothing compared to the annoyance they had with their younger sister's impatience. Adam tried to lighten the mood with a joke that didn't go over well, and then Violet tried to distract her by asking about her wedding plans, whether she had chosen a date or location. But just as the conversation was beginning to flow, they heard their father's voice in the foyer, followed by laughter from his female companion.

"Good morning, everyone," he greeted them, unusually cheerful. Then Morgan entered.

Violet's jaw would have hit the table if she didn't have such self-control. She recognized Morgan.

"I'm so sorry we kept you waiting," Morgan said. "A baby in the nursery at church threw up on me, and I had to change my clothes."

Did they go to church together? Dahlia wondered. Her dad hadn't been in a church since his wedding day. Alan introduced his daughters and son-in-law. Lily apologized that Brian couldn't be there, although no comment was made about his absence. Nobody knew him well enough to actually miss him.

Dahlia observed that Morgan was gorgeous with twisted black hair, rich brown skin, and almond-shaped eyes. She also couldn't help but notice that she was much younger than their father. Nobody said much as they began to fill their plates, but then Violet couldn't resist asking, "You're Morgan Vaughn, aren't you?" She hoped she was wrong, but she wasn't.

"Well, not for long," Morgan said as she smiled at Alan.

Alan was surprised. "How did you know that, Violet?"

"Because, dad, we went to high school together," she responded, sounding like she was stating an obvious fact, something she couldn't believe her father had missed as he'd gotten to know his fiancée. "She was a senior when I was a freshman."

That would make her thirty-six, Dahlia calculated.

"Oh!" Morgan was shocked also, really desiring to make a good impression on Alan's daughters. "I'm surprised you remember me, since we wouldn't have been in the same classes."

"You were captain of the cheerleading squad; I didn't need to be in your circle to know who you were," Violet explained, somewhat embarrassed.

"Oh." Morgan smiled awkwardly, ready to change the subject.

Alan was also. "So, Lily, I was thinking since both you and Morgan will be planning weddings, that you could do a lot of it together."

"Were you?" Lily glared at Alan. This was her special time, not to be shared with her father's new bride.

"Oh, I'm sure she doesn't need that, Alan," Morgan said. "She has two very capable sisters to help her plan her wedding."

"And a mother," Lily added while stuffing a piece of cantaloupe in her mouth.

Dahlia could see this was headed nowhere good. "Dad," she interceded, "Lily was talking about having her wedding here at your house, on the grounds. Perhaps on the front lawn?" Once she said it, she hoped Morgan wasn't envisioning something similar.

Both Alan and Morgan agreed that it was a wonderful idea. Morgan added, "I'm sure we'd love to have any of you stay with us this summer as you plan things."

"Yes, you all can help us transform one of the bedrooms into a nursery," Alan said enthusiastically.

The sisters looked at each other, almost certain this was their father's way of announcing that Morgan was pregnant. Adam recognized their confusion. "I think Alan is referring to his coming grandchild," Adam clarified, smiling at Violet and putting his arm around her shoulders. Everyone instantly relaxed.

Lily said to Morgan, "Your fiancé is old enough to be a grandfather."

Violet muttered, to herself, but loud enough for all to hear, "He's old enough to be your father."

"Hey, you two don't have to be rude," Alan said sharply. "You don't need to tell us things we already know either. We're quite aware of the age difference. Cut us some slack."

Besides experiencing constant pregnancy nausea, as an accountant, Violet was in the middle of tax season. She didn't have a lot of rope to give. She quickly apologized, but Lily wasn't finished.

"Well, she *is* young enough to be your daughter," Lily argued. "You never even told us and expect us to act like it's normal. Is she going to be our sister or our stepmom?"

Most of the time Violet and Dahlia would be embarrassed by Lily's brashness, but sometimes, when she said exactly what they were thinking, their hearts applauded. Not because they wanted to be rude to Morgan, but they wanted to be real about the situation.

"She's going to be *my wife,*" their father said firmly. "You all can figure out your relationships with her in time. But I will not tolerate you being hurtful."

"Dad, if we don't address the age difference, how can we move past it?" Dahlia asked.

"You should have told us about it last week, so we'd have time to adjust," Violet added.

Alan became defensive. "So what if there's an age difference? I've dated younger women before, and you never said anything."

"They were never our peers before, and you were never marrying them," Violet said, high school memories still running through her head.

Alan wasn't a man who was used to asking permission to do anything, at least not since his divorce. And his daughters had rarely had any comments about the previous women in his life, so, he didn't appreciate their criticism about the one he had chosen to marry. "Why can't you all just be happy for me?" he asked. "For *us*?"

"You just want us to accept it without any discussion, comments, or concerns?" Lily demanded.

"Yes."

Dahlia didn't care either way. Actually, she did care, but she convinced herself she didn't. She'd grown weary of being hurt by him and as a defense, long ago she had stopped emotionally investing herself in her father's decisions because he always did what he wanted regardless of how it affected others. But she hated the way he would leave things unspoken and ignore issues to avoid conflict. He was famous for not discussing the things that needed to be talked about. In that way, she wasn't like her father—she didn't fear the conflict, if it led to resolution. Violet and Lily were different; they started conflict, but rarely resolved it. Violet would let things build up in her mind, and she would talk about it to everyone except the person who needed to be addressed. Lily said whatever she wanted, whenever she wanted, until she felt defeated; then she would retreat with a cold shoulder.

After an uncomfortable silence, Morgan said, "I know that the age difference might seem awkward and uncomfortable for you all. It took me some getting used to as well, but I really love your father, and I would like the opportunity to get to know and love all of you as well."

Every one of them was surprised at her honesty and candor. None of their father's previous girlfriends had ever been invested in them. Dahlia could see that Morgan might be good for her father; she could soften his hard edges. Where he spoke with harshness, she took the time to empathize and speak with gentleness.

But Violet was still trying to reconcile the teenager she remembered with the woman who sat before her. Even though Morgan didn't remember it, Morgan was never very kind to her for the brief season they had been in the same circle, the few months when freshman Violet had dated a senior and attended all the same parties and events as Morgan. *It's been twenty years. People change,* she told herself. She would give Morgan the opportunity she was asking for, to get to know them.

When none of them responded immediately, Alan continued, "We plan to have a small wedding at the end of July. I know that's before your wedding, Lily, but it really will be something simple and small. Nothing in comparison to the grand extravaganza I know your day will be."

"Lily, will your mother be your florist?" Morgan asked.

"She most certainly won't be working the day of the wedding," Lily replied. "But I'm sure she will come up with some arrangements and her assistants will make them happen."

Morgan smiled. "I've heard her arrangements are stunning."

Where had she heard that? Dahlia wondered. Surely her father had not said anything so flattering about their mother's work. There was so much bitterness between them, neither of them ever said anything good about the other, at least not to her or her sisters. So, it always made Dahlia uneasy when her mother was mentioned in her father's presence. She decided to steer the conversation elsewhere. "So you two met online…?"

"Something like that," Morgan said. "We actually first made a connection because we both work in the medical field. I'm a nurse at a local doctor's office."

The remainder of their meal consisted of small talk, and it went smoothly—mostly because Lily didn't open her mouth again. Gail secretly listened from just inside the doorway, and while she had grown to respect Morgan, she knew it would take the rest of them some time. She was certainly not looking forward to the first encounter between the fiancée and the ex-wife at Lily's engagement party.

As soon as they pulled away from the house, Lily sent a group text to her mother and sisters. It simply said, "Dad's fiancée went to high school with Violet."

Violet fussed at her for sending it the entire drive home as their mother's responses came pouring in.

—

Dahlia stopped by Jina's apartment on her way home because her friend had requested all the details about Sunday brunch. Her phone buzzed so much on the drive home she felt compelled to silence it. Elaine had sent a million responses to Lily's message and then tried to video call all of them at once; her middle child had ignored it, not desiring to process out loud with them.

Dahlia knocked; Jina shouted for her to come in.

"How was church?" Dahlia asked.

"It was fine," Jina said. She was standing over the stove. "Umma brought a lot of food over yesterday. Do you want some?"

"I'm still full from brunch, but I'll definitely take some for later."

"How was brunch?"

Dahlia didn't say anything, but handed her phone to Jina with the text messages open for her to read. Jina removed the skillet from the burner and began scrolling through them, her eyes going wide from Lily's very first one. "She went to high school with Violet?" she asked in disbelief.

Dahlia just nodded, leaning against the counter. Watching Jina's facial expressions, she added, "I haven't read all of them, so I don't know how crazy mom got."

"She is…definitely not happy."

"Yeah. I think I saw the words *gold digger* in there somewhere."

"You did." Jina whistled like a bomb falling from the sky. "Elaine is fired up. Violet didn't say much."

"Yeah, I'm curious to talk to her alone. She seemed to have reservations about Morgan."

"What about you? What did you think of her?"

"From first impressions, she seemed genuine. But I'd like to talk to her alone too." Dahlia did better in one-on-one situations than group gatherings.

They sat on the couch while she explained things in more detail. Jina's parents' marriage had been a happy one, and when they did have conflict, it had always been discussed behind closed doors; they shielded Jina from it, and she had never felt stuck in the middle, never felt the pressure to choose sides. So, she always felt a little sad whenever she witnessed the reality of Dahlia's experience. Some divorced parents were amicable—Alan and Elaine, not so much.

Chapter Six

Jina didn't speak anymore about Daniel for the next few days, but he was never far from her thoughts—even though she wanted him to be. She wanted to forget any interest in him. Dahlia didn't mention his name either because she trusted her friend, with the Spirit as her counselor, to come to her own conclusions without any input from her. She couldn't possibly understand all the cultural complexities and potential conflict Jina could have with her mother, with her family, if she married a non-Korean, so she determined to be a supportive listener and faithful in prayer.

When Jina asked to go to Bible study again that Thursday evening, Dahlia didn't make any faces or insinuating comments about Daniel, even though she was certain it was at least part of Jina's motivation for wanting to attend. It was Erica's motivation too.

When they entered the room, Erica and Sasha—the girl who'd been so adamant about attending Josh and Maggie's wedding—were poorly attempting to engage Daniel and Andrew in conversation. Both of them had been disappointed with the lack of single men at the wedding, so they were resigned to try again with the only currently available options—not that they weren't excellent options. However, when Daniel saw Jina and Dahlia walk in, he soon found a way to politely excuse himself, leaving Andrew to fend for himself. Jina may have doubted he was interested in her, but it was obvious to anyone with an observant eye.

He greeted them with a huge, kind smile; Dahlia was convinced she had never seen a brighter, happier smile in her life, and she was delighted it was directed at her best friend. Andrew followed close behind, bothered that his cousin had abandoned him so abruptly, but grateful to see Dahlia and Jina. However, it was not obvious he felt either of these things, his face so stoic they would have never have guessed he was irritated with Daniel or glad to see them.

As they talked, out of the corner of her eye, Dahlia spied David coming in their direction, and she realized she could no longer delay introducing him to Jina. That was his sole design in entering their circle. He had already met the guys, and he knew from previous experience that Dahlia would not be wooed by his many charms. His hopes were that her friend would perhaps be more amiable. Of course, Jina knew a lot about David, and she thought he couldn't be nearly as bad as the stories she'd heard.

"Dahlia, who is your friend?" he asked, interrupting Andrew mid-sentence.

"This is Jina," she said dully. "Jina, this is David."

Jina held out her right arm to shake his hand, but he instead reached for her left hand, holding it awkwardly and making it extremely apparent he was checking for an engagement ring or wedding band, actually rubbing her ring finger with his thumb. When he saw none, he smiled broadly and said, "It is *very* nice to meet you."

She forced an uncomfortable, tight-lipped smile and pulled her hand away quickly even though he tried to maintain his grip. It made Dahlia angry when he approached new girls in this way, and she always become instantly protective. *Why does he have to be so cringe?* she thought. Andrew was thinking the same thing and feeling the same emotions, being more keenly aware of the general intentions of men than Dahlia.

"David, what do you say we go check out the food situation?" Andrew said, desiring to get him away from the ladies.

"I'm good, thanks." He would not be persuaded to take his eyes from Jina. "Unless, Jina would like to."

Dahlia had watched her friend squirm enough. "We're going to the bathroom." She grabbed her arm and began leading her away. "See you guys later."

"Did that really just happen?" Jina whispered, her cheeks flush, embarrassed. "In front of Daniel and everything."

"I know. I'm sorry. Poor guy just wants a wife." It was easier for her to be sympathetic when she wasn't in his presence and his attentions weren't directed at her.

"Then you volunteer," Jina threw back at her. The very thought made Dahlia shudder.

They waited in the bathroom until Chuck began speaking. Daniel tried to save seats for them, but he was too polite to refuse when people asked, so when they re-entered the room, they were forced to take the only empty seats on the front row. Jina was disappointed about missing out on talking with Daniel before the study began, but she had resigned herself to letting things play out however they were meant to, trusting whatever God had for her. Even if it meant a match made by her mother.

Dahlia was grateful Chuck had not decided to sync his lessons with the Sunday sermons during the marriage series. He knew his students were already inundated with constant thoughts on the topic; he wanted to focus on giving them solid truths to help them become more like Jesus, regardless of whether they ever obtained a spouse or not. It was one of the reasons Dahlia appreciated him as a teacher and didn't want to move to another group. After the lesson and prayer, Dahlia repeated her invitation for people to come help at Ms. Anna's that coming Saturday, but she downplayed the amount of work that was left because she secretly hoped to have the same small group as the previous weekend.

Ted stole Andrew and Daniel away immediately, wanting to introduce them to people they had not yet met. He didn't want them wasting their time with Dahlia's friend since Jina had said she wasn't waiting to be married. *There are plenty of other girls in the group who were ready now,* he reasoned. He kept them talking for so long, and while Dahlia and Jina waited, David appeared again.

"Jina," he said, choosing to ignore Dahlia who'd been so rude earlier. "I was wondering if you would like to get a cup of coffee with me?"

She was caught off guard. "Right now?"

"Yes."

"Uh, thanks for asking, but I really need to get to bed early. We have field day at school tomorrow."

"Plus," Dahlia interjected, "I'm her ride, and we're headed out." She looped her arm through Jina's. "Have a good night," she tossed over her shoulder as they walked away.

"Does he do that with every girl?" Jina whispered.

"Pretty much, but not usually so quickly. He must *really* like you," Dahlia teased.

"But if he does that with every girl, how could he expect them to feel *special*?"

"I don't think he's worried about special. Anyone will do."

Other than his odd personality, it was his desperation that made him even more unappealing.

"You would think he would have found someone to say yes by now," Jina mused.

"I always thought Erica should," Dahlia joked. They laughed at this idea. "She would eat him alive."

"Why doesn't he move on to the singles group they've been trying to put you in?"

"I overheard him in conversation once…he prefers to marry a younger woman who has plenty of childbearing years ahead of her to give him the large family he desires…"

Jina pretended to choke on vomit. "He must think I'm younger than I am."

On their way through the lobby, Dahlia spotted Marie coming out of Pastor Derek's office. "Here," she said, handing her keys to Jina. "Go on to the car. I'll be there in a sec. Just want to talk to someone real quick."

Marie had been Dahlia's favorite youth leader, but she'd stepped down from the position shortly after getting married. Over the years, she and Dahlia became friends and would still meet together every so often; Dahlia would even occasionally babysit her two children. But it had been a while since they'd spoken, and Dahlia wasn't sure what to say. She didn't have to say anything. As soon as Marie saw her coming, tears started running down her cheeks, and Dahlia simply wrapped her arms around the heartbroken woman.

"Greg left us," she said once she caught her breath and pulled away.

Dahlia wouldn't admit that she already knew, so she asked, "How long ago?"

"A few weeks back," she said. "Well, he emotionally and spiritually left us months ago, but physically a few weeks ago. I don't even know where he's living."

"I'm so sorry," Dahlia said and meant it. She knew Greg had been pulling away, but never expected he'd leave his family. He had also been a youth leader—that's how the couple met and fell in love.

"He wants his sin and the world and nothing to do with Jesus," Marie explained. "He said living with me is a constant reminder of what he doesn't want."

"Because you're faithful. Because you reflect Christ," Dahlia said, affirming her friend. "Don't change that for him."

Marie shook her head. "I won't. That's why he's gone."

"How are the kids?"

"They miss the dad they used to know," she said. "It's hard to know…was that who he really was, or is this who he really is?"

Dahlia remembered the youth leader who'd been so passionate about the gospel, who'd sown into the lives of so many young men. She remembered the vows he'd made at his wedding, the words he'd spoken when they had dedicated their children to the Lord, and the prayers he had prayed when she had shared meals at their table. But now he was choosing something completely different, abandoning not just his family, but the faith he'd professed for decades.

Dahlia was quiet for most of the ride home. She knew Jina was disappointed about the events of that evening, how she'd barely had any time to speak with Daniel, and she wanted to cheer her up, but she was overwhelmed by sadness and anger at Marie's current circumstances.

Eventually Jina broke the silence. "Did your mom say or do anything else about your dad's fiancée?"

"She has now changed the age preference on her dating profile to show she's interested in younger men."

Jina laughed. "Everybody watch out for Elaine! She's coming for our men."

"She can have them," Dahlia said with a touch of bitterness after hearing about Greg. "I think the date with the banker went well though. They went out again tonight."

"Good for her! Now maybe she'll stop worrying about your dating life."

"I doubt it." Dahlia could only pray for the day.

Jina's phone began ringing. She held it up for Dahlia to see, grinning from ear to ear. "It's Daniel."

"Well, answer it!"

Dahlia eavesdropped on their conversation the rest of the drive home, smiling with so much joy for her friend. Daniel apologized for not getting to talk to her afterwards and for failing to save seats for them. Then, he asked Jina out for a proper dinner date the following evening.

Her answer, of course, was yes.

—

On Marie's drive home, she turned the radio on and worshiped the Lord, even though her heart was heavy—no, *especially* because her heart was heavy. She had to worship. It was the only way to prevent bitterness, resentment, and anger from growing inside of her—not just against Greg, but against God too. If she worshiped Him, if she reminded herself of

His goodness, if she cried out her honest emotions to Him and remembered His truths, she could stand firm, she could find comfort.

Self-righteousness and self-doubt battled constantly within her. She thought she had always done everything right. She had loved Jesus from a young age. She had avoided dating through high school. She had never fallen into sexual sin, and she didn't have any relationship baggage. She had waited until she met a man who loved Jesus too and who seemed to be on the same path as her. All their church leaders and mentors had affirmed their engagement. Her marriage wasn't supposed to fail, and it wasn't failing because of anything she had done. She knew that was true, but still doubted.

One second she would tell herself she'd done nothing wrong, and the next second she would question if she *had* done something to cause this. Why did others, believers or not, get to have, not perfect, but successful marriages? Why did she, who had been faithful to the Lord and faithful to her husband, end up abandoned? When she felt strong, she thought, *I did nothing wrong.* When she felt weak, she asked, *What did I do wrong? What could I have done better?* Then she would become angry with Greg all over again. It was a cycle, feelings she kept surrendering and then picking back up. Only with her children did she know how to hold herself together.

When she pulled into the driveway, she wiped away her tears and made sure she appeared half-way decent in the rearview mirror. Her son would be sleeping, but her daughter would still be awake. Before she could go in the house, her friend Julie came out and met her on the porch.

Julie was almost thirty-five, still a youth leader, and still single. She loved a man who strung her along because he couldn't decide if he wanted to commit, if he wanted to be a husband and have a family. She had been there since the beginning of Greg and Marie's relationship. She and Marie had giggled through the early days of crushes and dating. She had been the maid of honor in their wedding. She had been there for the birth of their children; she was their Aunt Julie. And she felt like she was angrier at Greg than anyone else, a fire burning inside of her to find him and lay into him, not just for what he was doing to Marie, but especially to his children. She didn't feel the men of the church, the men from their small group, were doing enough to call Greg back, and she was ready to do it herself.

She didn't express any of this to Marie though; it stayed between her and Jesus. "How was the meeting?" she asked Marie.

"It was fine," she said, sounding exhausted. "How were the kids?"

Julie gave her a look that said, *Do you even need to ask?* "Perfect, as usual. Cole went to bed about thirty minutes ago. Abby's still working on her project, but almost done. Do you need anything before I go?"

"I'm good. Thanks for sitting with them."

"Anytime." They hugged. "Love you."

Marie said, "Love you too," as she went inside.

Her daughter Abby was at the kitchen table, working on a science experiment. She didn't look up as her mom hugged her and kissed her cheek. "Do you want any help?" Marie offered.

Abby shook her head, still concentrating. But then she said, "Dad called me today."

"He did?" Marie asked, surprised and concerned. He hadn't been in contact with anyone, ignoring calls and texts not just from his wife, but also from his parents, his friends, and his employer. "What did he say?"

Abby shrugged. "Nothing really. That he loves me. That we'll see each other soon." She still didn't look at her mom, but kept her eyes on the work in front of her, gluing two popsicle sticks together, attempting to build a contraption that, when dropped, would protect an egg from breaking. "He didn't sound good though."

"How did he sound?" Marie asked softly, taking a seat at the table.

"You know…" Abby said. Marie was pretty sure she knew, but wanted her to explain it. "Like he does when he's had too much to drink, but different. I said a prayer for him, and he cried and then got mad."

He sounded different because he wasn't drunk; he was high. Marie's first instinct was to forbid Abby from answering her father's calls, to protect her from all of it. But was it right to cut off their communication completely? She had never made hard parenting decisions without her husband; now she had to make hard decisions *because* of her husband. When Abby went to bed, Marie spent a long time on her face in prayer and lament. *Father, Your kindness leads to repentance, so please pour out Your kindness on Greg,* she pleaded.

Chapter Seven

Most days Dahlia and Jina would carpool to work. When Jina got into the car the next morning, she informed her friend that she and Daniel had stayed on the phone for hours. Dahlia hadn't seen Jina so excited about anyone in a long time, and she loved the smile on her friend's face. She approved of the match, so far anyway. Dahlia held a strong belief that a person's character needed to be tested over time; she had seen no red flags, but it had only been a week.

Jina had also invited Daniel and Andrew to help with the school field day. "They did say we were short on parent volunteers, didn't they?" she asked, wanting confirmation that it was all right.

Dahlia nodded and smiled.

"You don't mind them coming, do you?" Jina asked. "I know you aren't a huge fan of Andrew, but it felt weird not to include him."

"Of course, I don't mind," she assured her. "They'll be a great help. We can always use more male volunteers. Plus, I don't have anything against Andrew. He just doesn't speak much—and I always feel like he's judging me somehow."

"Really? I guess I haven't noticed. I've witnessed great discussions between him and Daniel. Maybe he's just quiet around people he doesn't know well. You're the same way. *Or* maybe he's just quiet around *you*," she teased.

"Why would he be?"

Dahlia was used to being the person everyone felt comfortable talking to; she'd always been told she was easy to talk to and a good listener, and because of it she often knew more secrets than she cared to know. Therefore, she concluded, if he couldn't talk to her, the problem was his—not hers.

Jina shrugged. "I couldn't say." She stared out the window, smiling peacefully and replaying all of the previous night's conversation in her head, and Dahlia decided not to interrupt her thoughts.

When they arrived at school, Jina immediately spotted Daniel and Andrew on the field with the rest of the volunteers, being directed by the gym teachers on the set up and rules for each event. They didn't have time to stop and chat, so they just waved. Anticipation was in the air, and the students were almost uncontrollable as their teachers passed out their field day t-shirts, every team from every grade wearing a different color. Dahlia's team wore blue, and as an elective teacher, Jina got to choose which team she would join. Of course, she had chosen her best friend's.

The office secretary finally made the announcement over the intercom that the blue team could proceed to their assigned bleachers on the field. Their bleachers, much to Jina's regret, were on the opposite side of the field from where Daniel stood at the frisbee toss station. Andrew was at the soccer relay. They had been assigned to separate activities. It was the teachers' responsibility to rotate their classes through the stations in the order they'd been given. Dahlia examined the clipboard firmly in her grip.

"We have the jump rope and hula hoop challenge first," she explained to Jina and the class.

"Robbie's looking at you," Jina said quietly without moving her lips. "It must be that shirt making your eyes glow from across the field."

"Oh, please. How can you even tell where he's looking from so far away?"

"Because he always has eyes just for you." Jina nodded her head in his direction. "And now he's coming over."

Dahlia looked behind her and then turned around and gave Jina an expression of exasperation. His tanned skin looked good with the bright neon green shirt, which he'd ordered a size smaller so that everyone could see his muscles. Dahlia was still grateful she had not seen him shirtless at Ms. Anna's house. She enjoyed his company, he was funny and fun to flirt with, but anytime his interest in her became too obvious, she could only think *if only he followed Jesus too.*

Nobody realized that Robbie wasn't the only one watching Dahlia. Andrew's attentions toward her had only increased since their first introduction. There was no doubt she was beautiful, but there were beautiful girls everywhere, and he had never been so intrigued by any of them. His first impression of her as a silly girl had quickly been replaced by the reality that she was intelligent and thoughtful. It was precisely her thoughts he wanted to discover, but it was extremely difficult to ever know what she was thinking, and most of the time he was too self-conscious to ask.

Robbie reached them. "Good morning, you guys. How's it going?" He nodded at Jina to acknowledge her, but like usual, he faced Dahlia, hoping to make his interest very clear.

"Going great," Dahlia said, focusing her eyes on the clipboard, repeatedly reading the same words. "How are you?"

"Good now that I'm talking to you." The moment he said it, he cringed inside. It was one of the most direct statements he'd made to her, and it sounded better in his head. Dahlia's face flushed, and from the corner of her eye, she could see Jina's lips pressed together, suppressing a laugh.

After a moment's pause, she said, "I think you should get back. Your class is waiting on you to start."

He glanced back over his shoulder and saw she was telling the truth, not just trying to get rid of him. Embarrassed and unable to read her response to his comment, he nodded at her and then jogged back to his group. Andrew, being stationed closer to them than Daniel, had observed the incident, and he took note of Jina's laughter and the look Dahlia gave her. Andrew had tried to figure out the dynamic between Dahlia and Robbie the previous Saturday, but they hadn't interacted enough to give him a clear picture. Now he wondered if that was intentional. Did Dahlia try to avoid Robbie? Certainly not in the same way that she tried to avoid David, but it hadn't escaped his notice that she'd seemed surprised to see Robbie at Ms. Anna's that morning.

Although the school day would be a short one, and the kids would be released to go home early, to Jina it felt so much longer. As much as she loved her students, she just wanted to talk to Daniel. They had only been able to pass a few, quick words between stations throughout the course of the morning. She was glad he was there to help, and whenever she watched him, he really seemed to be enjoying himself, but she'd invited him with the hope of spending time with him. *You have a date with him this evening. Quit being like this,* she told herself.

When the day finally ended with the blue team coming in third overall, but first in the seventh grade, and Dahlia and Jina had gotten all of their students on school buses or in cars, they returned to the field to help disassemble everything. Most of it was already done, but since parent volunteers had left with their kids, only a few remained to do the work. There was a boot camp obstacle course, which had been everyone's favorite activity. It was the last to be taken down, but when Dahlia and Jina reached the field, it was still standing. To their surprise, Robbie and Andrew were at the starting line, and Daniel was off to the side with a timer in his hand.

"On your marks, get set, go!" Daniel shouted.

Jina and Dahlia looked at each other, smiling, instantly wanting to challenge the guys to the course. "Let's see how good they are first," Dahlia said as they approached Daniel.

The intensity on the participants' faces made it clear that this wasn't just a friendly competition. But what had generated such ferocity was unclear to all the viewers, especially Dahlia and Jina who didn't even know how it had begun. They asked Daniel, but he didn't know and was too busy cheering for Andrew to say more than that.

They were halfway through the course, with Robbie in the lead, appearing overconfident, but Andrew wasn't far behind. The tunnels were a tight fit for both of them, not designed for their broad shoulders; they both almost got stuck, and the maneuvers they had to make to get out of them gave their audience a laugh. The hurdles were last; Andrew's height and long legs made those easy for him, and he beat Robbie by a couple of seconds.

Robbie was really winded, more than he wanted to be now that he realized Dahlia was there. Jina taunted him, "Looks like you could use more cardio and less weight lifting."

"Thanks for the advice." He waved her off and sat down on the bench to catch his breath.

Andrew sprawled out on the grass, his hat over his face to block the hot Georgia sun, inhaling deeply and enjoying the slight breeze that occasionally blew his way.

Jina and Daniel decided to try the course next, not in competition, but helping one another and taking their time. Dahlia knew it was partially an excuse for them to have some moments alone together, so she sat down at the opposite end of the bench from Robbie to watch them, Robbie hoping maybe she wanted to be near him. Since the previous Saturday, he'd felt a new boldness growing in him, something encouraging him to take a chance. He slid down closer to her, still leaving some space between them.

"So, Dahlia," Robbie began, trying not to sound nervous. Andrew's ears perked up to listen. "The other day you were talking about the new exhibit at the art museum, and I was wondering if you'd like to go see it this evening. We could grab dinner before, if you want."

Dahlia wiped her sweaty palms on her denim shorts. She liked Robbie, as a friend. She enjoyed his company, as a friend. She did want to see the art exhibit and try a new restaurant down the street from the museum. If she could have made it into a group event, she would have. Jina and Daniel were going on their first date. Erica was having dinner with her abuelos. Dahlia couldn't—she wouldn't—just go with Robbie and Andrew. *Is my circle really that small?* she asked herself as her mind ran through all the options.

She didn't want to lead him on, but also didn't want to outright reject him when Andrew could hear them. So, she said, "I think I have plans tonight."

"Really?" he asked, surprised. "With who? Daniel said he's taking Jina out tonight, and you said yesterday your mom has another date with some guy also."

Part of her was annoyed that he was questioning her, that he paid so much attention to her life, and part of her was embarrassed that even he knew how small her circle was. Andrew was on the verge of interrupting, to keep her from having to come up with an excuse, but Dahlia suddenly remembered she had sisters and that she should spend more time with them.

"I'm going to visit Violet," she said, relieved she had thought of something. And it wasn't a lie. She really had just determined to go see her older sister. "We haven't had any time to hang out since she announced her pregnancy, and I really should start working on plans for a baby shower. Maybe a group of us can go to the museum sometime soon."

Andrew was certain she had put an emphasis on the word *group*, and he was happy his hat was covering the huge smile on his face.

—

Violet and Adam lived in a cookie-cutter suburban neighborhood about thirty minutes away from Dahlia. They had been married for eight years, and had known each other since college. They were best friends, and their relationship was an easy one. Dahlia never minded being their third wheel, and they didn't mind having her around, so they weren't the least bit bothered or inconvenienced when she texted last minute about coming over for dinner.

"Come in, come in," Adam greeted her, opening the door before she knocked. "I'll be out back at the grill. Violet's in the baby's room." He flashed a big smile, so ready to enter the realms of fatherhood.

"Knock, knock," Dahlia said as she peered around the corner of the door frame to find Violet sitting in a rocking chair, staring out the window. As she took in the size of Violet's growing belly, she realized she had been absentminded, even uncaring —her entire family had. Why had none of them expressed more excitement at the pregnancy news? Internally, she was thrilled, but she hadn't fully shown that to her sister. "I'm sorry I didn't come sooner. I'm sorry everyone's been caught up in the two weddings," she said as she entered the room and sat on the floor at her sister's feet.

"They have been quite a distraction," Violet said with a light laugh.

"But this little one," Dahlia said, placing her hand on Violet's stomach, "is a much sweeter distraction."

"Yes. And let's hope this baby does not have a flair for the dramatic like mom or Lily."

"That will be my daily prayer."

After a moment, Violet asked, "What did you think of Morgan?"

"What did *you* think? You didn't say much in the group text with Lily and mom."

"And you didn't say *anything*." Violet gave her a look that sarcastically said *thanks for your help.*

"You know I'd rather avoid it when they both get going. Can't talk them both off a cliff. You just have to placate them, and make them think they're right. And I don't want to do that."

"Yeah…" Violet agreed. "But, they weren't completely wrong."

"What do you mean?"

"Dad should not be marrying someone young enough to be his daughter."

"Is that your only objection?" Dahlia asked. "Did anything happen between you two in high school? She didn't seem to remember you."

"She probably doesn't. We only talked twice at a couple of parties and both times she was completely wasted."

Dahlia was surprised. "I never knew you went to parties like that."

Violet was the only one of the Marshall sisters who had lived with their dad for a while and gone to the public high school. The relationship between Violet and her mother had suffered serious conflicts during her teenage years, so Violet had chosen to live in the quiet of her father's house where she wouldn't be constantly questioned or criticized—she also wouldn't be well-parented or supervised with Alan working long and late hours at the hospital. Dahlia and Lily weren't given an option and remained with their mother, attending the private Christian school—mainly because Elaine wanted Alan to keep paying for their educations. So, Dahlia didn't know much about Violet's high school days. They didn't have much of a relationship until Dahlia was in her early twenties; before that, she hadn't really known her sister at all.

Violet nodded. "For a few months my freshman year, I dated a senior. He took me to the parties. I did things I should have never done. I just made bad decisions during that time, and seeing Morgan reminds me of them."

Dahlia wanted to ask what kind of bad decisions, suddenly curious about the life her sister had lived when they'd been separated. She'd only ever seen Violet as the near-perfect, first born, honor student who excelled in all she attempted. But before Dahlia could decide whether to press for more information, Violet changed the subject, and they spent the rest of the evening discussing nursery design and baby shower themes.

—

Erica knew Dahlia and Jina viewed her as a boy-crazy younger sister. They never said that, but she could tell from their facial expressions and comments. But she wasn't as guy-obsessed as it may have seemed. She definitely wanted to find love—just like every other girl she knew—but even more than that she wanted to please her family, and what mattered to the family was building the family—through marriage and babies.

The summer she graduated from high school, her parents had moved to Mexico to start a non-profit ministry, so she lived in the apartment above her grandparents' garage. After class that Friday evening, she sat on the sofa in their house, holding her cousin's newborn. The baby slept soundly even with his siblings running around, screaming and hollering. She loved her nieces and nephews. She loved babies. But did she want her own already? Was she ready to be a mother? Would she even be a good wife? These were the questions she constantly wrestled with, and she never uttered them to anyone but Jesus. Because that's what everyone else told her she was called to do.

Her abuelo sat in his chair beside her, and she strained to hear his words over the playful, but shrill, shrieks of the children. She could only make out every few words, but that was enough for her to know he was telling her, again, it was time to settle down and start a family. It reminded her of a post she had just seen online. One of the teenagers from the church youth group had written a question asking older women what their one piece of advice would be for a woman in her early twenties. Erica fit that description, so she naturally paid attention. One of the first comments, from a thirty-something mother in the church, was: *marry young and start a family!*

When Erica read it, tears had immediately started running down her cheeks. She felt ridiculous for crying, but the pressure was too much. That advice was outside of a young woman's control. *A woman can't just decide she's ready to be married, and then a selection of potential grooms will appear for her to choose from,* Erica had argued in her head. *It doesn't always work out like that. Maybe it's not supposed to. God has different plans and purposes for everyone. A young woman should find out who she is in Christ, and let Him direct her steps, whether they included marriage and motherhood or not.* That's what she told herself, what she knew to be true, and what she was tempted to type in response to the older woman's advice. But the doubts and the pressure would always creep back in. Like when she had heard Daniel and Jina were going on a date. She did sincerely feel happy for Jina, but just a tinge sad for herself, once again feeling unchosen.

Erica's cousin was next to her on the couch, trying to console her fussy two-year-old. Even though she would never trade her husband or her children for anything, she secretly wanted to tell Erica to take her time. "Abuelo," she interrupted him, "how great is it that Erica's going to graduate from nursing school at the end of the year?"

Before he could respond, their abuela called from the kitchen. Dinner was ready.

Chapter Eight

Dahlia stayed up reading one of her favorite novels, springing up to peek out the window every time she heard a car door close in the hope that Jina was home. She wanted to hear everything about their first date. But when she hadn't returned by eleven, Dahlia texted to make sure she was all right—she was, of course, more than all right—and then went to bed so she could be up early to go to Ms. Anna's.

When Jina came knocking at six the next morning, Dahlia wondered if her friend had slept at all. "Very little," Jina admitted. "Got home at midnight, woke up at four. Tossed and turned all night. I was really just too wired to sleep. So, here. I brought you breakfast for waking you up this early."

With groggy eyes, Dahlia took the bagel and garden vegetable cream cheese, sat on the couch, and pulled a blanket over her lap. "Okay, you've got thirty minutes. Tell me everything."

Jina described their date in detail from beginning to end, never ceasing to smile. Dahlia thought her cheeks must be hurting. "First, we went to this delicious, gorgeous Italian restaurant for dinner. Then, we walked around downtown and just talked for a couple of hours, getting ice cream, visiting little shops, dancing in the square where some musicians were playing."

Dahlia couldn't help but smile too, imagining them slow dancing together. "I hope my texting didn't cause too much interruption," she apologized.

"Oh, no," Jina assured her. "It was good you messaged. It brought me back to reality, and we headed to the car shortly after that." She was quiet for a few moments, trying to remember what else she wanted to share, and Dahlia waited patiently, knowing new memories would surface for days to come as her friend repeated the date over and over in her mind, memorizing every detail. Finally, she said, "Oh! Did you know their grandmother is Korean?"

Dahlia gave her a doubtful look. "They certainly don't *look* Korean."

Jina laughed. "Their *step*-grandmother, but she's been around all of their lives. After their grandparents divorced, their grandfather was stationed in South Korea for a while, and he came home with a new wife. No wonder Daniel knew so much about Korean food and culture."

"That's interesting," Dahlia mused. "So, Daniel and Andrew's dads are brothers? I saw they have the same last name on their volunteer forms yesterday."

"Yes, that's right. Sommer. Jina Han Sommer, has a nice flow to it."

Dahlia narrowed her eyes at her best friend. "Be careful. Don't get too far ahead. It's only been a week."

"I know," Jina said. "I'm trying not to. Why do girls have to be like this—dreaming of weddings before first dates?"

Dahlia shrugged her shoulders. "I don't know." She really didn't, and she hated it. Any time she caught such thoughts in her head, she would squash them quickly, pray them away, and then try to focus on something else. Luckily, she hadn't struggled with that in a long time; it had been years since she'd met a man who inspired her to try his last name with her first. "I don't know if we *have* to be like this," she added. "But I don't know any of us who aren't."

Jina sighed, desperately trying not to like Daniel too much too soon. Especially when her mother was always in the back of her mind, reminding her of Steve's impending visit.

—

As they pulled up to Ms. Anna's house, Jina asked, "Do you think Robbie will come today? I mean, after you *rejected* him." She said it with a lighthearted smile, but it made Dahlia uneasy.

"Please don't say it like that," Dahlia said. "I didn't want to reject him or hurt him in any way."

"I know. I didn't mean it. He never called it a date, and we'll just hope it doesn't come up again. Otherwise, our lunches are going to become really uncomfortable."

Dahlia's eyes went wide at the thought of it. "Please, Lord Jesus, let him be content just as a friend."

As Daniel approached the car, it was plain the date had a similar effect on him. He didn't appear to have gotten much sleep, but somehow his eyes were bright, and his cheerful disposition was still intact. Daniel and Andrew went to work on the roof, repairing a few small sections. After their grandfather had retired from the military, Jina explained, he had started a construction company, and he had passed on his skills to all his grandchildren, male and female. Chris and Jina wanted to learn, so they helped them, and it almost gave Ms. Anna a heart attack to see Chris on the roof.

Dahlia helped her mother and Erica with the rest of the flowerbeds and bushes. On observing Jina and Daniel, they both demanded an explanation from Dahlia. Elaine wanted to know because it would make her happy to see Jina finding romance; Erica wanted to know because it would make her sad that she had not. "Are they in love or something?" Erica asked sarcastically.

Dahlia smiled and joked, "Maybe. They had their first date last night."

Ms. Anna, overhearing from her spot on the porch, asked, "Who did?"

"Jina and Daniel," Erica said without enthusiasm.

"Oh, well isn't that something," she said in her soothing voice. "It's always nice to fall in love in the springtime."

Dahlia smiled at the old woman she loved and admired. "Is that when you and Mr. Thompson fell in love?"

"Oh, yes," she said, the wrinkles around her eyes and mouth becoming more prominent with the big grin on her face. "And we were married a few months later in the heat of summer."

Elaine said, "Dahlia's father and I married too quickly too."

"Oh, honey," Ms. Anna said with a chuckle, "it wasn't quick enough for me." All three of her listeners blushed and laughed.

When they took a break for lunch, Jina, Daniel, and Andrew were sitting at the kitchen table eating sandwiches. Daniel and Jina were carrying on their own discussion, almost forgetting anyone else was in the room, but Andrew didn't feel left out. He was more interested in the conversation happening at the counter behind him where Ms. Anna was asking Dahlia about meeting her father's fiancée.

"Well, there is quite an age gap," Dahlia was explaining. "She's only a few years older than Violet, and they actually went to the same high school, so that's a little strange. I'm sure it will be interesting, but she seemed nice enough, so far."

"Don't let the age thing cause problems," Ms. Anna cautioned. "You know my George was several years older than me."

"I know." Dahlia smiled. "I've seen your wedding pictures. He wasn't old enough to be your father though. It was just surprising. I don't really have a problem with it, I guess."

"Well, I do!" exclaimed Elaine as she entered the room, fanning herself and dabbing sweat from her brow. "Who does he think he is? Going after some young woman in her thirties! I *know* why he likes her, but what in the world could she see in him?"

Jina was paying attention to their conversation now too, knowing her friend would be so embarrassed.

"Now Elaine," Ms. Anna said, "he must have some good qualities or you would have never married him yourself."

"His good qualities were all physical, and they blinded me from seeing his bad ones for too many years. I mean, look at Dahlia," she stood behind her daughter and caressed her wavy hair. "Her dark hair and blue eyes. At least his physical qualities got passed on to this one. I *can't wait* to meet his new lady at Lily's engagement party, so I can fill her in on what she's getting herself into."

At this remark Dahlia had heard enough. She was so frustrated and mortified that the knife she was using slipped and cut her palm. She cried out, more in shock than pain. Tears welled up in her eyes, not from the cut, but from her mother's words. She blinked them back even though it burned to do so.

Andrew jumped quickly to his feet and grabbed a bunch of paper towels, taking her hand and applying pressure to try and stop the bleeding, while Ms. Anna left to retrieve her first aid kit. After Elaine examined it and saw that it wouldn't require stitches, she grabbed the glasses of lemonade she had originally come inside to get, and then she left. But not without saying, "Dahlia, please be more careful."

Andrew was still holding Dahlia's hand when the screen door slammed shut behind her mother. Blood had already soaked through every layer of paper towels. "Are you okay?" Jina asked, coming to stand beside her.

Dahlia nodded. "I've got it, thanks," she said as she pulled her hand from Andrew, turning away so he could not see her face, not in the mood to be scrutinized by him.

When Ms. Anna returned to bandage her up, Andrew decided to go outside and find Chris. The kitchen was too small for so many people. He had not been that close to Dahlia before, and he was overwhelmed by how much he realized he liked her. He had been acutely aware of the way she flinched when her mother started playing with her hair, and the tears in her blue eyes—even though she'd tried to hide them—and the fact that Elaine's comments always seemed to upset her.

—

The next afternoon while Jina, Daniel, Andrew and Erica went to lunch after church, Dahlia was scheduled to meet her mother and sisters at the bridal shop to find Lily a wedding dress. The entire drive she prayed there would be no drama or harsh words; she asked instead for a peaceful, happy time with her family, which was rare, but possible.

Dahlia met Violet in the parking lot as they saw Lily's car pull into a spot.

"What's Brian doing with her?" Violet asked.

Dahlia shrugged. "Maybe he's just dropping her off."

But they both exited the car, holding hands as they approached and greeted the two sisters.

"Is Brian staying?" Violet asked, clearly trying not to sound rude with her tone, but Dahlia knew how traditional Violet was about the groom not seeing the wedding dress before the ceremony.

"Yeah," Lily said. "He wants to help."

With his arm around her shoulder and a sloppy kiss on her cheek, Brian added, "Gotta make sure my girl looks good."

Before she could stop herself, Dahlia said, "And you don't think she can do that on her own?"

It wasn't that she cared about tradition like Violet. She didn't care if grooms came to be supportive, but she felt like, for Brian, it was possibly just a way to exert control.

"Hey, if Lily wants me here, I'm gonna be here," he said.

Dahlia didn't think Lily really wanted him there. She had always talked about surprising her future husband when she walked down the aisle, but Lily smiled and assured Brian that she was happy for him to come to the appointment. Her two older sisters looked at each other, doubtful, as they all entered the building. Their mother was sitting in the waiting area.

When Brian excused himself to the bathroom, Elaine asked, "Have you talked to your father about the wedding budget and how much he is paying?"

Lily hesitated. "No…I assumed it would be the same as with Violet's wedding."

They were all silent for a moment, then Violet said, "Adam and I paid for our wedding."

"What?" Lily asked, surprised. "Daddy didn't pay for your wedding?"

"Well, he offered…but we wanted to do it ourselves."

Lily looked like she might cry. "Did you realize what kind of precedent you were setting for me and Dahlia? Brian and I can't afford to pay for the whole wedding."

"I'm sure he won't expect you to," Dahlia said, putting a hand on Lily's shoulder. "He'll offer to help, just like he did with Violet."

"I doubt it," Lily said, resentful. "He has his own wedding to pay for now."

Dahlia and Violet exchanged glances, fearing the appointment was going downhill before it even began and annoyed that their mother had waited until then to ask about the budget.

"Oh, he'll pay for this wedding," Elaine said with a determination all of them dreaded when it came to their parents communicating. "I'll make sure of it."

"You won't need to," Violet said firmly. "I'm certain he will help on his own without a word from you. If you find a dress today, you only need to put down a deposit, and *we* can talk to dad later about the budget." The *we* was intended to exclude their mother, and Violet gave her a look that told her so.

Just then Brian returned from the bathroom and plopped down in the seat beside Lily. "They haven't called us back yet? The appointment should have started ten minutes ago."

Elaine shushed him, embarrassed by his words and how loud he was with them. She networked with the bridal shop, and the owners and consultants recommended her as a florist to all of their brides. They had specifically made time for Lily that day even though they were fully booked.

The consultant took them back, and she pulled a few dresses with varying silhouettes so Lily could figure out what she liked best, but Dahlia knew her younger sister's princess heart was drawn to ballgowns; she had talked about them for years. When Lily appeared in the ballgown, her face was bright, her smile almost hesitant—she wanted everyone else to love it as much as she did. All of the women thought she looked stunning, exactly how they'd always imagined she would look on her wedding day, but Brian said, "Oh, no. This one doesn't flatter you at all."

Instantly, in unison all the women's necks snapped in his direction, as they looked at him in disbelief and shock. But he ignored their stares and stood to examine Lily more closely. "You don't think so?" she asked him, running her hands over the skirt.

"You look absolutely beautiful, Lily," Elaine said and her daughters spoke up in agreement. They agreed on something.

"It's fine," Brian said. "But you can't see her figure."

Lily had a curvier figure than both her sisters, and he wanted it to show.

"So, you want to try something more form-fitting?" the consultant asked Lily. "We can do that next."

She tried on a dozen dresses, but Brian had something critical to say about every one of them. It solidified Violet's opinion that the groom should *not* be there, but Dahlia just thought that *Lily's* groom shouldn't be there. Elaine had to bite her tongue more than once, but she did fuss with Brian a good deal, arguing with his opinions. And in the end, Lily was thoroughly confused. She had known what she wanted, but too many voices had muddled her own.

As the appointment was drawing to a close, Brian stood up and said he had to leave. "Where are you going?" Lily asked, caught off guard at his abrupt departure.

"I've gotta meet up with Eric to talk about our next work project," he said. "I can take your car, right?"

"How will I get home?"

He gestured to her mother and sisters. "One of them can take you, can't they?"

She looked from him to her family, feeling embarrassed. Dahlia could tell, so she said, "I'll take you home."

"Okay, great." He stepped up to where Lily stood, still in a slinky silk wedding gown, and kissed her before heading toward the front entrance. Lily disappeared to get changed before anyone could say anything.

They didn't even speak to each other in her absence, although they all had plenty of thoughts.

Violet and Dahlia didn't want to say anything that would trigger their mother to go on a tangent, and Elaine was trying her best to respect her daughter's fiancé even though she was frustrated with him.

On the ride home, Lily asked, "Do you think I'll find the right dress? Was I being too picky?"

Your fiancé was, Dahlia thought. And she hated that his comments had left a typically confident Lily feeling insecure. "We'll find you the right dress," she assured her. *If Brian doesn't come again,* she added in her head. Dahlia figured now was the best time to have a serious conversation with Lily. She was strapped in a moving vehicle, couldn't leave, and couldn't avoid it.

"Lily, does Brian consider himself a Christian?" she asked.

"What do you mean?" Lily asked. "I wouldn't date someone who wasn't Christian."

"But…how strong is his relationship with Jesus?" Dahlia asked gently. She knew Lily's relationship with Jesus was lukewarm at best and nominal at worst, but was she marrying a man who would bring her closer to Him? From what she had just observed, she didn't think so.

"He grew up going to church. His parents' pastor is officiating the wedding…" she said. "I don't know why you're asking these questions."

"Have y'all talked about spiritual things?"

Instead of answering, Lily asked, "Do you not *like* Brian?"

"I barely know him. But I don't *like* the way he treated you today."

"How did he treat me?" she asked defensively. "Everything was fine. You just don't understand him. That's just who he is."

"Is he always that critical?" She wanted to add that he was rude and arrogant too, but she didn't.

"Really, Dahlia?" Lily asked in anger. "Aren't you the one being critical? Judge not, that you be not judged."

"Don't take that verse out of context," Dahlia said. "Jesus is instructing us on how to judge rightly—he's not saying *not* to judge. And I *will* judge the man who's going to marry my little sister."

"Well…then maybe you won't be in the wedding party, if you can't be supportive."

"Really?" Dahlia asked. "Because I'm asking questions to make sure you're marrying the right person? Because I don't want to see you end up in an unhealthy marriage? Or divorced like our parents? Because I don't want you to get married just because you think that's the next step? Because I love you and want the best for you?"

Lily threw herself back against her seat and crossed her arms, staring out the window. "Everyone else likes him. You're the only one with a problem."

Dahlia remained silent. She doubted whether everyone else liked him. Even her mom had seemed bothered by him at times, and although their dad said he liked Brian, he had only met him once or twice. She could tell from her Violet's facial expressions during the appointment that she also had similar doubts about his character.

The only thing Lily said was, "Thanks for the ride," when she slammed the car door behind her.

Chapter Nine

Lily didn't speak to Dahlia the rest of the week. Whenever her mother or sisters would send something in their group text, Lily would respond separately to Violet and Elaine only. It took a while for their mother to pick up on it, but when she did, she would not stop asking about what happened, why Lily was mad at Dahlia, and when Lily finally broke down and told her, she was furious with her middle child. Elaine called Dahlia while she was at work and left an angry voicemail, yelling about how she had no right to question another person's religious beliefs and how dare she ruin this special time for Lily.

That day Jina found Dahlia crying in her classroom after school. "What happened?" she asked with concern. Dahlia replayed the voicemail for her to listen. Jina had known Elaine almost her entire life, so she wasn't surprised by anything she heard, but she knew how much it hurt Dahlia not to have any immediate family members who understood her and her faith. Any time she tried to have conversations about it and encourage them in *their* faith, they took it as judgment or criticism. It was moments like these Jina was grateful to be an only child. She said softly, "I'm sorry, friend."

Dahlia shrugged, wiping her tears away. "They just don't *get it*. They don't get *me*," she said, and she internally decided she wouldn't say another word about Jesus to them unless they asked—unless the Spirit commanded it. She would just try her best, by the power of the Spirit, to show Him to them through her actions. She'd had to do that several times over the years—say a few things and then retreat—because they never seemed able to receive truth from her, like she wasn't the right person to give them the message. She never said it right, or they always heard it wrong.

She didn't call her mother back—she didn't know what to say to her—and Elaine hadn't asked her to. But she did send a text to Lily, apologizing for anything she said that may have hurt her and explaining that her intentions had only been to care for and protect her sister. All Lily replied was, "Ok."

But when Saturday rolled around, all three sisters were scheduled to meet Morgan at a bridal shop in Rome to get fitted for bridesmaids dresses. Even though Morgan barely knew them, and even though her wedding was going to be very small, she still wanted to include them and hoped it would be a bonding experience for all of them. She was unaware that, at that moment, Lily was not interested in bonding with Dahlia. Though Violet *was* aware, she stayed out of it. She didn't understand why Dahlia had found it necessary to ask questions about Brian's beliefs, but she also didn't really care for Brian either, so she remained neutral and maneuvered her way through the tension.

When they entered the salon, they didn't expect to find the groomsmen there also—their father's two brothers, Uncle Bob and Uncle Pat, both of whom were adored by their nieces, and Morgan's brother, Michael. Lily nudged Violet, and whispered, "Did you go to high school with him too?"

Violet shook her head. "Maybe, but I don't remember him."

Michael overheard them, and with a smile said, "You wouldn't. I'm seven years younger than Morgan."

"And he always likes to remind me of it," she said, pushing his shoulder.

Michael was tall and fit with blond hair and blue eyes—the complete opposite of his sister.

"I'm just wondering…but…" Lily began, not sure how to ask her question.

"Why is he white?" Morgan finished it for her. "I'm sure he asks himself that all the time." She laughed, and Michael rolled his eyes. Dahlia was amused at the interaction between them. After a moment, Morgan explained, "My parents couldn't have children, so they adopted me from Haiti. But seven years later, they were blessed with a pregnancy, and along came Michael." She said it kindly, but it was obvious she had spent her whole life repeating those same sentences, explaining their differences.

Michael was easy to talk to, because he did most of the talking. He had a friendly openness and sense of humor that quickly brought levity to the event, which would have otherwise been tense, and he made all the party members feel comfortable with one another almost immediately. All of the Marshall girls were delighted to make his acquaintance.

The men were taken to one side of the store; the women were ushered in the other direction. Their biggest concern was for Violet and her growing stomach. "By your wedding, Morgan, I will be five months," she said. "And by yours, Lily, I may barely be able to walk, let alone feel comfortable in a bridesmaid's dress."

"Well, we can't do it any sooner," Lily declared. "Brian's parents won't be back from France until then, and if we do it any later, it will be too cold."

"I wasn't suggesting you change the date," Violet said. "But maybe I shouldn't be in the wedding party."

Lily's eyes got huge at this idea. "I already have one sister who may work herself out of the wedding party, so you most definitely have to be in it, even if we have to push you down the aisle in a wheelchair."

Violet shook her head. "That won't be necessary. We'll make it work."

Dahlia wanted to come to her defense, to tell Lily how selfish she sounded, but it would only make things worse. Lily hadn't said a word to her, and Violet didn't like when Dahlia interfered in their interactions. Trying to smooth out the friction, Morgan said, "You'll look beautiful in these dresses with your pregnant belly. You're tall with so much space for the baby, I don't think your belly will get that big anyway."

Violet smiled politely. "I hope you're right."

After everyone was measured for their individual wedding attire, Morgan invited them all to come back to the house for the rest of the afternoon to hang out and have dinner. "But I need to go to the grocery store to get some things that I forgot," she said.

"I can do that for you," Dahlia said. "Just tell me what you need."

As Morgan rummaged through her purse for the tiny piece of paper, Michael also offered to help. "I'll come with you."

Violet and Lily gave each other insinuating looks. Dahlia noticed, narrowed her eyes and shook her head at them, definitely not romantically interested in her future stepmother's brother.

—

The entire ride to the store was full of easy conversation and laughter. Michael was quick-witted with a funny and charming sense of humor. And Dahlia loved to laugh, which made him feel very good about himself. She thought he would be a welcome addition to future family gatherings.

While they waited at the butcher's counter for the specific cuts of meat Morgan had requested, Michael became impatient, though he hid it well, and Dahlia didn't notice at all. He was full of energy and wanted to get back to the house. "Let me get whatever else we need while you wait here," he suggested.

"All we have left are these salad dressings." She showed him the list; he glanced at it for a second and walked off with the basket in hand.

A few moments later, someone called her name. "Dahlia."

She knew the voice and turned around. "Andrew. Hi. What brings you here?" It was strange seeing him there. The people from her *home* life rarely overlapped with the people from her *Rome* life.

"Just visiting family for the weekend. You?" He was happy to run into her. He hadn't been able to attend the Thursday night study and had missed seeing her, had missed an opportunity to know her better.

"Pretty much the same," she said. "Had to help my dad's fiancée with some wedding stuff."

"Oh. How's that going?"

She understood he was inquiring not about the wedding planning, but about how she was dealing with the new family dynamics. But before she could answer him, Michael came around the corner with two different bottles of salad dressing, asking which one was correct. When he looked up and saw Andrew, he froze for a second. Andrew also appeared shocked, his jaw clinched, a stern and confused expression on his face.

Michael recovered first. "Hey man, how's it going?" He reached out to shake Andrew's hand, but Andrew simply looked at him, ignoring his outstretched arm. After an awkward moment, he turned to Dahlia and repeated his question about the salad dressing, and then walked off quickly to return the wrong bottle, grateful for an excuse to leave.

Once he was out of sight, Andrew relaxed slightly. "What are you doing with him?" he demanded, his tone catching Dahlia off guard.

"His sister is marrying my dad," she replied, more timidly than she wanted. "We're just getting some things for dinner tonight." *Why do I have to explain myself to him, and what does he have against Michael?* she wondered.

"*Morgan* is marrying your dad?" His eyes widened in surprise.

Dahlia nodded, and they were silent for a long moment, neither sure what to say next.

Finally, he spoke a warning. "Be careful around him."

"Why?" she asked, genuinely curious.

Michael was coming back down the aisle from the opposite end, hoping Andrew would take the hint and get lost. Andrew didn't have time, nor did he want, to answer her question, so he simply said, "It was good seeing you," and then headed toward the frozen food section.

When Michael came up beside her, he asked, "Do you know that guy?"

"Yeah, and he seems to know you," she said, suddenly suspicious and on edge, feeling the need to *be careful*.

"We used to know each other, a long time ago. We grew up down the street from one another." When she didn't respond, he added, "Why? What did he tell you?"

"Nothing really," she said, now unsure about trusting Michael. "How come you two seem to hate each other?"

"I don't hate him. I just think he feels bad," he confessed. "He hates himself for what he did to me."

She asked slowly, "What did he do to you?"

"Like I said, we grew up together, went to high school together, were on the same soccer team. He was angry with me because the girl he liked wanted to date me, so one day during practice, he came at me really hard, permanently injured my knee. I wasn't able to get a scholarship to play in college."

"Wow, I'm sorry that happened," Dahlia said.

"Hey, it's all in the past now. I've forgiven him. I just don't think he can forgive himself."

"Well, did you end up going to college?"

"No. My parents couldn't afford it after they blew all their money on a divorce, and my grades weren't good enough for an academic scholarship."

"What do you do now?" she asked.

"I did some odd jobs for a few years until I became a personal trainer. Even if I had gone to college, I still think this is where I would have ended up. So, in the long run, it saved time and money." He smiled, and it seemed genuine.

"I'm glad you can be so positive about it, and that you have forgiven Andrew." She was quiet for a moment before adding, "He had no right to be so rude to you back there."

"Oh, you know Andrew! A man of few words."

"That's no excuse."

Michael desired to change the subject. "You know, I'll be your step uncle in a couple of months!"

"That won't be weird at all," Dahlia said sarcastically.

When they got back to her father's house, Brian was also pulling into the driveway. From Brian's demeanor it was clear Lily had told him everything Dahlia had said, although Dahlia was sure it had been shared in a twisted and dramatic way, out of context, the intentions of her heart not properly conveyed. Michael seemed to notice there was something odd between them, and he quickly introduced himself and began talking to Brian like they were old friends; Dahlia realized that was what it was about Michael that made people comfortable so quickly—his easy manner made you feel like you had known him forever.

They wasted no time joining everyone else on the back patio; in fact, Dahlia carried the groceries in by herself because they walked off, perhaps forgetting about her, but when Michael winked at her over his shoulder, she realized it was his way of sparing her from Brian. Morgan greeted her in the kitchen, apologizing for her brother's lack of assistance. "I'm used to doing things on my own. It's no problem," she said. *He did me a favor*, she thought.

Dahlia helped Morgan make a salad and prepare the food for the grill. Then she brought it outside for her father to cook. He gave her a big hug, more affectionate than usual. "I just want to thank you," he said quietly, "for being so kind and helpful to Morgan. She and I both appreciate it."

—

After dinner, everyone walked around the property, surveying the grounds and talking about possible layouts for Lily's wedding, while Dahlia stayed behind to help Morgan work on her wedding invitations.

As she addressed an envelope to Morgan's mother, she said, "Michael mentioned your parents are divorced too."

"Yes," she admitted with a solemn face. "They divorced when I was in high school. I was nervous when Violet said she knew me from those days—I don't remember her—but I don't think she has a good opinion of me. I was awful back then, acting out against my parents. I know I developed a bad reputation, and I continued to make horrible mistakes into my early twenties."

"Violet hasn't said anything about your bad reputation," Dahlia assured her. *She just mentioned her own bad mistakes,* Dahlia thought. "I always think it was probably a good thing my parents divorced when I was younger, or maybe I would have acted the same way you did."

"Divorce isn't pretty no matter what age you are," she said, speaking from experience. "Thankfully Jesus was able to help me heal not only from my parents' divorce, but also from my own."

Her remark took Dahlia by surprise. Her father never talked about God, and aside from his specialty handcrafted nativity scenes at Christmas time, he didn't appear to care much for Jesus. But here he was, marrying a woman who naturally brought Him up in conversation.

"Morgan, you mentioned last week that you went to church?"

She nodded. "You know, I even got your father to go to with me the past few Sundays."

"Really? I bet he hated it." She had practically begged him to come to her baptism several years earlier.

"Oh, I don't know. He's not so against it as you may think. He speaks very highly of your faith and relationship with Christ. Not that he would use those words."

"He's never expressed that to me." Dahlia was deep in thought about these new revelations. A couple minutes passed in silence as they continued stuffing and stamping envelopes. "Morgan, do you mind if I ask you a question? And, I mean no judgment by it."

"Shoot."

"Why would you marry my father when he doesn't share your beliefs?"

"Dahlia, do you know how your father and I met?"

"Y'all said through an online dating site."

"Sort of," she paused, hesitant if she should tell Dahlia so much. "Alan was meeting a woman for lunch at the restaurant where I where I was working on the weekends. He was meeting a woman he had met online, but she never showed. I watched him sit at that table for two hours waiting for someone who never came. So, when my shift ended, I asked if I could join him, to keep him company while he waited. That's the excuse I gave him, anyway. Really it just made me sad to see him alone, knowing that lady, whoever she was, wasn't coming. We ended up talking for hours. I don't want you to think your father was trolling the online dating sites looking for younger women. He wasn't. He's a respectable, good man.

"As for him not sharing our beliefs, I have high hopes that he will in time. We've had great discussions, and he's very open to the Truth." She paused, listening to make sure nobody was around, "I'm only telling you this because I trust you will keep it to yourself. Alan thought it might upset the others. We are already married. I made it clear I wouldn't live with him unless we were married, so we did it at the courthouse the day before I moved in here."

Dahlia's eyes widened in surprise. "Wow. I was not expecting that."

"Yeah. I wasn't expecting to tell you, but I'm glad I did. I hope you won't tell your sisters. Or your mother. Not that I want to sow secrets in your family.

If you feel the need to tell them, you can—we can deal with any consequences."

"Definitely not." Dahlia shook her head. She would tell no one. It wasn't her secret to share.

"Thank you." Morgan smiled, her bright white teeth gleaming.

They were quiet for a few more minutes, and then Dahlia asked, "Do you plan to have children with my dad?"

"No." She paused, then added, "I can't have children."

"Oh," Dahlia felt bad for asking. "I'm sorry."

"Don't feel bad. I've known for years, so I've accepted it." She decided to tell her more. "Like I said, I was married once before, in my early twenties. It was an abusive relationship, and when we learned I couldn't have children, he left me. Not being able to get pregnant actually saved me; I probably never would have left him. I didn't think I could live without him. It was after that when I realized the only person I can't live without is Jesus."

Dahlia felt special that Morgan found her worthy to know these details about her life. "Thank you for sharing that with me," she said with sincere gratitude.

"Of course. You're easy to talk to, and I think you're the only one here who can fully appreciate what I've said."

Dahlia nodded in understanding, delighted from the bottom of her soul that there was going to be a member of her family that she could talk to about Christ and know that they were on the same page, someone who *would* get her.

Everyone returned from outside, bringing their loudness with them, disturbing the peaceful quiet moments that the two believers had just shared.

Before they all left for the evening, Lily issued an invitation to her engagement party to Michael. "You must come," she insisted, then narrowing her eyes at Dahlia, "because I know my sister is not going to bring a date like I requested, so you can be her dance partner!"

He agreed to be in attendance and spare Dahlia the shame of being solo for every dance.

"Thanks, uncle!" she said sarcastically as she clapped him on the shoulder.

"Anytime," he smiled.

Dahlia decided she liked Morgan—and her brother.

Chapter Ten

During the weeks following their first date, Jina and Daniel saw each other several more times, often just the two of them, sometimes with Dahlia and Andrew in tow. Dahlia firmly believed that it didn't matter if Jina's future husband was Korean or not—the only non-negotiable for him was that he loved and followed Jesus. But Jina still worried about whether her mother would approve, and she knew their relationship was coming to a decision-making point. She hadn't told her mother about Daniel—honestly, she didn't know how to even begin the conversation—and thankfully, Ms. Yoon hadn't stopped by unannounced any time during their courtship. Whenever Ms. Yoon spoke eagerly of her daughter's impending meeting with doctor Steve, Jina was always quiet, neither encouraging nor discouraging her.

"What have you told Daniel about your mom's matchmaking?" Dahlia asked her.

"He knows that she has introduced me to people before and sent me on blind dates. But I haven't mentioned Steve."

"What are you planning on doing?" Dahlia was anxious not just for Jina's feelings, but also for Daniel's. She now considered him a friend and didn't want to see him hurt either.

"At this point, Daniel and I haven't discussed being exclusive. So, I can just have dinner with Steve and tell him it's not going to work out." She paused, in thought. "Mama will be disappointed, but I'm used to disappointing her."

"And if Daniel asks you to be exclusive before then?" Dahlia asked. Personally, she felt like he should know about Steve either way.

"Then I'll have to cancel the meeting with Steve."

Both of them sat in silence as they imagined how upset Ms. Yoon would be after weeks of anticipation and planning.

Jina asked, "You don't think there's any way Lily or your mom would have invited my mom to the engagement party, do you?"

"No, although she probably should have been invited..." Dahlia said. "I helped with the guest list and invitations. Your mom wasn't on it, and I can't see how she'd know about it unless you told her."

"I didn't." She sighed, relieved. "I asked Daniel to be my date."

"Okay..." Dahlia was hesitant, concerned Jina was being too careless.

"What?" Jina demanded. "You don't think I should have?"

"If Daniel is someone you want to have a future with, and I can see that you do, you need to tell your mom. I know that when I have something to tell my mom that she won't like, it's better to tell her in advance, so she has time to adjust to the idea."

Jina didn't say a word. She knew Dahlia was right. She also knew her mother could be frightening to oppose. When it came to her mother, she knew she had too much fear of man, and that was where she found herself in constant repentance. Dahlia said no more on the subject, trusting that if her friend cared for Daniel the way she thought she did, she would do what was necessary sooner rather than later.

Throughout this time, whenever Andrew and Dahlia were brought together by the desires of his cousin and her friend, Andrew's admiration for Dahlia continued to increase. The silliness he'd first judged harshly, he now enjoyed; her laughter made him smile. Hearing her laugh was so much better than seeing tears in her eyes. He appreciated the passion with which she spoke about Jesus and the care she expressed for her students, her family, and her community.

She was completely unaware of this, and she found it hard to reconcile the young man from Michael's account with the man who sat across the table from her. Michael had forgiven his wrongdoing, so she couldn't hold the offense against him, but it did affect her opinion of him, and she still held to her first impressions of him being judgmental and hard to read. When she caught him staring at her, she took it as scrutiny—not admiration—and she tried her best not to be self-conscious about his opinion of her.

—

The night before Lily and Brian's engagement party, Elaine invited Violet and Dahlia to her house for dinner. She wanted them to meet her new boyfriend Walter and to assist with decorating for the event. Before they could ring the doorbell, their mother opened the front door. "Come in, come in," she greeted them, rushing them inside. "Walter isn't here yet, and I need help finishing dinner."

The sisters glanced at each other with surprise. "Mom, are you really cooking?" Violet asked. Elaine wasn't known for her skills in the kitchen; she was much better with garden tools than cooking utensils. Usually if she wanted to impress someone, she ordered out.

"Yes, I'm cooking," she said. "Don't look so shocked. I've been practicing."

"You really like this guy, huh, mom?" Dahlia teased.

"You wouldn't be meeting him if I didn't, but don't make such a big deal out of it," she said as she practically fluttered into the kitchen. Dahlia and Violet laughed at the hypocrisy of that statement. All the time, Dahlia only wished she could tell her mother not to make such a big deal out of things. "Dahlia, please show me how you make your green beans!" She held up a bowl of fresh cut beans. "And, Violet, please tell me what you add to your mashed potatoes to make them so good."

They both obliged their mother, happy to see her in such a good mood, being so teachable and willing to listen. She proved to be a quick student, and it made both Violet and Dahlia feel good that she wanted to learn something from them. Dahlia wondered if the dynamic was different because Lily wasn't there to add to any drama or because their mother was in such a good mood because of Walter. Either way, she was happy about it.

Just as Elaine put the last place setting on the table, they heard a knock on the door. Elaine nearly jumped up and down with excitement and nerves; the girls had never seen their mother respond like that to anyone. After hearing years of bitter and angry remarks about their father, they were finally getting a glimpse of the woman she might have been at the beginning of their relationship.

When Walter entered the room, he had flowers for each of them—two small bouquets for the sisters and a much larger, elaborate one for Elaine. He had learned immediately that the best way to Elaine's heart was with beautiful flowers. She had never received such gifts from Alan—because he had always assumed she had enough flowers in her garden, the house overflowing with vases full of her own arrangements; she had assumed he would know what she wanted without having to open her mouth and tell him. A million wrong assumptions contributed to the disintegration of their marriage.

Walter had gentle eyes and a deep, soft voice, which instantly made Dahlia and Violet feel at ease. He was what Elaine referred to as a silver fox, and it was so obvious how smitten she was with him that the girls could hardly contain their smiles. Just as Dahlia had seen that Morgan had a good effect on her father, she concluded that Walter had a similar effect on her mother. It wasn't in Dahlia's nature to want to change the past or ask *what if* questions, but she couldn't help wondering for a split second why her parents couldn't have had these effects on each other and remained married.

Walter was delighted to finally meet Elaine's two oldest daughters; he had met Lily earlier in the week. He was a widower and had four grown children of his own, all were married and none lived in the same state as their father. He loved the prospect of having found a local family to be part of. The dinner was excellent, all the compliments paid to Elaine who did not bother to share any of the credit. Her daughters didn't mind as long as the huge smile remained on her face. It had been a rare occurrence throughout their childhood and adolescence to see such happiness in their mother's eyes and to hear such genuinely positive words from her lips; they would not say or do anything to jeopardize it.

But Elaine would. "Dahlia, since you won't try any dating apps, what about one of those guys who helped at Ms. Anna's house?" she asked. "Andrew seemed kind of stuffy, but what about Robbie?"

"He's my co-worker."

"Exactly. You must have a lot in common. You're both teachers, and you both clearly love your students from the way you both interacted with Chris. He's very cute too."

Dahlia didn't want to explain that they weren't compatible with their beliefs. Elaine's angry voicemail about Brian was still fresh in her mind, and she didn't want to give her mother any reason to revisit it or to accuse her of being judgmental, especially in front of Walter. So instead she said, "I'm just not interested in him like that. We're friends, that's all."

Before Elaine could say more, Violet interrupted. "Mama, let Dahlia make her own decisions about men, just like you did with me and Lily."

Elaine took a deep breath and nodded with a tight-lipped smile. She also didn't want to press further or cause any conflict with Walter present. Dahlia mouthed a thank you to Violet when their mother wasn't looking.

After dinner, they followed their mother's instructions perfectly while setting up the backyard for the engagement party. Walter did most of the heavy lifting, moving the tables and chairs to the exact locations on Elaine's floor plan. Dahlia hung the lights and arranged centerpieces, while Violet hooked up the sound system and organized the playlists. Aside from the questions about Robbie, the sisters completely enjoyed themselves that night, feeling more peace around their mother than they had in a long time. And perhaps because of Violet's words at dinner or Walter's presence, much to Dahlia's surprise and relief, Elaine never once mentioned her not having a date for the following evening. She could only wonder how long it would last.

—

Elaine's backyard always looked like a floral wonderland, but that night, beneath the string lights and lanterns, it looked magical, just as Lily dreamed it would. Everything was perfect except for the few relational issues the girls needed to monitor. All three

Marshall sisters were concerned about their parents meeting—they had not seen each other since Violet's wedding years earlier, at which point they barely maintained civility. They knew their father wouldn't say anything unless provoked, but it didn't take much to provoke him; he had a very short temper when it came to his ex-wife—and she knew it. Now that he was engaged to a much younger woman, the sisters could only imagine the kind of backhanded insults their mother might throw at him.

Other than Dahlia's prayers that everything would go smoothly, the only hope they had was that Walter would keep Elaine so distracted she would have no time to pay attention to Alan and Morgan. The only person more anxious for the evening than the girls was Morgan herself; she had even suggested she not attend, but her husband—er, fiancé—adamantly refused to accept the idea. He argued that she was part of the family now.

They also had to consider Brian's parents. His mother and father usually put on a good show, but it was no secret to his future wife's family, that their marriage stood on rocky ground. In some ways it made Lily feel better about her own dysfunctional family, but there was always concern that Brian's father would drink too much and cause a scene. Dahlia gave her dad, who was a recovered alcoholic, this information, so that he could help with Brian's dad, if necessary. All the children, including Jina, Erica, and Daniel, rallied around and came up with diversions and strategies for intervening if situations appeared to be brewing. Violet also filled Walter in on the family dynamics, knowing he would probably be the best one to intercede with Elaine.

Violet and Dahlia stood near the back gate, ready to greet guests as they entered.

"Is this how it's going to be at the wedding?" Violet whispered to Dahlia.

"Don't you remember your wedding?" Dahlia shuddered at the flashbacks.

Violet shook her head. "I mean, yes I remember my wedding, but not all the behind-the-scenes stuff."

"Well, unless you expect our parents to become best friends before October, yes, this is how it will be. But you'll be so pregnant, I'm sure nobody will bring any problems to you. When are you finding out the sex of the baby?"

"In June." They smiled at each other with giddy anticipation.

Lily and Brian were seated at a small table designed for just the two of them. Elaine and Walter were bringing the last trays of food from the kitchen. Adam swiped a couple appetizers from Elaine as she walked by him, and if she'd had a free hand, she would have playfully smacked his arm for messing up her arrangements.

Guests began piling through the gate. Dahlia hadn't realized so many names had been on the list, and she and Violet discussed whether the yard could fit them all. Elaine ordered her daughters to switch positions with her; they could maintain the food table, while she welcomed people to her home. Their father and Morgan had not arrived yet, so they really didn't want to leave their post, but Walter assured them with a wink of his eye that he would be there to make sure things went okay. They reluctantly retreated to the buffet.

Alan and Morgan appeared shortly afterward, and while Dahlia could not hear what was spoken, she observed facial expressions and tried to read lips. Elaine was definitely forcing a smile, but Morgan's was genuine. Alan and Walter shook hands, and then they moved on through.

"Hey girls," Morgan said. "How are y'all?"

Their father hugged them before going to greet Lily.

Morgan began making plates for herself and Alan, trying to make small talk with Violet about the baby. It was evident from Violet's demeanor that she was still uneasy about her, and Dahlia wished she could reveal pieces of her previous conversation with Morgan, so that perhaps her sister could see that Morgan was different than the girl she remembered from high school. Plates full, she walked off to join their father. Then Erica ran up to them.

Dahlia glanced back at her mother; she was having a loud discussion with David. "What's David doing here?" she asked.

"He's my date," Erica said in a voice that dared anyone to ridicule her.

"You brought *David*?" Dahlia asked incredulously, trying to suppress laughter.

"Yes," Erica replied firmly. "And, don't laugh. You came *alone*. I did ask somebody else first, but he turned me down."

"Who?"

It pained her to admit it, but she slowly answered, "Andrew."

"*Really*? Did he give a reason?"

"He said that since Daniel is coming with Jina, he had to stay home with his cousin because she's been having some complications and might go into early labor. I *guess* that's a good enough reason."

Jina and Daniel had just arrived and approached them. "What's David doing here?" Jina asked quietly, sounding like Dahlia's echo.

"He's my date, thanks to you," Erica said and stormed off, leaving Dahlia to explain how it could possibly be Jina's fault.

"Oops," Jina replied, not able to truly feel bad when she glanced over at the man on her arm. She wouldn't have canceled with Daniel for anything in the world. "Pretty sure he doesn't like to dance. I don't think they would have fun together anyway."

"I'm not sure she and David will either," Dahlia quipped, nodding in their direction and laughing. He was clearly already irritating her with whatever he was saying, but she dragged him onto the dance floor anyway. Nobody was dancing yet, but Erica didn't care—when there was a beat, she had to move. Immediately, they witnessed that David didn't know how to move, so Dahlia and Jina knew whenever they needed a laugh that evening, they need only to watch him on the dance floor.

When it appeared that all the guests were in attendance, Elaine clinked her wine glass to get everyone's attention. "Good evening everyone. I would just like to take a moment and thank you all for coming to this dinner party. It is no ordinary occasion though, and I would like to invite my ex-husband Alan to join me." She looked around. "Alan, where are you?"

He stood up slowly from a table in the back corner, unprepared for whatever Elaine was planning, and he nervously made his way to her side. All their daughters gave each other worried glances and held a collective breath.

Elaine continued, "As most of you know, we have three beautiful daughters together. And the reason for tonight's event is to celebrate the engagement of our youngest daughter, Lily to Brian Wallace." Everyone clapped and cheered. "Would you two please stand up?"

They obeyed, and Elaine smiled at them. "I just want to say congratulations and welcome to the family, Brian." She gave them both hugs. Alan shook Brian's hand and kissed Lily on the cheek. "I only hope that you two will have a much more successful marriage than we did." The listeners were silent, unsure if Elaine was being serious or funny. She realized their confusion. "It's a joke. You can laugh."

They all laughed, most of them only to appease her. But Brian's dad roared with laughter, having arrived half-drunk and having already thrown back a few more drinks since then.

Elaine wasn't finished yet. "Also, I wanted to add that we still have one daughter who is available. If any young men would like to talk to her, she is over by the punch bowl." She pointed directly at Dahlia, who desperately wanted to disappear, as the crowd looked in her direction and laughed at her expense. Violet squeezed her elbow in support.

After the announcement was made, everyone was in the clear to enjoy themselves because their parents didn't have any more reasons to interact. But Dahlia still kept an eye on all of them. She knew the number of drinks Brian's dad had, and that every time he crossed paths with his wife, they exchanged unkind words. She was aware that Lily was slightly embarrassed by her mother's attempt at a joke. She could tell that Erica was enjoying the attention she was receiving from David, but that she wasn't really into him.

And then there was Jina and Daniel, dancing and laughing at their goofy dance moves, probably the only couple in sight who were truly content and excited to be with one another. But then again, she realized that her mother and Walter looked pretty happy, as did Alan and Morgan, even if they were in an uncomfortable setting.

"Hey there," a voice interrupted her thoughts.

She looked up, "Michael. How are you?"

"Late, as usual. What'd I miss?"

"Just a very amazing speech by my mother."

"Oh, man. Think she'll do it again for me? Let me ask her." He pretended to turn away to find Elaine.

"No, no," Dahlia stopped him, grabbing his arm. "That's okay. It wasn't *that* amazing."

She handed him a glass of punch. Erica came rushing over from the dance floor, leaving David mid-hip thrust. "Dahlia, I thought you didn't have a date," Erica accused, smiling at Michael.

"I don't. This is my…" she paused, thinking how to introduce him, "…uncle."

She and Michael laughed, and Erica looked confused. "Really?"

"Yes." He reached to shake her hand. "I'm Morgan's brother, Michael."

It was obvious Erica found him attractive; she was always obvious. "Well, since he's not your date, you won't mind if I steal him for a dance."

She didn't wait for a response, but grabbed his arm and began pulling him away. He gave Dahlia a *what's a guy to do* sort of look and handed her his drink, nearly splashing some of it on her dress; she took a step back in time to miss it. He didn't notice.

"Dahlia," Elaine came up behind her, making her jump. "Who was that young man you were just talking to? Looks like my last announcement worked, huh?"

"Actually, mom, that's Morgan's brother, Michael."

"What's he doing here?" she asked, sounding ready to kick him out.

"Lily invited him."

"Oh, okay. If the guest of honor wants him here, then it's okay." She was quiet for a moment. "You know, he is rather cute. You should go out with him."

She didn't wait for Dahlia to reply before leaving to join Walter for a dance.

Violet leaned over and said, "Now *that* would be awkward and dysfunctional."

Dahlia laughed and nodded in agreement, but she didn't completely disagree with her mother—he was rather cute.

Chapter Eleven

Jina deep cleaned her apartment vigorously while her mother cooked in the kitchen. The day of Steve's visit had finally arrived, and Jina wanted it to be over with as quickly as possible. But her mother had other thoughts. "If you like each other, maybe you two can get together again before he goes home," Ms. Yoon suggested. "He will be in Atlanta for a week. You know, after your appa and I met, we went on another date the very next day. He couldn't wait to see me again." Her eyes misted over at the memory.

Jina's father and mother had been introduced by their parents. Ms. Yoon believed it was her responsibility to do the same for her only child, and she took pride in making a successful match. She had married the second man her parents set her up with, and she didn't understand why it was so hard with Jina. *Is Jina the one being difficult, or am I a bad matchmaker?* she often wondered. She also often wished her husband was there to help her. He always had a way with Jina and had been good at knowing which men she would actually like—because they were usually the ones he would like. So, that is how she tried to choose men—which of them would her husband like? Jina would still reject them. Ms. Yoon was at a loss, but she had a good feeling about Steve.

But as Jina scrubbed the bathroom sink, she was feeling guilty, because she knew that all of it—the cleaning, the cooking, the preparation, the anticipation—was for nothing. She knew at the end of it all, she was going to tell her mother she wasn't interested in Steve. She knew she would have to scrutinize him, to find all his flaws so she could use them as good excuses for turning him down. They needed to be things that would bother her mother too. Jina hated to do it because he was probably a perfectly nice guy. But her heart was already with someone else. *And, if I wasn't so cowardly,* she thought, *I would have already told umma about him.*

"Umma, I'm done cleaning," she said, entering the kitchen. "Can I help you with anything?"

"No, no." Her mother shooed her away. "You need to clean yourself up now. Wear something nice. Braid your hair so pretty, like you do."

Jina stared at her reflection in the mirror, brushing her hair, replaying all the moments with Daniel from the past several weeks. She had tried to maintain some boundaries, to not let things move too quickly—like not staying up to talk on the phone past a certain hour or not going on more than X amount of dates in one week—but it had been hard because she was so drawn to him and had never felt such a strong connection in previous relationships. Even though she didn't believe she was technically doing anything wrong by having dinner with Steve, she still felt insincere because Daniel was the only one she wanted to be having a meal with. Could she muster the courage to tell her mother that? She quickly shook the thought away. *There's no reason to tell her anything unless we're exclusive,* she assured herself. *I don't even know if Daniel likes me as much as I like him.*

While setting the table, there was a knock at the door. It was time. Jina had never been so nervous for one of these meetings. She had always been hopeful that perhaps she would meet her future husband—but she'd never had another man in her life who had already captured her affections. Her mother opened the door while Jina stood a few feet back, her hands clasped politely in front of her. She caught a glimpse of Steve, standing behind his aunt—he was handsome, looking even better than he did in the pictures her mother had shown her, and when he greeted them, his voice was deep and soothing, and his smile was kind—like Daniel's. But he wasn't Daniel.

—

Dahlia had spent the evening at Violet's, knowing she would be too nervous about Jina's blind date to sit at home by herself. When she pulled into the parking lot of her apartment complex, her hopes of going immediately to Jina's were dashed when she observed Ms. Yoon's vehicle was still there. But when she closed her car door, she recognized Daniel pacing back and forth along the sidewalk in front of Jina's apartment. Internally, she panicked—he shouldn't have been there.

Unsure what to do, she walked over to him slowly. "Hey, Daniel. Whatcha doin' out here?" she asked.

He had been staring at the ground, his lips moving as he recited the words he wanted to say to Jina, so Dahlia's stealth approach startled him, and he jumped. "Whoa, Dahlia. You scared me," he whispered.

"I'm sorry." Their conversation continued in whispers.

"I'm just working up the nerve to knock on the door."

"Is Jina expecting you?" she asked, even though she knew her friend wasn't. She knew at least Ms. Yoon was still there, if not Steve and his aunt as well.

"No. That's the beauty of a surprise."

"Right." Dahlia wasn't sure what to say. She desperately wanted to prevent anything bad from happening, but she couldn't lie. At the exact moment when she was about to explain to him that inside the apartment, Jina was having dinner with another man, her phone rang. Very loud. The loudest it had ever rung. She searched with urgency the depths of her huge purse for the phone. Rather than putting it in its assigned front pocket when she left Violet's house, she had just tossed it into the chaos.

Daniel's eyes were wide. "Find the phone before she hears it," he pleaded, still in a whisper.

"I'm trying!" she said louder than intended.

Jina's apartment door flew open. Daniel turned quickly, hiding the bouquet of flowers behind his back, a huge smile plastered on his face. But it soon dissipated under the stern eyes of Ms. Yoon.

"What is going on out here?" she demanded.

Jina stood behind her mother, shocked to see Daniel there. Steve and his aunt could be seen seated at the table behind, curiously staring out the door also.

"Dahlia, what are you doing?" Ms. Yoon continued. "You know this is an important night for us." She turned her attention to Daniel, examining him from head to foot. Then she returned her gaze to Dahlia, who had finally found her phone, even though it had stopped ringing long before. "You and your boyfriend, please leave now."

"Oh, I'm not her—" Daniel began to say, but Dahlia immediately put her hand over his mouth and grabbed his elbow.

"Yes, Ms. Yoon," Dahlia said, pulling Daniel away from Jina's apartment. "We are so sorry for disrupting your evening." Dahlia bowed slightly to show her respect. Ms. Yoon didn't respond, but shut the door—Dahlia noticed Jina's worried expression through the crack before she disappeared.

When Daniel and Dahlia were around the corner, standing in the breezeway, she removed her hands from him. "What's going on?" he asked, brushing the hair away from his forehead. "Jina said she was having dinner with her mom, so when I saw her car in the parking lot, I figured she had already made it home."

Dahlia hesitated. "Would you like to come upstairs for some coffee or tea? We can talk. You can wait for Jina."

Daniel shook his head. "I just want to know what's going on. Is her mom setting her up with someone again? Because she clearly doesn't know about me. Who was that guy at the table?"

"Yes, she is introducing her to someone. He is a doctor from Washington that her mom wanted her to meet while he's in town visiting his aunt."

"And he's Korean. Is that a non-negotiable for her mom?"

Dahlia nodded slowly. "I think so…" She had never actually heard Ms. Yoon say that.

"Why didn't Jina tell me?" His voice sounded dejected as he leaned against the brick wall.

Dahlia was asking herself the same question, irritated that her friend hadn't taken her advice. "I'm so sorry she didn't tell you, but her mother has done this before. Several times. So, I think she thought it would be like that. They'd meet, have dinner, he'd go home, and nothing would come of it." She wanted to explain further, to tell Daniel how much Jina really liked him, but she knew it wasn't her place to expose her friend's innermost feelings.

After a moment, he said, "Thanks for your honesty," and handed her the flowers. "Do whatever you want with these."

As he walked to his car, head hung low, shoulders hunched, she didn't know if she should try to stop him, try to persuade him to wait in her apartment until Jina's guests left for the night, so they could talk things through—so Jina could properly apologize. She had never seen Daniel without a smile on his face. In the six weeks since they had met, she had never seen him without his cheerful disposition. His feelings for Jina had taken him so high, and now brought him low.

After he left, Dahlia continued to mentally examine the events of the past hour. At first she felt guilty, like it was her fault because her cell phone rang. But regardless of whether she had come along,

Daniel had been determined to knock on Jina's door. It would have happened anyway and could have been much worse.

Then she became angry with her friend. Why had Jina not listened to her weeks ago? Now, exactly what she had feared would happen had happened. Daniel was hurt and betrayed, and he didn't even seem like he wanted to talk to Jina. Dahlia waited up for her, knowing she would come over immediately after her dinner guests departed.

—

After the meal, the two older women suggested Jina and Steve go outside and sit on the bench in the community garden for a few minutes. They obliged, happy to be away from the matchmakers, walking in silence until they sat down on opposite ends of the bench.

"So, you're in town for a residency interview?" Jina asked, unable to think of talking point.

He chuckled softly. "I think my aunt covered that topic enough at dinner."

She gave a closed-mouth smile. "You're right."

"I noticed your whole demeanor changed after your friends came to the door," Steve said after a moment of silence. "If you don't mind me asking, is that guy *your* boyfriend—not Dahlia's?"

Jina wrung her hands, aware that he was watching her. *How is he so perceptive?* she wondered. "Not officially," she said slowly. She turned toward Steve in earnestness. "I'm so sorry I wasted your time."

He shrugged. "It wasn't a waste. I got to have a good meal with good company." He was, as she had predicted he would be, a perfectly nice guy. After a few more quiet moments, he said, "Your mom doesn't know about him. Be careful with that. I've been there—it's rough."

Jina nodded. "Did your parents eventually accept her?"

"They…*tolerated* her. Of course it didn't work out, or I wouldn't be here with you."

The thought of her umma only *tolerating* Daniel made her heart hurt. *Lord, please let it be better than that*, she prayed, now determined to be honest with her mother.

"I'll tell my aunt we aren't compatible," he said, even though he thought they could have been, even though he considered her very beautiful and sweet. "You can tell your mom the same. Don't make up anything too bad though…don't want rumors being spread among the matchmakers." He laughed. "Tell her I'm allergic to your cat."

"Are you?"

"No." He loved cats, and they loved him.

"I'm really sorry," she apologized again.

"It's all right. But if it doesn't work out with that guy, you know where to find me. But only message me if I'm still single. I don't need any kind of emotional conflict and drama," he joked.

"Yeah, it's no fun," she said softly.

Once they all left her apartment and she saw their cars pull out of the parking lot, she dashed upstairs to see Dahlia, sure that she would be waiting for her, sure that she had properly explained things to Daniel for her. She knocked softly and waited for Dahlia to unlock and open the door.

"Is Daniel still here?" Jina asked, hopeful, peering around Dahlia's shoulder.

"No. But those are the flowers he brought for you," she said, pointing at the peonies she had arranged in a vase on the counter.

As they both took their usual seats on the couch, Jina said, "He's not answering my texts or calls. Maybe he's sleeping, but he doesn't usually go to bed this early...When did he leave here?"

"Just a few minutes after your mom shut the door. He didn't come up here."

"Why were y'all outside my apartment?"

"I don't know why he was there. I was just coming home from Violet's and saw him outside your door. I thought I might distract him or tell him the truth or something. *Something* other than what happened."

Jina sighed. "So, what did you tell him?"

"The truth." Dahlia recounted word-for-word their conversation for Jina.

After some silence, Jina said, "I should have told my mom about Daniel weeks ago."

Dahlia didn't want to be an I-told-you-so friend, and she was trying not to be angry on Daniel's behalf, but she still couldn't stop herself from asking, "Why didn't you?"

"Because I'm an idiot, Dahlia. Because I lack wisdom and courage. Is that what you want to hear?" she cried. "I messed up. I know I did."

"I'm sorry. You can cry." Dahlia wrapped her in an embrace, pulling her closer on the couch. "Did Steve or his aunt realize what was going on?"

"I think his aunt believed that you two were just my friends who stopped by unannounced, like my mom told them. But Steve guessed that Daniel was there to see me, and he was so nice about it, which makes me feel worse about the whole thing. Do you think Daniel will talk to me again?"

"I hope he will. Maybe just give him some time."

Jina nodded. "Well, I'm not giving up. I'll keep trying to text and call him, and if he still won't answer, I'm going to church with you on Sunday.

Even if he no longer wants us to see each other, I would at least like to apologize to him in person."

Dahlia didn't say it, although Jina was already thinking it, that Daniel may not want a potential future mother-in-law who wouldn't support their relationship, and he definitely wouldn't want to come between Jina and her mother.

Jina didn't want to go home, didn't want to be alone, didn't want to clean up or wash the dishes from the dinner that appeared to have ended her relationship with Daniel, so she stayed with Dahlia that night.

Chapter Twelve

When Pastor Derek finished reading the very familiar passage from 1 Corinthians regarding the unmarried and widowed, Dahlia couldn't help thinking that Peter was right when he wrote that some of the things in Paul's letters are hard to understand. And when he wrote about marriage, she often wondered how well Paul really knew the minds of women—but she always appreciated that he made a distinction between his own judgment and commands from the Lord. Erica heard the passage and couldn't help thinking how contrary Paul's advice seemed to be in comparison with what she had heard in the church her entire life. When Jina heard it, all she could think was, *I don't want to remain as I am anymore, now that I've met Daniel.* But at present, she would have to. Daniel never returned her calls and texts, and he wasn't at church that morning. If it weren't for her friends knowing him, she might have thought he never existed, that she had imagined him.

Andrew wasn't there either, and Dahlia wondered if her prediction was correct—that Andrew had only been attending their church because Daniel wanted to keep coming. Erica asked where "the guys" were, but Jina wasn't ready to tell her what happened—and she didn't *really* know if that was the reason for their absence—so they just shrugged their shoulders in response.

After service, one of the older women approached them. "Good morning, ladies, how are y'all doing?" She gave them a second to respond before launching into her real reason for talking to them. "I'm going to be co-leading the women's Bible study this summer. The topic will be God, Marriage, and Family, and I would love for each of you to join us." They had already heard her make the announcement at the beginning of service, but she wanted to personally invite them. Even without knowing them well, she genuinely thought she knew what was best for them. When they didn't seem immediately enthusiastic, she added, "I know we just finished the marriage sermon series, but you can never have enough preparation. I mean, what could it hurt?"

They were all thinking, to one degree or another, that it could hurt. They felt they had "prepared" enough for the marriages they may or may not ever experience. Whatever else they needed to learn they would learn in action, after they were married. The last time Dahlia was part of a Bible study like that she overheard one of the newly married women talking about how she no longer had anything in common with her single friends, how she could no longer relate to them. As the only single woman there, she'd been made to feel like she didn't belong, even though she had always thought that when believers were together, they had everything in common.

Dahlia said, "I'm sorry, but I'll be spending much of the summer at my dad's house, out of town."

Jina added, "I have a Bible study at my church on Wednesday nights."

Erica didn't know what to say because she hadn't solidified any summer plans, but she knew *that* women's Bible study was not going to be part of them. She had attended the one the previous summer and always felt like an outsider, someone nobody really wanted to get to know—the young married women just wanted to be friends with other married women. Plus, the woman who was inviting them was the same woman who had posted online about her advice for young women: to marry young and start a family. Erica forced a smile and honestly said, "I'll be taking summer classes, and I'm not sure what my plans are yet, but thanks for inviting us."

"Well, I would still love to see all of you there," the woman said excitedly as she began to walk away. "Wednesday evenings, 7 p.m., in two weeks."

On their way through the parking lot, they ran into Marie. "Was Bea asking y'all to come to the women's Bible study?" she asked them, curious if they would take part because she wasn't sure if she would.

"Yes, but we probably won't be there. Are you planning to go?" Dahlia asked.

Marie shook her head. "I just don't think I can handle it right now. I'm sure it will be a great study—I just don't think I can talk about what a godly marriage and family should look like…every week."

"That's understandable," Dahlia said. "If you need help with the kids over the summer, don't hesitate to ask. I'll be back and forth between my place and my dad's."

"Same here," Erica quickly added. "I'm happy to help in any way."

Marie thanked them, appreciative of those who were supporting her through this time. The next day, she had a meeting with the lawyers and her husband—if he showed up—to discuss custody and visitation. She didn't know if her husband would get sober, repent, and choose Jesus again. She didn't know if he would choose her and the children. She could only control her own choices, and she was choosing to faithfully wait on the Lord to guide her steps, every second of every day. Dahlia watched her drive away and imagined what she must be going through, trying not to be angry at the man who had promised to love and cherish her.

—

Robbie had been distant since field day. He still sat with them at lunch, but he no longer stopped by Dahlia's classroom in the mornings or brought her coffee, and he didn't speak directly to her unless she spoke to him first. Dahlia didn't know if it was because she had hurt and offended him, or if they were all simply too busy finishing up the final two weeks of school. The school had assigned Dahlia a new classroom for the next year, so at the end of the last day, after the final bell rang and her students rushed out with whoops and cheers, she wasted no time packing up her stuff.

Robbie knocked on the open door. "Need any help?" he asked.

Since Jina had not arrived to help yet, she smiled gratefully and said, "Sure."

Robbie was still working on only considering her a friend—he had gotten the hint at field day—but when she smiled at him like that, it didn't help. For her, it was just a normal smile—and he knew that, even if he wanted it to mean more. He was hoping not seeing her daily would take away the feelings.

"Can you grab those boxes on top of the cabinet, please?" she asked.

He did what she asked, and as they began removing posters from the walls, he asked, "So, anything fun planned for the break?"

"Only if you consider wedding planning fun."

He laughed. "Not particularly."

"I'll also do some online tutoring. You're going abroad this summer, right?"

"Yeah. I've decided to backpack through New Zealand and Australia for a month. Then I'll visit my parents in Maine for a couple weeks before coming back here."

"Oh, good destination choices!" Dahlia wished she had thought about planning a vacation, but she was honestly such a homebody, someone who enjoyed her routine and her community, that going back and forth to her dad's house would be plenty of travel for her.

They cleared everything out quickly, and Robbie helped carry the boxes to her car. She said goodbye to him in the parking lot, wishing him a great summer, before she went back to the classroom for one more look. She ran into Jina in the hallway.

"Sorry I'm late," Jina apologized. "I had an unexpected phone interview."

"Interview for what?" Dahlia asked.

"Well, a few weeks ago Daniel convinced me to apply to be a teacher and counselor at a camp in the mountains where he volunteers every summer." It hadn't taken much convincing.

"Are you still gonna do it?"

"I think it will be a good opportunity. The director was very encouraging."

"And…?" Dahlia prompted, guessing her friend's underlying motive.

Jina hesitated before admitting, "What if it's the only way I can see him again?"

"How long is this camp?" Dahlia asked, wanting to have more details before offering her thoughts—if Jina wanted to hear them.

"Six weeks…which means I'll miss your birthday." She frowned slightly.

Dahlia didn't care about her birthday. She cared about how awkward and hurtful it would be for Jina to be at camp if Daniel didn't want her there, if he ignored her for a month and a half. Although, it was hard to imagine him doing that. Dahlia didn't want to be mean, but she had to say it. "What if he doesn't want to see you? Do you want to put yourself in that position?"

"Then I'll leave him alone and just focus on my job. It sounds like a really amazing place, and I really do want to work with the kids. Training starts next week."

Dahlia knew there was no changing Jina's mind once it was made up, so she supported her the best she could—by praying, promising to write, and taking care of her cat while she was gone. To maintain some sense of unity, they committed to memorizing the same passages of scripture while they were apart.

Part Two: Summer

Chapter Thirteen

The following week when Adam was out of town on business, Dahlia met Violet at the hospital for her ultrasound appointment. The hospital always reminded Dahlia of her childhood, of the time before her parents divorced, because her father used to work there, and she would play in his office occasionally. She and her sisters had been born there, and now it would be the place to welcome Violet's baby into the world too. The appointment went smoothly, everything was great, and seeing the baby on the screen, hearing his or her heartbeat, gave Dahlia a deep sense of anticipation and responsibility as an aunt-to-be.

As they were walking down the hallway, on their way out, Dahlia asked her sister, "Have you heard much from Lily lately?"

Violet glanced at Dahlia and then averted her eyes regretfully. "Yeah…she's still been messaging mom and me in a separate group text."

"Oh," was all Dahlia could manage to say. She had already apologized to Lily for offending her, even though she really believed she had only been showing concern.

"She hasn't said anything important that you need to know, or I would have shared it with you," Violet assured her. "I think she just doesn't feel comfortable talking to you about Brian because she doesn't think you like him."

"Do you like him?" Dahlia asked.

She hesitated. "He's not exactly…great, but I wouldn't say that to her. It's her decision."

"It is her decision," Dahlia agreed. "And I only asked her questions so that she would think more wisely about her decision."

Violet shrugged, not wanting to get caught in the middle of their conflict, avoiding any extra stress. She agreed with Dahlia to an extent because she thought Brian was rude and potentially controlling, but she never fully understood the "religious" aspect of Dahlia's life or why she felt the need to ask questions about Brian's beliefs. Because she had lived with their dad through her high school years, she had never attended the church or youth group with Dahlia and Lily. If asked, she would have identified herself as a Christian, even though she didn't really know what she believed or if she really wanted to "follow Jesus" the way Dahlia did.

"Maybe you two can patch things up when you spend some time together at dad's house," Violet suggested.

"Yes, I hope so." Dahlia gave Violet a goodbye hug at the hospital entrance. "Thanks for letting me come today. Can't wait 'til we get to hold this baby." She smiled and placed a hand on her sister's growing belly.

"Me too. I'll see you at your birthday, if not sooner," she said as she walked in the direction of her car.

As Dahlia turned to go the other way, she caught a glimpse of someone in the parking lot who looked familiar. At second glance, she confirmed that it *was* Andrew, and he was holding the arm of a pregnant woman she assumed was his cousin and Daniel's sister. She froze in place, unsure whether to quickly disappear or wait for them to approach. Up until the day Jina left for camp, she hadn't heard from Daniel, and Dahlia wasn't sure what Andrew knew about what happened. *This will be awkward*, she thought, still trying to decide whether to walk away. But she took too long—he saw her first.

And as he saw her, the bag on his shoulder slipped down his arm, and some of its contents spilled out the side pocket. Dahlia rushed to pick them up. "Here, let me help," she said, taking the bag from him.

"Thanks, Dahlia," he said. "This is Katherine. She decided to go into labor this morning."

"It's about time," Katherine said in between breaths. She looked and sounded like Daniel, and seemed to have his same easygoing nature.

"Did your water break?" Dahlia asked.

"It did," she said. "They told us to come in directly. I was scheduled to be induced tomorrow if he didn't come before then." They entered the cool, air-conditioned hospital, and headed toward the elevator.

As they waited for it, Dahlia asked, "Is Daniel on his way? Do you need me to contact anyone for you?"

Katherine laughed softly. "We don't know where Daniel is."

Dahlia met Andrew's eyes with a questioning look, so he explained, "He just packed a bag, asked me to take care of Katherine, and said he had to go somewhere. Wouldn't say where."

"How long ago?" Dahlia asked.

"Almost two weeks," Andrew said.

That means right after he almost knocked on Jina's door, Dahlia calculated. "Are y'all worried?" she asked.

"All's I'm worried about is having this baby," Katherine said. "My brother's a grown man—he can take care of himself with the Lord's help." Dahlia couldn't tell if Katherine was mad at her brother for abandoning her in her time of need or if it was just her sense of humor, but she admired her transparency and the way she remained so calm in the middle of what seemed to be very painful contractions.

Dahlia wondered if Daniel was at camp. *But surely he would have told them about that,* she argued mentally. Jina wasn't allowed her cell phone at camp, so she hadn't been able to let Dahlia know if he had arrived there.

Inside the elevator, Andrew was uneasy—though no one would have known by his body language or facial expression—because Dahlia was present to witness him in a moment when he felt completely incompetent. Katherine's husband was deployed with the military. Daniel and Andrew were staying with her to help through the birth of the baby and through the summer until her husband came home. But Daniel was the one who had taken the birth classes with his sister. He was the one who was supposed to be in the room during labor and delivery—not Andrew.

"My uncle and his wife don't have a flight until tomorrow," he said, realizing it really was all on him.

That's right. Daniel's mom died when he was a teenager, she remembered. Jina had told her that. They both had lost a parent. "I don't mind helping, however you need," Dahlia said, giving them both an encouraging smile. "I assisted a midwife for a couple months on a summer mission trip. So, even though I'm a complete stranger, I'm comfortable helping however you want or need."

They had reached the check-in desk, and a nurse offered Katherine a wheelchair. When they disappeared down the hallway to get settled in a room, Dahlia decided to wait a little while, just in case they needed anything. And as she waited, she couldn't help thinking about the amazing moments Katherine's husband was going to miss; he'd been sent on mission and wouldn't even be able to video chat. And as she thought of this, she remembered she had the camera in her car—the one she planned to use to record her dad and Morgan's wedding ceremony—so she rushed out to the parking lot to grab it.

When she returned, she knocked gently on the door of the hospital room and waited for permission to enter. Katherine had already changed into a gown and was settled in the bed under the sheets, while a nurse was starting her IV. Andrew had been sitting in a chair in the corner, but stood when she came through the curtain just inside the door. Dahlia didn't want to be an intruder or push herself upon them, so she just said with a smile, "I don't know if you want to record anything for your husband, but I had my camera in the car. I'm happy to record for you, or I can show you how to use it and leave it here with y'all."

Katherine's blue eyes welled up with tears, heartbroken that her husband wouldn't be able to join them live, as they had hoped, and grateful that Dahlia offered them another option. She nodded, smiling through watery eyes. "Yes, please stay and record everything."

"Everything?" Dahlia asked with an insinuating look and smile.

"Only if you're comfortable with that."

"I don't mind at all. It's what *you're* comfortable with that matters."

"On that note," Andrew finally spoke, "are you sure you're comfortable with me here?"

He was embarrassed. Even though he knew Dahlia had just met Katherine, and she had no obligation to stay and help, he also knew she would be a better birth companion than he could ever be. Katherine didn't have any close female relatives, and while she could have asked a friend from church to be there during the birth, her brother and her cousin had always been her best friends. She had already discussed keeping things as covered and private as possible with her birth team. Katherine smiled sweetly. "Andrew, you're staying. Daniel asked you to, and I know he told you everything you need to know, and I want you to be here. It will be good for you to learn how capable you are in this situation."

At that moment she had an excruciating contraction that nearly caused her to cry out, but she stopped herself and breathed through it. Andrew's eyes went wide—that was the worst one yet. "Should you really use your labor as a teaching experience? I don't think I'm as capable as you think I am."

"The Lord will make you capable and competent, and you'll be fine." She turned to Dahlia. "Thank you for being so thoughtful. It's hard without Ben here, but you've made it a little better. I'm glad I finally got to meet you. You are everything the guys have said you are. I know this is definitely not how you planned to spend your day."

They all laughed softly, but Katherine's last comment reminded Dahlia she needed to cancel her tutor session for that afternoon. And her second to last comment made Dahlia wonder what exactly the guys had been saying about her. Andrew smiled with what Dahlia thought was gratitude, like he was glad he wouldn't be alone through the process. Dahlia turned the camera on so Katherine could give an opening message to her husband who couldn't be there and her son who would soon be in her arms.

And then they had to wait until Katherine's body was prepared, until she was fully dilated and ready to push. She made easy conversation—another trait she shared with her brother—between contractions, and sometimes they all sat in what Dahlia considered comfortable silence. Whether Andrew thought it was comfortable, she couldn't tell. At one point, she turned the camera on him, unconcerned with whether he liked it or not, amused that she had the chance to "interview" him.

"Andrew, how are you feeling today?" she asked.

He cut his eyes to her before turning his head and realizing she was filming. He didn't want to talk to her about his feelings. The only people who rarely asked him about his feelings were Daniel and Katherine. "Inadequate," he said, staring into her eyes, not at the camera.

Her heart fluttered slightly under his gaze, but she didn't allow herself to notice. She smiled and said, "Inadequacy is where the Lord often does His best work."

She always knows the perfect things to say, he thought, unsure how to respond.

When the hour finally arrived, He did do a good work. Andrew held his cousin's hand and wiped the hair from her brow and supported her weight when necessary—all while keeping his head turned away or his eyes averted, sometimes closed. He was able to be there for her, just as Daniel would have been, without crossing any personal boundaries. He didn't see anything he shouldn't have seen. That was left up to Dahlia, as she recorded *everything*, every moment of baby Caleb's new life coming into the world, all seven pounds, two ounces of him, all the voices cheering Katherine on as she gave one final push, all the smiles and happy tears as she held him for the first time.

While mother and baby bonded, waiting for the lactation specialist to visit, Dahlia and Andrew went downstairs to the cafeteria to grab some dinner before it closed. It was the first time they were having a meal together, just the two of them, and while it wasn't awkward, especially after the experience they had just shared, Dahlia couldn't help trying to reconcile the man Andrew seemed to be with the story Michael had told her. The perfect combination of gentleness and strength she had witnessed as he had helped his cousin had softened her opinion of him—for the moment—and she could only conclude that he had changed and matured a lot in the last ten years, as he should have. *As we all should have*, she added, considering the ways she had changed as well.

"Thank you so much for staying today," Andrew said, sitting across the table from her. He truly believed it was God's perfect provision that they had run into her that morning.

"It really was a pleasure," she said. "I enjoyed it. One of the things I love about having my summer days free is the ability to be flexible and interrupted. Caleb's birth was a welcome and beautiful interruption."

Again, he was stunned by her words. He simply smiled, nodded, and said, "It was."

"Will he call you uncle?" she asked.

"Yeah…and you'll be an aunt soon."

"I can't wait," she said, shaking her fists in excitement.

He smiled softly. "What's one thing you can't wait to teach your niece or nephew?"

"Well…" she hesitated. "I know it will sound hyper-spiritual, but honestly I just want to teach him or her about Jesus. I don't want him or her to ever remember a day not knowing Him. I'm not sure my sister or brother-in-law consider that a priority. What about you, with Caleb?"

"Well, your answer, most definitely. But also, I can't wait to teach him soccer. His dad will teach him basketball, but I can teach him soccer."

"You played in high school, right?"

"I did. How'd you know that?"

"Michael mentioned it."

His face became hard at the sound of that name. "Michael," he said.

Dahlia couldn't determine if it was a question or a statement, so she added, "Michael Vaughn. You saw us at the grocery store together."

"I remember." The thought of them *together* for any reason made him uneasy. "I don't know what Michael told you, but *I* told you to be careful around him. I wouldn't trust his honesty or sincerity."

"But I can trust you?" she asked frankly, not rude, but direct. She really wanted to trust him, to trust them both, as she always tended to trust people until they gave her a reason not to. Andrew usually waited for his trust to be earned, so he instantly understood why she might doubt him, but not why she wouldn't doubt Michael as well.

Before he could answer, his name was being called from across the room. At first, he was confused as his Uncle Tim, Katherine's father, approached them. "We were able to get an earlier flight," he explained, almost out of breath. "Sheila is upstairs with Katherine now."

From conversations they had had throughout the day, Dahlia knew that Katherine wasn't completely comfortable with Sheila—they were kind with one another, but there was still some tension. She nudged Andrew's foot under the table and said, "Y'all should get back up there. I'm going to head out."

Andrew stood when she did. "You're right. I need to find out what food she wants delivered."

Tim reached to shake Dahlia's hand. "Thanks for everything today. My daughter said you were such a blessing—her words, not mine." He laughed, clearly unsure about calling anything a *blessing,* as he thought it was a very "spiritual" word, and he was not a very "spiritual" person, which was one of the reasons he moved away from the Bible belt as soon as his children were grown.

"It was great," Dahlia said. "Congratulations on your grandson! He's perfect." To Andrew she said, "Please tell Katherine I'll get the video footage edited by tomorrow and email it."

Andrew nodded. "I'll walk you out."

She shook her head. "I'm good. Get back up there." Knowing Katherine was exhausted and probably feeling vulnerable, Dahlia didn't want her to be alone with Sheila any longer than she had to be.

Dahlia walked to her car as the sun was setting, and she wished nothing more than to be able to call Jina. Two hours away in the mountains, Jina had just finished her first official day of camp, and she was wishing the very same thing, tempted to break the rules and call her friend. Even if she did, there was no cell service—she'd checked. She just wanted to tell Dahlia that Daniel had never arrived at camp.

Chapter Fourteen

Alan traveled out of town for a medical conference that weekend, and he asked Dahlia to stay with Morgan, and she invited Erica along, so that it wouldn't just be the two of them—for although she liked Morgan, she wanted someone she knew well to be there too. They watched movies, spent time by the pool, talked about life and Jesus, and decided they would host a weekly women's Bible study for the summer. It thrilled Erica's heart, not only because she would genuinely enjoy it, but also because it gave her a good excuse not to attend the women's Bible study about marriage and motherhood at their home church. Dahlia wondered if she'd be able to get Violet and Lily to come.

Sunday morning they went to church with Morgan. Erica was always interested in visiting other churches, curious to see if the situation was any different elsewhere, but she always found the same thing—an abundance of single women and very few, if any, single men. Though there was a large college-age crowd at Morgan's church, most of them seemed to already be coupled up, and it was difficult for Erica to determine how many of the guys were available as she scanned every room they entered. It wasn't that Dahlia didn't pay attention to these things—she took note of it all as well—but she just didn't talk about it or share her thoughts, so Erica assumed it was never on her mind. Morgan had been thinking about whether there were any guys she could introduce Dahlia to, but most of the single ones she knew were closer to Erica's age.

While it may seem like that's all they thought about, it wasn't. They really did pay attention to the sermon. They really did focus their hearts and minds on the Lord during worship. They really did love Christ the most. Thinking about marriage or desiring a spouse did not mean they lacked faith or contentment, as some had told them, and they had learned they could never please everyone. Some people complained they didn't think about dating and marriage enough, and others would make them feel like they thought about it too much. Morgan had told them the day before, "As a single person, there's nothing wrong with being aware of the options in a room." Erica clung to those words. Because she was always aware.

After the service, Morgan needed to discuss her serving schedule with the childcare director, so Dahlia and Erica waited in the crowded lobby as some people filed past them and exited into the bright sunshine and others congregated in smaller groups to chat. They were suddenly approached by a beautiful young woman with light brown hair and piercing hazel eyes. "Hi, I'm Sera," she said with a smile. They shook her hand and introduced themselves. "Are you two new here?"

"We're visiting from out of town and came with a friend," Dahlia said. She really didn't want to explain her connection to Morgan and hoped Sera wouldn't ask, for although she was learning to accept the age gap between Morgan and her father, it was still weird to tell others.

"A friend? Shouldn't we call Morgan your soon-to-be stepmom?" Erica asked, half-serious, half-playful.

There were just some moments when Dahlia didn't appreciate Erica's lack of a filter. She felt her cheeks go hot, and she cringed at the idea of calling Morgan her stepmom. She was only six or seven years older than her. "Let's just call her my dad's wife," she said.

"But they aren't married yet," Erica countered. Sometimes, like a younger sister, she enjoyed getting on Dahlia's nerves.

Yes, they are, Dahlia thought, but remained silent and gave Sera a closed-mouth smile, trying to be polite, but already wanting to end the conversation, ready for Morgan to come so they could leave.

"Oh, I heard about Morgan's engagement," Sera said. "That's exciting! She's great, and I'm sure you'll enjoy having her as *your dad's wife*." She used the words Dahlia preferred to try to ease any embarrassment.

"Yes, she is great," Dahlia agreed.

"Look, Andrew's here," Erica said softly, nudging Dahlia's arm, and pointing in his direction.

Sera's eyes went wide with surprise. "How do you two know Andrew?" she asked.

"Do you think Daniel's with him?" Erica asked, looking past Sera, not answering her question.

Dahlia smiled at Sera. "We met them at our church when they've visited the last several weeks."

"Oh. So, that's where they have been recently," Sera said, more to herself than them. And Dahlia took note that Sera had noticed they had been gone, and she wondered if she had been missing them, or at least one of them. At that moment, Andrew's eyes met Dahlia's, and he excused himself from his current conversation and headed toward them.

"Hey, y'all," he said.

Sera gave him a side hug. "I hear you've been church hopping," she said with a smile and a tinge of accusation.

"You know I'm staying with Katherine this summer," he said. "So, we found a local church to attend."

"How are Katherine and Caleb doing?" Dahlia asked, strangely eager to see them again.

"They're well. She loves the video you sent." He smiled. "I think she watches it just so she can cry."

"You've met Katherine and the baby?" Sera asked. She'd been one of Andrew's closest girl friends for years, and she hadn't even met the baby yet. She'd also hoped for years that she could be more than just his friend, so she, like most women would, was trying to assess the relationship that had formed between Andrew and Dahlia.

"She was there when he was born," Andrew said. "She filmed the birth."

"Oh, so you're a videographer?" Sera asked.

"Oh, no." Dahlia shook her head. "I was just in the right place at the right time with my camera."

"Oh." Sera still didn't fully understand. To Andrew she said, "The group's heading out the door. Ready to go to lunch?"

"Yeah. You two want to join us?" Andrew invited Dahlia and Erica.

"Sure!" Erica said without hesitation.

"We came with Morgan though," Dahlia said, "so we don't have a car."

"You two can ride with me," Sera said immediately before Andrew could offer. She grabbed their arms, pulling them with her towards the door, and said to Andrew over her shoulder, "We'll see you there!"

Dahlia didn't like being dragged along, especially when she hadn't actually agreed to lunch, and she didn't want to leave Morgan behind. She searched the crowd for her father's wife, but instead she had to settle for sending her a text message from the backseat of Sera's car.

"Ugh, David messaged me again, asking why I wasn't at church," Erica complained to Dahlia, turning to look at her in the backseat.

"You shouldn't have brought him to the engagement party," Dahlia said bluntly. "Now you've encouraged him."

Erica frowned. "Lily said I had to bring a date, and Andrew said no. I told David it was *just as friends*."

Dahlia had forgotten that Erica had asked Andrew to be her date. She shook her head at her friend and stared out the window, saying, "But you're not even his friend." Sometimes she liked picking on Erica too.

Sera listened, attentive. Andrew had turned Erica down, so she could at least rule her out as a potential relationship interest. But Dahlia, she wasn't sure about yet. Sera was wonderful and would make an excellent wife. But so would Dahlia and Jina and Erica and Julie and all the other single Christian women they knew. There wasn't an issue that disqualified them; it was the lack of men, and that sometimes made it feel like a competition, sometimes made them feel like they couldn't measure up, sometimes made them have to remind themselves, especially when they liked someone, that all their worth is in Christ.

At the restaurant they met up with two young couples. The four of them sat across from each other at one end of the table, Andrew sat beside one of the guys, and Sera made sure to grab the seat beside him —she had missed him very much—leaving Dahlia and Erica the two seats across from them. Dahlia thought she was probably the oldest one there. She would be thirty in a few days, wasn't sure how she felt about it, and hoped it wouldn't come up in conversation.

"It's weird to see you without Daniel," Erica said to Andrew.

"When will y'all be back in Rome?" Sera asked him.

"Assuming we pass the bar, we'll be back to work at my dad's law firm in the fall."

"Of course you'll pass," she said. "Will Daniel be back in time?"

He shrugged. Erica asked, "You really don't know where he is?" She had been intrigued about the mystery from the moment Dahlia had told her he was gone. But Dahlia had left out the part about him coming to Jina's place; she was still curious if Andrew knew about that.

He shook his head. "No, I really don't." And he hadn't realized he was going to be constantly asked about it, and it almost felt like nobody believed him —his uncle, his father, his friends. He was so annoyed with Daniel.

Dahlia wasn't saying much, and he wondered what she was thinking. Ever since their meal at the hospital, her question had been replaying in his mind —*But I can trust you?* He'd been considering all the ways he could earn her trust, be worthy of it, without having to share things about Michael which weren't his to share. Besides, it was in the past, maybe Michael had changed; he didn't want to ruin the reputation of a changed man. But he still wanted Dahlia to be cautious around him—because what if he *hadn't* changed?

Andrew's tone sounded like he didn't want to talk about Daniel, so Erica decided to change the topic. "How long have you two known each other?"

Sera said, "Since high school, but I wouldn't say we were good friends until maybe…four years ago?" She glanced at him with a questioning look, and he nodded casually. It seemed to Dahlia that Sera wanted to assert that *she* knew him best, which wasn't being disputed, but she couldn't understand why there was even a tiny piece of her that cared. *Perhaps because I'm having such a hard time figuring him out*, she mused as she took another bite.

She was always quieter in groups, especially with people she had just met—it's why she often tried to bring a friend along. Erica was perfect for these situations; she carried the conversation well with her naturally outgoing and inquisitive nature. Sometimes she said more than Dahlia would have liked, but it was a small price to pay for the comfort it brought. She and Sera did most of the talking on their end of the table, and she even invited Sera to the weekly women's Bible study they were starting Thursday night. Morgan had said to invite whoever they wanted, and Erica took that seriously.

As the meal was ending, Andrew was disappointed he hadn't heard more from Dahlia, that he hadn't made more effort himself, so he asked her, "How's your mom doing?" Right when he said it, he doubted whether it was the best thing he could have asked, but she didn't seem bothered, and he breathed a sigh of relief.

"She's good," Dahlia said. "She's on a cruise this week."

"Are you bothered that she's missing your birthday?" Erica asked. She only asked because birthdays were a big deal in her family, and it always bothered *her* that her parents couldn't be there. But birthdays weren't like that for Dahlia, so she just shook her head. She was used to spending her birthdays with one parent or the other, or having two separate celebrations. And even if it *had* bothered her, she would never have admitted it in front of any of the people present.

"Oh, happy early birthday," Sera said. "How old are you going to be?"

Her mother not being there didn't bother her, but that question did. "Thirty," she said with a slight smile and little emotion, trying not to make it seem like a big deal. But she could tell Sera and the other two young women seemed surprised.

"You don't look thirty at all," one of them said.

"I can't imagine turning thirty," another one added. "It seems so old. Not that you're old. I thought you were around our ages."

One of the guys asked jokingly, "Aren't you not supposed to ask a woman's age? What's wrong with you girls?"

"They don't know any better," the other guy added. The girls playfully took offense.

"I'll be thirty soon enough," Andrew said. "Here's to being older and wiser." He clinked his glass with Dahlia's and smiled. And then he quickly started talking to the guys about sports until the women got bored and wanted to leave.

Sera had to go immediately to the pastor's house to babysit their kids, so she couldn't give Dahlia and Erica a ride home. Andrew was happy to hear it and pleased to do it. As Sera watched them drive away, she was no closer to deciphering if Andrew was interested in Dahlia or if he would one day ever be interested in her. She could say she had been waiting for him for years, but there also had not been anyone else to come along and win her heart. Sometimes she wondered if she had tunnel vision and couldn't see anyone else, but then when she intentionally looked around her at the options—like Erica constantly did—she didn't find any who compared with Andrew.

The three of them rode home to the sound of the radio. Even Erica had grown tired of talking, and she had given Dahlia the front seat this time. When they pulled into the driveway, Erica thanked him for the ride and rushed inside. Dahlia lingered a moment at the passenger side window and issued him an invitation to her birthday party.

—

Because it was Sunday evening and because she had promised to mail a letter to Jina every Monday morning, Dahlia sat down at the small desk in her bedroom, pen in hand.

Dear Ji,

The most interesting, and unexpected, things have happened this week. After Violet's ultrasound, I ran into Andrew and his cousin Katherine at the hospital —she was in labor. I ended up staying with them all day and recording the birth. I know you must be wondering—where was Daniel? Or perhaps you aren't wondering that because he's there with you. Is he there with you? They said he left and would not tell them where he was going. I can't imagine he would have missed the birth without having a very important reason.

I stayed at my dad's house this weekend, and Erica stayed with me. We went to church with Morgan this morning, where I, once again, ran into Andrew. We ended up having lunch with him and a group of his friends. It's strange to be around him without you and Daniel there as well. I invited him to my birthday party, but I also mentioned that Michael will be there; he seemed to tense up the same way he always does when Michael's name is brought up, so I don't think he'll come to the party. That's probably for the best. You know how I have an aversion to friend drama; all my family drama is enough for one person.

Which reminds me—Lily still hasn't spoken to me about anything of value. I'll do my best to make amends at the party. Wish you could be there, but hope you're enjoying camp. Talk soon. Love you.

> *P.S. Artemis misses you, but he is good. I'll go by in the morning to give him pets, food, and water. Do you think I'd be a good birth videographer? You'll have to watch the video—if Katherine gives permission—and offer me your honest opinion. My favorite verse from this week's scripture memory: This is the message we have heard from him and proclaim to you, that God is light, and in him is no darkness at all.*

Chapter Fifteen

Dahlia spent a few days at home, and a few hours each day cuddling Jina's cat, before returning to her father's house on Thursday for their first Bible study meeting. She and Morgan were going to co-lead, but had decided the first gathering would just be a time for all the women to get to know each other, assuming they would be more willing to participate in discussion if they felt comfortable with one another—at least that's what Dahlia preferred.

Morgan had invited several women from her church, all from various ages and stages of life. Dahlia had texted both of her sisters and wondered if either would show up. Erica had made sure to message Sera the night before—Dahlia had never realized they'd exchanged numbers—to remind her about the meeting.

As Dahlia helped Morgan prepare a charcuterie board and dessert tray, her father lingered in the kitchen, leaning against the countertop and stealing the snacks, one sneaky bite at a time. "Would you stop that?" Morgan asked as she swatted at his hand. "I already made you a plate and set it in your office."

"You did?" He sounded pleasantly surprised. It had been a long time since anyone but Gail, the housekeeper, had taken care of him or thoughtfully prepared food for him.

"Well, it was the least I could do since I'm messing up your usual evening routine," she said with a hint of apology.

He came up behind her and wrapped his arms around her waist while she cut an apple. "Yes, what will I do without my reading chair?" he asked teasingly in her ear, breathing her in.

Dahlia could feel the blood rushing up her neck and into her cheeks as she witnessed the affection between them. She wanted to be unaffected by it, but she hadn't seen her dad with a woman since she was a teenager, so she quickly grabbed the trash bag and headed out the back door. She'd never even seen her parents so affectionate with each other, not that she could remember. What she remembered were the arguments. Most of them revolved around how Elaine had been supportive of Alan's career and life goals, but she'd never felt he'd done the same for her. But with Morgan, he was supportive; she'd told Dahlia that he had been so enthusiastic when she asked him about hosting the Bible study at the house.

As the trash bag thudded at the bottom of the garbage bin, she saw Erica's car pulling into the driveway. When she stepped out of the vehicle, she carried a large bouquet of flowers.

"For me?" Dahlia joked. "You shouldn't have."

Erica rolled her eyes. "David sent these to my house."

"How does he know where you live?"

"He picked me up for the engagement party."

"You let him pick you up?" Dahlia asked incredulously.

"Yeah. I know. It was stupid," Erica said flatly. "You don't have to tell me."

"Well, you need to tell him you're not interested."

"Believe me, I will. Abuelo saw these, and now he's preparing for my wedding."

Because Erica lived in the apartment above their garage, Abuelo *missed nothing*. His chair was positioned by the window, and he could click through the TV channels and keep a watch on all the comings and goings outside.

Dahlia tried not to laugh. "How is your abuelo?"

"Since he retired, he pays attention to *everything* in my life."

"He just loves you."

"He'd love me more if I was married with a baby on the way. Mateo gets to study abroad in Spain and do whatever he wants with his life because he's just his grand*son*."

Dahlia imagined if she was his granddaughter, she would be an even bigger disappointment to him. She only had one living grandparent, and he lived across the country. It was enough just to disappoint her mother. Returning to the previous subject, she asked, "Did David send a note with the flowers?"

"It said *thinking of you*." Erica's body shivered as she cringed from repeating the words.

This time Dahlia didn't suppress her laughter, but in sincerity said, "If he keeps bothering you after you talk to him, let me know."

"What will you do?"

Dahlia shrugged. "Get Chuck to talk to him, or maybe one of the elders."

"Oh, don't do that." Erica shook her head. "They are far too busy to deal with something like this. I'll talk to him and make him understand."

When they entered the house, Alan had already retreated to his office, and Morgan had the kitchen island spread with trays and bowls of food. Dahlia grabbed a vase and added Erica's flowers to the display. And then they waited to see who would arrive. When Dahlia glimpsed Lily's car out front, she felt like she might cry and expressed her gratitude to the Lord. "I'm so glad you made it," she said as she opened the front door for her sister.

"I only came because I was already in town," Lily replied, hanging her purse on the coatrack. She had softened, but still had an edge of hostility toward Dahlia.

"What were you in town for?" Erica asked.

"I had the first fitting for my dress at a cute little shop not far from here."

"You already found a dress?" Dahlia asked. Nobody had told her about any more bridal appointments. Hadn't Violet said she would let her know about these things if she was excluded from the communication? Was Lily really going to leave her out of the wedding planning?

"Yes," Lily said. "After the first appointment, I went a second time with just Brian, and that wasn't any better. So, I decided to go in secret, by myself, so no one could influence my decision."

Dahlia breathed a sigh of relief knowing she hadn't been the only one left out. "That was a really good idea," she commended Lily. Her younger sister always had a hard time making decisions when there were too many voices involved, because she wanted to please them all and didn't know how to hear herself. "Are you in love with the dress you found?"

Erica quickly asked, "What does it look like?"

"I am in love with it, and I'm not telling anyone what it looks like. It will be a surprise!"

Morgan appeared, having heard the conversation, and said, "I know you'll be stunning."

The compliment caught Lily off guard, but she smiled and mumbled her thanks.

Several more women arrived. Morgan formally introduced everyone, opened the evening with a word of prayer, and then freed everyone to continue socializing. Most of them already knew each other, and they mingled throughout the kitchen and living room, remarking on how beautiful the house was and catching up on each other's lives. Morgan specifically engaged Sera in conversation because she had never had an opportunity to get to know her. A middle-aged woman was busy asking Lily all about her wedding plans. And Dahlia moved among the groups, listening to bits here and there.

A much older woman—Ms. Cynthia, Morgan's mentor—talked quietly with Erica in one corner. As Dahlia passed by, Ms. Cynthia was telling Erica, "When you have a husband, the two of you will truly honor one another." She stopped and listened more closely to their conversation, and in Ms. Cynthia she found a woman whose feet she'd like to sit at, soaking up all the wisdom and knowledge she could, realizing these were the things she missed by not having an *abuela*. These were the things she sought after and gleaned from Ms. Anna, and she made a mental note to stop by and see the old woman soon.

Toward the end of the evening when everyone else was in the living room, Dahlia and Sera stood across from each other at the kitchen counter, grazing on the food. Sera said, "I was able to see Katherine and baby Caleb this week. She couldn't stop talking about how happy she is with the video you made." She had made it a point to text Katherine as soon as she left the restaurant after Sunday lunch, and she visited them the very next day.

"Oh, good," Dahlia said with a smile. "I'm just glad I could capture the moments for them, especially with her husband overseas. How are they doing?"

"Good. Her dad and stepmom went home a couple days ago, but Andrew has been a great help. But, I'm still kind of mad at Daniel for not being there too."

"Yeah…" Dahlia hesitated before saying more. "I wonder where he's gone off to, and I hope he's okay."

"They seem to think it has something to do with the girl he was dating…even though, from the beginning, Andrew had warned him against pursuing her."

Dahlia tried to maintain her composure, attempted to keep her face expressionless, as her fingertips gripped the granite countertop. "Why did he warn against her? Did he not like her?"

"They didn't say exactly. It was hard to get them to say anything at all—they're always tight-lipped about any kind of potential gossip, which is a good thing, but then it's hard to know what's going on. It seemed like it may have had something to do with her family. That's all I know." Sera popped a grape into her mouth.

Her family? What could be wrong with her family? It was just Jina and her mother. And what did Andrew know about her mother that he could form any objections, *from the beginning*? So, Daniel had dated Jina against the judgment of his cousin, his closest confidant? Had Katherine felt the same way, even though she'd never met Jina? What did she know about Jina, and did she have a bad opinion of her? So many questions and a lot of anger ran through Dahlia's mind; she was mad that Andrew would consider Jina not worthy of pursuit and upset with herself for deciding to trust him against *her* better judgment. She didn't know what to say, and before she could think of anything, all the women began funneling into the room to grab their last morsels before saying their farewells, all of them excited to begin studying the Word the following week.

Dahlia spoke to no one about what Sera had revealed—she certainly didn't write about it to Jina—but she pondered over it for the next two days leading up to her birthday party, and she was almost positive she no longer wanted Andrew to be there and prayed he wouldn't show up.

—

When Dahlia opened her eyes to the Saturday morning sun cascading through the window, she didn't feel any older. She didn't feel weighed down by the number thirty, like so many other women seemed to. They weren't really weighed down by the number though; they were weighed down by the desires and expectations—of the church, of society, and of themselves—they had to meet by the time they reached that number. But Dahlia woke up that birthday morning feeling light and confident. She predicted that would all change when she encountered her family and friends and their comments and jokes, but so long as she spent those quiet moments with Jesus, she felt sure of her place in life and His plans for her.

When she went downstairs, her father and Morgan were still asleep, but Gail was in the kitchen, baking her favorite cinnamon rolls. As was her birthday tradition, Gail rested her hands on top of Dahlia's head, closed her eyes, and said, "The Lord bless you and keep. The Lord make his face to shine upon you and be gracious to you. The Lord lift up his countenance upon you and give you his peace." She kissed her forehead and added, "Happy birthday, child."

Dahlia smiled and thanked her. She had always been grateful for Gail's stable and reassuring presence as a child and even into adulthood. Now that Morgan had moved into the house and assumed some of the responsibilities, Gail worked less hours —which was good for her aging bones—but Alan paid her just the same. She was like family, and he wanted to ensure she had provision for the rest of her days.

"Gail, you shouldn't be here on a Saturday," Dahlia said as took a finger scoop of the leftover icing into her mouth.

"It's been years since you've been here in the morning on your birthday. I wasn't gonna miss the chance to make your breakfast," she said. "Don't worry. I'm only staying for a few hours. Gotta prepare for my grandbaby's birthday party too."

"How old is he turning?"

"Twelve."

"That's right. He was born the summer I graduated high school."

"Seems like yesterday," Gail said, her eyes staring into a faraway place as she remembered.

Did high school seem like yesterday? It did, and it didn't. Dahlia could think about events that happened then and immediately feel those same emotions rising in her chest, the same ones she felt as a teenager—the embarrassment or the excitement or the jealousy. And when she felt those things, thirty-year-old Dahlia thought how silly and stupid her younger self was, hoping nobody remembered her as she remembered herself. She didn't still live in those emotions; they were fleeting. She tried to figure out why Andrew seemed to still live in his feelings against Michael. Shouldn't he have moved on from that by now? Shouldn't he be able to think how silly and stupid his younger self was?

She was not only struggling to understand what he had against Michael, but mostly what he had against Jina. Sera had said it was her family, but that didn't make sense to Dahlia. He'd never met her family. She could understand if he perhaps had something against *her* family—after all, he had met *her* mother, had heard about her parents' messy relationship and divorce, had heard about her father marrying a much younger woman, the sister of one of his schoolmates. That would make more sense to her. She knew whoever she married, if she married, would have to be willing to lovingly take on her crazy family too.

Morgan and her father entered the kitchen, singing happy birthday to her in unison, interrupting her thoughts, and she decided to put those thoughts away, to focus on investing in the people around her. A few of those people were Marie and her children, Abby and Cole. Dahlia had invited them to the party, but asked them to come a couple hours earlier so the kids could swim while she caught up with their mother. Dahlia donned a French blue sundress—Morgan's birthday gift to her—and twisted her dark hair into a bun shortly before they arrived.

Marie and Dahlia sat in the sunroom where they could enjoy the cool air, keep an eye on the kids, and talk without them overhearing.

"How are things going?" Dahlia asked, pouring them both a glass of raspberry lemonade.

Marie shrugged. "Greg gets visitation with supervision, which isn't ideal, but at least they get to see their dad. Cole's been acting out more—he's angry at Greg, but takes it out on everyone but him."

"And Abby?"

"She's being a typical first born, trying to take care of everyone, make everything run smoothly, acting like she's fine."

"So…a lot like you then?" Dahlia asked, a sad smile on her face.

"But I'm the mother. It's my job to be fine for them."

And it's Greg's job too, Dahlia thought. She asked instead, "What is Greg saying or thinking? Do you know?"

Marie sighed. "He seems to think he's doing what's best for all of us…and I guess if he won't get sober, then he's right."

Dahlia nodded. There had been a few years when her father had lost himself in alcohol, and nothing his ex-wife or his children said could persuade him to stop. If Dahlia hadn't already known Jesus at that time, she was sure it would have greatly affected how she saw her own worth, like she wasn't enough reason for her father to choose sobriety. It wasn't until he almost lost his medical license that he had his last drink and went to his first meeting. Marie had been there for her then, constantly speaking truth to her. Dahlia prayed she could give Marie the same kind of love and support. The kids joined them for a swim break, the serious talk ceased, and the room overflowed with laughter until the other party guests began to arrive.

Erica, then Violet and Adam, and then, though most of her had hoped he wouldn't come, Andrew arrived, and what was worse, he brought a gift. Dahlia welcomed him and introduced him to everyone, but she didn't really want to talk to him because she didn't know how to do that without confronting him about Jina—and she didn't want to do that at her birthday party. For his part, he simply thought she had never looked more beautiful and hoped she would like his gift.

It was a while later when Dahlia saw Lily's car pull up, and she went through the house to welcome her, but Violet got there first. They were in the formal living room, and Dahlia paused in the hallway to listen when she heard their voices.

"Why are you so late?" Violet asked. "We've been waiting on you to do the cake and presents."

"Because of Brian," Lily said in frustration. "I kept waiting on him to get ready, and then he finally said he wasn't coming. He doesn't want to celebrate Dahlia."

Violet sighed. "You should never have told him about your conversation with her. She didn't mean any harm. In her own way, even if we don't understand, she was just looking out for you."

"I know she was." From the tone of Lily's voice, it sounded like she really did know, like she understood and had forgiven her sister. "But I can't get Brian to let it go."

Dahlia walked past the entrance to the living room, so they could see her, toward the front door.

"Dahlia, what are you doing?" Violet asked.

"I thought I heard the doorbell."

"No, you didn't." Violet narrowed her eyes like she didn't believe her. "Are you expecting anyone else?"

Dahlia thought quickly. "Well, Michael isn't here yet."

"Does he ring the doorbell?" Violet was like a detective, sure that Dahlia had been eavesdropping.

"Well, he most certainly should! This isn't his house," Lily declared. She rushed forward to hug Dahlia, saying, "Happy birthday!"

Lily hoped Dahlia hadn't heard their conversation; Dahlia was glad she did. She embraced Lily tightly, relishing the first hug she'd received from her in months, and she decided if Brian was the man Lily was determined to marry, she would have to figure out a way to make things right with him.

"I'm so sorry I'm late. Traffic was terrible. Let's do cake and presents!" Lily said, clapping her hands excitedly.

They brought out the cake and sang to her on the back patio, and she blew out all thirty candles in one breath. Then, Morgan began handing presents to her. Dahlia was most nervous to open Andrew's gift in front of everyone; truth be told, he was too. She guessed from the shape of it that it was probably a book, and when she pulled the pretty floral wrapping paper away—she wondered if he wrapped it himself—she found a small, leather bound copy of *The Valley of Vision.* She had briefly mentioned in conversation with Katherine at the hospital how she gave her copy of the book away while on a mission trip; she had said that she needed to buy another one for herself. As she traced the engraved gold letters of the title with her fingers, her blue eyes met Andrew's green ones, she smiled and said thank you.

All the women watched this exchange closely, analyzing it to the best of their abilities. It was hard to decipher because Andrew nodded, but he didn't really smile back—not a real smile anyway, just a slight, closed-lip smile, the smallest upturn to the corners of his mouth. And Dahlia, while her smile and gratitude seemed sincere, there was something like distrust or confusion in her eyes.

So when Marie spotted Dahlia alone a short time later, as everyone was preparing to leave, she approached her to find out more information. Marie had watched Andrew playing with Cole all afternoon and was curious about him. "So, you invited a *boy*?" she asked quietly, almost whispering the words with a smirk and raised eyebrows. She hated they had only discussed her marital problems earlier in the day, and she hadn't asked Dahlia about her life.

Dahlia rolled her eyes and shook her head. "I thought he was a new friend, but now I'm not so sure."

"Well, he's here, isn't he? He gave you a good gift. And he's entertained my son for more than an hour. I think he *at least* wants to be your friend."

Dahlia knew she had been intentionally avoiding Andrew the entire time, but he hadn't noticed at all. He chocked it up to there being so many people, and he didn't make any ploys for her attention, content to observe everything and kick the ball around with the children. He was just happy she had invited him, glad he had decided to come, and grateful Michael had not shown up.

It wasn't until everyone, except Erica, had gone home that Michael came knocking on the front door. It was dark, Alan had gone to bed, and the three women were watching a movie in the family room. They didn't hear the knocking, and Michael called his sister's phone to get their attention. She was not thrilled when she opened the door. "The party's over. What are you doing here?"

"Aw, sis," he said, coming inside and wrapping his arms around her, resting his chin—and most of his weight—on her shoulder. "I'm sorry I missed it."

"Have you been drinking?" she asked. She hoped the girls wouldn't be able to tell that he had; she could always tell from the subtle differences in his voice and mannerisms, but didn't think the girls knew him well enough to notice.

He pulled back, and putting his thumb and pointer finger about an inch apart, said, "Just a little."

"But you drove here?" she asked. She knew it'd been more than a little.

He hated when she used her stern voice. He straightened himself up. "I'm fine, really. Just because you don't drink anymore, doesn't mean the rest of us can't. Where's the birthday girl?" He followed the sound of the television, and Dahlia paused the movie when he appeared. "Happy birthday!" he told her with a giant smile. "Did you save me any cake?"

"I don't think you deserve any," Erica said playfully. She had been looking forward to seeing him.

"Come on, are you that mad?" he asked Dahlia who was curled up in her usual comfy armchair.

She shook her head. "I'm not mad at all." She honestly hadn't thought about his absence except for when she used him as an excuse to open the front door.

"See, Erica?" He plopped down on the couch beside her. "And for the record, *everyone* deserves cake."

Morgan knew her brother wouldn't stop talking about cake and that he needed to eat something, so she brought him a piece and then instructed him to be quiet while they finished the movie. A minute later when the cake was gone, and he couldn't stop himself from asking questions, Morgan shushed him, and soon he was asleep, his head on Erica's shoulder as he breathed heavily in her ear. She didn't mind it.

Chapter Sixteen

"Do y'all have to go to church this morning?" Michael asked as they sat at the kitchen table eating breakfast. "Let's just hang out at the pool all day."

Morgan gave him a hard look. "We did that yesterday, but you weren't here."

"Oh, come on. Dahlia here," he put a hand on her shoulder and gave it a squeeze, "hasn't given me any fuss about it, but you and Erica won't let it go."

"That's because we're the ones who missed you," Erica teased with a smile as she spread jam on her toast.

Michael feigned shock. "Is that true? Dahlia, did you not miss me?"

She side-eyed him, smirked, and then nodded. "It's true."

He yawned loudly. "Guess I need to work on being more missable."

"I think that's a good goal," Morgan agreed.

As Alan took a seat at the table, he asked, "Why don't you come to church with us? The girls have talked me into going. Could be good for all of us." It was strange, but wonderful, for Dahlia to hear her father say those words.

Michael pretended to think about it. "Hmm…I'll pass. Morgan's church is too much for me."

So, they left him behind at the house to enjoy the amenities at his own leisure. Dahlia thought about how he needed a Christian man to help him see the truth and teach him the ways of Jesus; she thought that if Andrew didn't hold such a grudge, he could have done it years ago. The idea that they had ever been friends still perplexed her, and she marveled that the man who refused to attend church had practiced the act of forgiving, while the man who attended church refused humility and an apology. She hoped Andrew would be back at Katherine's house, so she wouldn't see him that morning.

Morgan's church had been going through 1 Corinthians, and the pastor had finally reached chapter seven—principles for marriage. It felt like déjà vu, since Pastor Derek had touched on the same passage at the end of his marriage sermon series. But this time, Morgan's pastor said something new, something liberating. He said, "Paul writes about how it is good for the single people to remain single, as they are, if they can maintain self-control. Some commentators will say this was specific advice for the members of the church in Corinth in that specific time with whatever hardships they were currently facing. And, that may be true, but I think it's also important to note that Paul knew the scriptures. He knew the verse in Genesis, which states that it's not good for the man to be alone. Many use this verse to tease the single man about being unmarried, that it's not good for him to be without a wife. But, here in Corinthians, that's exactly what Paul says—that's it's good to remain unmarried, if you can. So, are the scriptures contradicting themselves? Is Paul contradicting Genesis? Of course not. We need to remove the idolatry of marriage from our churches, from our interpretations of the scripture. It is not good for the man to be alone means it's not good for him to be *without community*, without relationships, without other people. That community could come in the form of a spouse, and that is perhaps the ultimate earthly community, but we can all attest to needing a greater, wider community than that—it's why the body of believers exists, knit together by the Spirit. Paul never married, but he *always* had community, always had companions living and traveling with him. It is not good for man—or woman—to be without community."

It was exactly what Dahlia had been needing to hear, something to help release all the pressure. She felt light as she stood from her seat after service, felt like she could take on anything so long as she had her community around her. But then she spotted Andrew at the back of the sanctuary and her chest instantly felt heavy again. Their eyes had met, and then he started heading toward her. Could she pretend she hadn't noticed him and flee in the other direction?

Her dad called out to Andrew and greeted him before there was a chance to bolt. She could tell her dad liked him; they had spent plenty of time chatting around the grill the previous evening at her birthday party. Alan had even mentioned his name at the breakfast table that morning, and Dahlia was certain she had seen a slight flicker of worry cross Michael's face before he covered it up with a blank stare and dug into his grits. Even though he had forgiven Andrew, it didn't mean he wanted to be around him.

Forgiveness doesn't always mean reconciliation. She concluded he must have been relieved about not being at her party after finding out that Andrew had been in attendance.

Erica went to chat with the young women they had previously gone to lunch with. Morgan let the men talk for a minute, but then pulled Alan away to introduce him to someone. She gave Dahlia a discreet wink as she went; Dahlia was instantly confused about what it was supposed to mean. Did Morgan think something was happening between them? It was awkward for a moment, but then Andrew spoke, "Thanks again for inviting me yesterday. It was fun."

"Yeah, thanks for the book. I appreciate it, really."

"Of course, you're welcome." He was distracted by how loud it was in the sanctuary, the buzz of so many conversations, and he desired a private moment with her. "Can we step outside to talk for a minute?"

Stepping outside with him had not been on her agenda for the day; just minutes ago she'd wanted to dodge his company by slipping outside—by herself. But she politely nodded and followed where he led, into a small, quiet courtyard enclosed with a tall brick wall. There was a little fountain, a bench, and well-tended stone flower pots. She hadn't known the place existed, but instantly imagined herself sitting there, reading for hours. Even though it called to her, she decided not to take a seat because the bench was too small, and he would be too close if he sat beside her. She waited for him to speak.

Before he could lose all his coherent thoughts in her blue eyes, he got straight to the point. "So, I'm really grateful to have met you this year, and I've enjoyed getting to know you these past few months…I wanted to ask if you would go on a date with me?"

He called it a date because he wanted to be very clear about his intentions, leave nothing open for interpretation. He didn't want to *hang out*. He didn't want to *get together* or *hook up*. He didn't want to just get her number and end up texting forever without taking any steps forward. He had been witness to Robbie asking her out at field day; he didn't want to make the same mistake of not being direct and clear. He had been praying about the right time to ask her—even though he honestly wasn't sure how she really felt about him—but the fact that she had invited him to her party had boosted his confidence.

However, it was quickly deflating as he tried to understand the cycle of expressions on her face.

She questioned whether she had heard him correctly; he'd spoken so fast, the words almost merging together, like he was nervous, trying to say it before he lost the courage. That's how it sounded it her, and it was the last thing she had expected him to say. When he had asked her to step outside, she wasn't sure what he wanted to talk about, but a date certainly had not crossed her mind. She had hoped perhaps he was going to finish their conversation from the hospital, that he would explain why she shouldn't trust Michael—and why she should trust him, for that matter. Instead, he'd asked her on a date, and she simply wanted to disappear.

When she didn't say anything after several seconds, he asked, "What are you thinking?"

"I think…you don't really know me, and I don't know you."

"Well, that's the point. I want to know you more." He almost added more *deeply*, but that seemed like a bit much for her at the moment.

She wanted to avoid saying anything mean or hurtful, and after what felt like an eternity, she asked,

"Do you realize I've been harboring anger towards you?"

With a furrowed brow, confusion flashed in his eyes. "Anger? No, I hadn't noticed. Why are you angry with me? Have I done something wrong?"

She weighed whether she really wanted the conversation, the confrontation, before asking, "Did you counsel Daniel not to date Jina?"

"Who told you that?" he asked calmly.

She ignored his question. "Is it true?"

He hesitated. "Yes. But I had my reasons."

"I'm sure you did. Just like you had your reasons for hurting Michael too?"

His body stiffened, his jaw tightened, his eyes narrowed. He always had a visceral response at the mention of Michael. "I *did* have my reasons," he said firmly.

"What—" Dahlia began, but she was interrupted by Sera.

"There you are!" Sera said as she approached. "I've been looking for you everywhere." Even though she liked Dahlia, she loved Andrew, and her words were aimed at him. "Everybody's waiting on you to go to lunch." After a moment she added with a smile, "Dahlia, you can come too, if you want."

Dahlia declined. "Thanks, but I actually need to get back. I'll see you on Thursday, Sera." She made sure to add her name, not wanting Andrew to think she was agreeing to any kind of date with him.

She went to the car and waited for her dad, Morgan, and Erica to arrive, preferring to bake in the heat than have to talk to anyone else. She needed to be alone with her thoughts. But when they got on the road, her dad had other ideas. The sermon had given Alan a lot to think about, stuff he had never considered before. Every time he went to church with Morgan, he came away bemused and contemplative; he was hearing things he had never heard before, and hearing old things in new ways. He hadn't given much thought to Morgan being a "church girl" when he fell for her, but as he learned more about the thing she loved most—Jesus—he could feel himself begin to change, little by little. He could see the way this Jesus had knitted his wife and his middle daughter together in a way he didn't think anything else could, and it intrigued him.

That morning while the pastor spoke about marriage and singleness, Alan couldn't help but think of Dahlia. He remembered all the comments he used to make to her about dating and boyfriends, and now he regretted them. He had always assumed he was being encouraging, but he realized he had never really asked her how she felt, never tried to understand what she thought about relationships, especially since he could fully admit that she hadn't had a good example of a healthy one with his first marriage. So, on the car ride home, he asked Dahlia and Erica, "What did you two think of the sermon?"

But Dahlia didn't want to talk; her mind was too consumed with the conversation in the courtyard, replaying over and over as she analyzed each word. She was certain her cheeks were still burning, whether from anger or embarrassment she couldn't say—probably both. Had she been too harsh, too unfair, too unkind? She was angry, but she didn't want to sin in her anger. She let Erica answer her dad's questions, while she reflected and waited for the Spirit to give her clarity. Alan's intentions were good, but his timing was not, though he could have never known that.

When they arrived at the house, Dahlia was ready to go home. She had already packed her bag that morning and planned to leave directly after church, but it was obvious Erica wanted to stay a while, to spend some time at the pool, as Michael had proposed that morning. Dahlia felt weird leaving Erica there without her, but Morgan assured her it was fine, claiming Erica was her friend now too.

The entire drive home Dahlia was fueling her anger as she thought about how easily Andrew had confessed to both her accusations, without any hint of remorse for his actions, like he truly believed he had done the right things. And she even became angry with Sera for showing up at the wrong moment, so they weren't able to resolve anything, so that she couldn't hear all about his *reasons* and then argue against them. She couldn't think of any good reason he should ever have rejected Jina. She spent time with Jina's cat, did some planning for the upcoming school year, and went to bed early.

When she checked her e-mail in the morning, she had a message from Andrew.

Dear Dahlia,

I hope it's okay to send this to you. I got your email address from Katherine from when you sent her the birth video. Our conversations always get interrupted, and I express myself better in writing, so I hope to offer you an explanation for the things we spoke about this afternoon.

Regarding your first accusation, it is true that I did warn Daniel against pursuing Jina—not because she isn't a wonderful person or worthy of his affections, but because one day at Ms. Anna's, I heard Erica teasing her about how she had to marry a Korean man. I simply cautioned Daniel not to get too attached because it might not work out, and I didn't want to see him hurt. I apologize if that has hurt her or you, but I was only doing what I thought was in the best interest of my cousin. Please forgive me if my assumptions about her family's expectations were incorrect. If it's any consolation, I don't believe my words had any bearing on his decision; he still chose to pursue her, though I have no idea about the current state of their relationship.

Regarding Michael, I'm not sure what he's told you, though I'm almost certain it wasn't honest. We were friends most of our childhoods, but began to drift apart in high school, even though we were on the soccer team together. At a party, where I was not in attendance, he assaulted a mutual friend, and when I found out, I did attack him. She wouldn't come forward to report him, but the rage inside of me wanted to hold him accountable—not that anything I did could undo what he'd done.

It's something I've been conflicted about all these years, something I have had to continually bring to the Lord. I mean…am I supposed to feel sorry for what I did? I never do. For a split second I might regret injuring him permanently, but then I think about my friend and how he injured her permanently, more than just physically. She can try to heal, she can move on, but it will always be with her, always creep into her mind in dark moments. Perhaps my only regret is not telling you this sooner. Then maybe you would have understood why I wanted you to be careful around him, and maybe you would have a better opinion of me. Or perhaps this confession is only making me sound worse for lacking the conviction and repentance of my actions toward him. What I can honestly admit, is that I do repeatedly practice forgiveness every time it resurfaces, every time I see him or hear his name, every time I hear my friend share her story with other women who've been hurt, every time I think about you or any other woman being near him.

I hope this offers you the clarity you need. Andrew

She read it countless times, nearly memorizing his words, and although she should have responded, she didn't. Her pride wouldn't let her. She could admit only to herself that he was right.

Chapter Seventeen

To be honest, Morgan would have liked to have had her wedding on the grounds at their home. But the moment Lily expressed her desire to do the same thing, Morgan knew she'd have to make alternate plans. She knew she'd have to allow the youngest daughter to have her dream wedding at her daddy's house. And she was okay with that if it meant she and Lily could begin their relationship without any added conflict. But it meant finding—and paying for—another venue, and even though Alan assured her he was able to pay for both Lily's wedding and their own, Morgan wanted to stick to a small budget and a small guest list. And a part of her didn't want to have a wedding at all because they were already married, but Alan insisted since she'd only had a courthouse wedding with her first marriage as well. So, she decided to get married on a weekday evening in the chapel at her church—the Saturdays were already booked.

When the wedding day arrived, Dahlia's dad and uncles used the carriage house to get ready and left the main house to Morgan. Gail was there to prepare snacks and make sure they were all well-fed before the event. Morgan's maid of honor, her childhood friend, was flying in and planned to meet them at the church, as would Violet and Lily, so for most of the day it was just Morgan, Dahlia, and Gail. The bride plaited her hair into a halo braid, placing a few small flowers in it, and she did her own makeup as well. She was calm and ready, and she didn't get nervous until about thirty minutes before her mother, Patricia, was scheduled to arrive.

"Do you two have a good relationship?" Dahlia asked.

"It's fine," Morgan said. "We've come a long way from where we used to be. But there does always seem to be more work to do." Dahlia nodded in complete empathetic understanding. "I'm just nervous because I want her to love the groom and the dress."

Dahlia tilted her head in confusion. "She has met my dad, right?"

"Yes, only a couple of times though. My first wedding was an elopement, a run-away-from-home kind of decision. She didn't get to be a part of it—or the marriage really. This time, I want her to feel welcome."

And when her mother arrived, she did feel welcome. The men were piling into their cars to head to the church, so she was able to talk with them in the driveway for a few minutes. Patricia didn't quite understand why Morgan wanted to marry someone who was nearly as old as she was, but she assessed that Alan genuinely loved her daughter, and he was certainly able to provide for her, so she never contested the match—even if it didn't make sense to her. After Morgan's divorce, and before Alan came along, she feared her daughter would always be alone. *She* was always alone; that was the life she had chosen, and enjoyed, since her divorce. But she knew it wasn't what Morgan wanted, so she was happy for her oldest child and only daughter.

After leaving Patricia and Morgan alone for a while, Dahlia went to check on them. Patricia had helped her into her gown, and even though everyone says it about every woman on her wedding day, Dahlia truly believed she had never seen a more beautiful bride. Morgan had splurged a little more on the dress than she budgeted, but she couldn't envision herself walking down the aisle in any other gown. Her smooth brown skin was stunning against the blush-colored satin, her neck and shoulders so elegantly displayed with the bateau neckline. The dress didn't need any embellishments—and it didn't have any. Morgan was all it needed.

Morgan had dressed the bridesmaids in floral watercolor maxi dresses that they could wear again for other occasions. Dahlia would never had declared it, but she felt beautiful too. When they arrived to the church, Dahlia saw Michael outside before the ceremony began, and she couldn't stop thinking about Andrew's email. She hardly knew Michael, so she couldn't say he wasn't capable of things of which he'd been accused. But she also felt like she didn't know Andrew either. She had never had so much trouble reading a person as she did with him; it still frustrated her to remember their previous interaction. But she brushed all those thoughts away as the music began and she reached out for Michael's elbow; she had been assigned to walk down the aisle with him. She tried not to feel weird about it. The ceremony was short, sweet, and simple, just as

Morgan wanted, and then they all moved into the fellowship hall for dinner, cake, and dancing.

Since overhearing Violet and Lily's conversation at her birthday party, Dahlia had been determined to fix things with Brian, if only for her sister's sake, if only for her family's peace. So, when she saw Brian exiting the room, she followed him, in the hope of having a moment alone where she could apologize to him face-to-face. In the hallway, she called his name. He stopped and then slowly turned around with an annoyed expression on his face. His tie was loosened, his shirt disheveled, his hair sweaty—he and Lily had been dancing hard. "What?" he demanded as she reached him.

She almost took a step back and hesitated to speak because of his harsh tone. *God does not give me a spirit of fear*, she told herself. When she found her voice, she said, "I just wanted a moment to talk to you, to say I'm sorry for any way I have offended or hurt you."

He smirked. "And what about what I want? What if I don't want to talk to you?"

She took a deep breath. "In a few months we'll be family, and it would be best for everyone if we could work past this."

"Oh, really?" he asked with attitude. "Why do you always think you know what's best for everyone?"

The prideful voice inside of her wanted to say, "Because I usually do," but she refrained. Instead, she said, "I'm very sorry that's the impression I've given you." Even if it was an accurate impression. Because he clearly couldn't handle it, couldn't handle her being right.

"That's the impression you give everyone. All high and mighty."

She immediately began to question whether that was true, her confidence faltering. It was always one of her chief concerns when she self-reflected—did she not represent Jesus well? Did she draw people to him, or push them away? She was always trying to find the perfect balance of truth and love, and often feeling like a failure. Was he just being mean, or was that really what everyone thought of her? She could feel her eyes beginning to fill with water, but she rapidly blinked it away. He would not see her cry. She wanted to walk away, but instead pressed on, reminding herself that God gives her a spirit of power and of love.

"I'm really very sorry," she apologized for a third time, just hoping to make peace. "I only asked Lily those questions because I barely know you, and I was curious about your beliefs. It wasn't to judge you as a person."

"No. You wanted to judge me as Lily's future husband."

She paused for a moment, and then asked, "Well, isn't that what family and friends are supposed to do? Wouldn't you do the same for your sister?"

He came toward her, and she attempted to step back, not liking him so close, but he grabbed her arm, his fingers wrapped tightly, digging into her skin. He stared down at her, his face only inches from hers, not quite the face-to-face conversation she had imagined. She really just wanted to get out of his grasp, without causing a scene, without causing him physical harm, without a knee to his groin. Finally, he said, "No, I wouldn't. My sister's a grown woman who can make her own decisions. Next time you have any questions about me, you can ask me directly. Do you understand?"

She swallowed hard, glaring back at him, ready to bring her knee up—if she could in that dress—when suddenly Michael appeared. "Hey, what's going on?" he asked good-naturedly, attempting to ease the tension he perceived.

Brian released her wrist and smiled at Michael. "Nothing, man. Just having a chat with my future sis."

"Well, come back to the dance floor. You're missing all the good songs. We need your energy."

As the two men walked back to the reception, Michael threw Dahlia a smile and a wink over his shoulder, as though she should be grateful he had "saved" her from Brian once again. Why was her sister marrying a man from whom she needed saving? Lily needed saving from him too. Dahlia turned away, rubbing her wrist and letting the tears fall. Did she really have no choice but to let Lily marry him? She instantly had so many more questions about him, the first one being whether he had ever been violent with Lily—physically or otherwise? She wanted to walk right up to him on the dance floor and ask him *that* directly, in front of witnesses.

But she didn't. It was her father's wedding day.

She wanted to talk to him and Morgan about what had just happened.

But she didn't. They didn't need to worry about anything while on their honeymoon.

She considered telling Violet and Adam about it, but her older sister already hated being in the middle of the situation, and being pregnant, she didn't need any added stress. Adam strategically kept her away from family drama as much as possible, especially now that there was a baby on the way. Dahlia spotted them across the room, sitting alone at one of the tables, and they looked like they were getting ready to leave. Most of her dad's work colleagues were also seated, and seemed like they were ready to head out at any moment, but her crazy uncles were sweating on the dance floor with the younger crowd. Her dad tried his best to keep up with Morgan. They really didn't *look* like they belonged together, but somehow it worked.

Elaine had told Dahlia to keep any eye out for any young, single men. There weren't any. Except Michael. The fact that she had ever thought he was cute was lost on her now. She spent the rest of the evening sitting with Ms. Cynthia from their Bible study group, talking and observing everyone else. Looking at Patricia, Dahlia could see the resemblance to Michael, and she wondered what it must have been like for Morgan to grow up in that blond-haired, blue-eyed family, without anyone who looked like her. For six years, she had probably been the center of her parents' world, but then they had miraculously conceived Michael; she wondered how the dynamics had changed.

Since it was a Tuesday night, the bride and groom made their exit somewhat early, driving off into the night towards a luxurious mountain cabin. A few minutes later all the guests hopped into their cars as well. Only Patricia stayed behind to help Dahlia clean and load up her car. They packed the wedding gifts in the back seat and the flowers in the trunk; Dahlia planned to visit a local cemetery the next day and leave them on the most neglected-looking graves. She was tired and ready for a quiet night alone in her father's house.

After her head had hit the pillow and she was just about to drift off to sleep, she heard a loud noise, a bang, something falling. She had set the alarm, but it hadn't gone off. Who was in the house who knew the security code? Had her father and Morgan come back for some reason? She threw on her robe—one she only wore to be appropriately covered, not because it was cold in July—tucked her phone into the pocket, and tiptoed down the stairs, flipping on lights as she went, her heart racing as she tried to think of all the potential weapons in the house. There was a second thud as she reached the bottom of the staircase. It was coming from the kitchen. "Who's there?" she asked, her voice sounding more timid than she liked.

She didn't get a response, but when she was almost to the kitchen entrance, she heard a string of cuss words. It was Michael's voice. She let out a relieved sigh that it wasn't a burglar, but then felt uneasy that it was him. Why did he have access to the house whenever he wanted? She turned the corner and saw him in the glow of the refrigerator light before she flipped on the overhead light. He had spilled food all over the floor in front of the fridge, food Gail had prepared for Dahlia to have for the next couple of days. He was trying to clean it up, but only making a bigger mess.

"What are you doing here?" she demanded, taking the rag from him and attempting to scoop the bits of pasta salad together.

He stood up, but didn't seem steady on his feet. "Thanks, Dahlia," he said. When he spoke, she could tell he had been drinking. "I couldn't drive back to the city, so I had the driver drop me here to crash for the night." He grabbed a fork from the drawer, sat on a barstool, and proceeded to eat whatever food remained in the container he had dropped.

She dumped the fallen food in the trashcan and then ran the rag under the faucet so she could wipe down the floor. "You didn't go home after the wedding?" she asked.

"Dry weddings are the worst," he complained. "I had to hit up a couple bars, which weren't that great on a weekday night." He took a bite of pasta and thought for a moment. "You know, Morgan used to be fun. We'd drink together…smoke a little weed sometimes." He let out a breathy laugh at the memory. "But she's different now." He paused to take another bite. "I guess I'm happy for her, but it's not the same."

Dahlia didn't know what to say. Well, she had plenty to say, but didn't think she should say it. She didn't know what kind of drunk he was, if he would be easily provoked to anger or violence, so she remained silent. If he was a sad drunk, she didn't want to lead him down memory lane and end up sitting up with him and his emotions for hours. Maybe she lacked compassion. Maybe she should have shared Jesus with him. But it had always been her experience that the drunk person either didn't receive it well, or received and agreed with all of it, only to not remember in the morning. Maybe she just didn't present it well enough, say the right words—Brian's accusations were still causing her to doubt whether she was a good witness at all.

When Michael didn't say anything for at least thirty seconds and continued stuffing his face, Dahlia took the opportunity to excuse herself. "I'm going back to bed," she said. "You can have the downstairs guest room."

"I'll probably just pass out on the couch."

For some reason, all she could think about was the drool she'd have to scrub off the sofa pillows and cushions. She prayed he wouldn't throw up anywhere, though she was somewhat sure he wasn't that kind of drunk, that he could hold his liquor. Even though he had never made her feel threatened, when she arrived to her bedroom, she shut and locked the door, still unsure what he was capable of, Andrew's email still running through her mind.

Chapter Eighteen

Dahlia kept up with the whereabouts of her mother by Elaine's posts on social media. When their Mediterranean cruise docked in Greece, rather than fly home, Elaine and Walter decided to spend a couple more weeks traveling around Europe. Her daughters were thrilled for their mother because she'd never had a chance to explore the world—they hadn't either, really—but they were equally surprised that she was willing to leave so many of her summer events, especially the weddings, in the hands of her assistants. Walter certainly had a freeing effect on her. These days, she let things go in ways her daughters had never known.

Elaine called Dahlia a couple days after her return home and invited her to dinner, so they could have a late birthday celebration. "Wear a pretty dress, so we can take some good pictures, and meet me at the restaurant at seven," she said in the voicemail. Dahlia had been in the middle of leading the Thursday night Bible study when she missed the call.

She did as her mother commanded and wore a coral and white striped sundress she bought with the gift card Jina had sent her for her birthday. When she arrived at the restaurant, she didn't see her mother. But she did see another familiar face. From a table in the back, he smiled and raised his hand, motioning for her to join him. Dahlia raised her own hand as if to say, "Just a minute," as she turned away and dialed her mother's number.

Elaine answered the phone with, "Surprise! Are you at the restaurant?"

"Mom, what's going on?" Dahlia asked. "Where are you and why is Robbie here, waving at me?"

"Well, don't keep him waving. Get on in there! A date with a nice, handsome man is my birthday gift to you."

"I told you he's a coworker and friend, nothing more."

"That's because you're just scared to let it be something more," Elaine said. "Go, and enjoy yourself."

No, her mother was wrong. She wasn't scared. Not in the way Elaine meant it. Dahlia wasn't scared of a relationship, at least she didn't think she was. *No, I'm not scared at all,* she determined. She was cautious to let herself be interested in a man who didn't love Jesus too—she'd done that once. It had been a heartbroken disaster, and she had no desire to do it again. She had known from the beginning how easy it would be to like Robbie; he was very likeable, good-looking, and funny. That's why she'd given herself mental boundaries, not even allowing herself the option to consider him anything more than a friend. That was wise. She knew it was.

As she watched him waiting for her, she wanted to turn around and leave. But she wouldn't treat a friend that way, and she had never agreed to this being a date. It was a dinner between friends—that was all. When she approached the table and he stood, that's exactly what she told him. "This isn't a date," she said. "I'm not sure what my mom told you, but we're just friends."

He seemed surprised. "Is nobody else coming?"

"What do you mean?"

"When I ran into your mom at the store, she gave the impression this was a birthday dinner for you. I assumed she would at least be here, if not others."

"No," Dahlia said. "I just called her. This is her way of setting us up on a date."

"Oh." He laughed softly, nervously. He would have embraced it to being a date. "Well, just dinner between friends, then. We can catch up on our summers."

The tension in Dahlia's shoulders dissipated as she slid into the booth and he sat in the chair across the table from her. He was easygoing—another quality she liked about him. *No, I like when any person is easygoing. It's nothing special about him,* she argued with herself.

"That would be wonderful," she said. "I'd love to hear all about Australia and New Zealand."

And that is what they talked about for most of the meal. He would ask her questions about her summer break, she'd give brief answers, and then deflect the conversation back to his travels. It was a habit of hers, and she rarely realized she was doing it—choosing not to talk about herself. Robbie *had* noticed it though, which is why he always asked her direct questions, straining to know her better, to break through her defenses.

After dinner, Robbie suggested they walk to the square across the street, and they ended up sitting on one of the benches near the fountain. It was the same square Jina and Daniel had walked to after their first date, the place where they'd had their first dance. Dahlia couldn't help thinking of them as she stared at the fountain, entranced by the water trickling down the three layers, landing in the pool below. She hadn't heard from Jina in a couple weeks, and she wondered if either of them would ever hear from Daniel again. He hadn't even posted on his social media accounts—Dahlia had checked many times, for Jina's sake and her own curiosity. There was nothing new. He'd just vanished.

"What are you thinking about?" Robbie asked.

She covered her mouth to hide a yawn. "Just wondering how Jina's doing. I think this is the longest we've ever been apart."

"It's crazy to think you've had such a long friendship."

"Do you not have any? Long friendships, I mean."

He shook his head. "I guess just with my brother. We moved around a lot."

"Do you intend to continue that trend—move around a lot?"

"I guess it depends if I have a reason to stay somewhere."

"Interesting. You would leave unless there's a reason to stay, and I would rather stay unless there's a reason to leave."

To him, the oppressive Georgia heat and humidity was reason enough to leave. But, she could be a good reason to stay. He took a deep breath and decided to take his chance. "I know you said this isn't a date, but would you ever consider going on a real date with me?"

Immediately, she mentally slapped herself for agreeing to sit by the fountain. Of course the romantic setting would lead to this. They should have said goodbye at the restaurant.

"I think it's best we just remain friends." She hoped that would be sufficient.

But he wanted more. "Is there something I've done to offend you? Do I have some glaring flaws I'm not aware of?"

You don't love Jesus, she thought, but didn't say. "No, it's nothing like that. You haven't offended me."

"Then what is it? Your mom must think we'd be a good match."

If he kept pressing, especially bringing up her mother, she thought she might actually take offense. She explained, "Unfortunately, because we're so different, my mom doesn't always know what's best for me…She thinks she knows what will make me happy—because it's what would make her happy—but she's not often right."

"So, you don't think I could make you happy?" he asked, as if he was ready to accept the challenge.

She didn't say anything for a long, quiet moment. Suddenly the voices of the children on the playground sounded very loud to her as she thought about all the ways Robbie could make her happy. But she knew the happiness would be so brief, fleeting—it wasn't worth it. She wanted to be honest, but she didn't want to encourage him. Finally, she said, "Maybe temporarily, but not long term. Besides, I'm more concerned with holiness than happiness."

He looked confused. "What does that mean?"

She had expected the third degree from her mother that evening—not from Robbie.

"Look," she said firmly, finally turning to look at him, "we just wouldn't work because we have different beliefs."

"You mean spiritually? I don't see why that's a problem," he said. "I can respect your beliefs."

"Can you?" she asked. The previous guy, from years earlier, had actually claimed to believe the same things she did, and even *he* couldn't respect her beliefs.

He nodded. "Yes, I don't care if you go to church on Sundays or want to celebrate Easter and Christmas."

"Do you know how lonely it would be in a relationship with someone who didn't share my beliefs? We couldn't pray or read the scriptures together..."

"You have your friends for that."

"We don't even think about the world in the same way."

"How?" he asked. "I want to understand."

Part of her wanted to say that he didn't *have* to understand, that she didn't *have* to explain herself, that he just needed to accept *no* as an answer. But the other part of her wanted to make it really clear and practical for this *man*—so she went to the subject she knew he would get. She had once heard him mention living with an ex-girlfriend, and she was sure he would have certain expectations, ones that she wouldn't meet.

"Okay," she said. "Tell me this. When you're in a dating relationship, at what point in the relationship do you have sex?"

"Whoa, I was not expecting you to go *there*," he said with an amused smile. Dahlia was annoyed that he'd made her go *there*. She stared at him blankly, waiting for his response. He cleared his throat and said, "I guess when we both decide it's the right time…when we're in a mutually exclusive relationship."

"See, that doesn't work for me," she said. "I won't be having sex until I'm married."

He was quiet for several seconds—nine to be exact. Dahlia counted them. Then he said, "I've known plenty of Christian girls who still have sex before marriage."

Dahlia didn't want to comment on the sex lives of any Christian girls he might have known, so she simply said, "Not this one."

"So, are you saying you've *never…*"

"Nope." She shook her head, not at all feeling mortified like she thought she would.

"But, you just turned *thirty*, Dahlia."

She shrugged her shoulders, not at all feeling inadequate because he couldn't understand.

"But, what if you never get married?"

She narrowed her eyes at him. "Thanks for the vote of confidence. But even so, I'd be fine. Would you quit acting so surprised?"

"I'm sorry," he said, trying to suppress a smile. "I've just never known anyone but priests to abstain from sex."

"Well, we do exist, plenty of us, and it's not that big a deal."

He sat there, dumbfounded. "You only say that because you don't know what you're missing."

"Maybe. But you don't know what you're missing by not following Jesus."

"Sounds like we could both help each other out then," he said with a charming smile, moving his eyebrows up and down flirtatiously. Yep, he would definitely be a temptation.

"Oh wow. You really do need Jesus," she said with an embarrassed laugh.

He smirked and shook his head. "I don't need some guy who's been dead for two thousand years."

"Well, that's the whole point. He's not dead. He's very much alive."

He stared at her like she was talking nonsense, as if he couldn't believe she would actually believe something like that. And she looked at him, hoping one day he would recognize it as truth. Standing, she said, "Let's just be co-workers and friends, and leave it at that."

He stood and said, "I guess I'll have to reactivate my dating apps. Maybe I'll find Mrs. Herd's daughter on one of them."

Dahlia laughed. "You may run into similar issues. Mrs. Herd and her children really love the Lord."

He looked at the darkening sky, and cried dramatically, jokingly, "God, why did I end up in this place?"

"Maybe so He can save you," Dahlia said lightheartedly, though in her heart she prayed He would.

"I don't need saving."

"We all do."

—

When she pulled into the parking space at her apartment complex, she sat there for a minute, replaying the events of the evening. After mulling over what she should tell her mother, she texted her, "Thanks for the gift, but I returned it," with a smile emoji. She was only then beginning to feel a little mortified about bringing up the sex talk with Robbie. But it had worked—he had left it alone after that, walked her to her car, and said he would see her again when school started.

Her spirits lifted when she glimpsed the light on in Jina's apartment. She rushed to the door and did their secret knock. Jina threw the door and her arms open wide, and they hugged for a good long minute, relieved to be back together again.

When Jina stepped back and actually looked at her friend, she asked, "Why are you dressed so fancy? Were you on a date?"

"No…and yes," Dahlia said, plopping down on the couch and wrapping a blanket around herself, even covering her head, ready to hide from the world.

Jina's mouth dropped open as she sat beside her. "With who? You didn't tell me you met anyone!"

She pulled the blanket back so she could see her friend. "Well, I was supposed to be having dinner with my mom, to celebrate my birthday. But instead, she set me up on a date, which she thought was a wonderful gift. Want to guess who she set me up with?"

Jina's eyes narrowed in suspicion. "Do I know him?"

Dahlia nodded.

After a pause she guessed, "…David?"

Dahlia's eyes went wide and she burst into laughter, momentarily covering her face with the blanket again. "Oh, my goodness. It *really* could have been worse!" She had forgotten how her mom had met David at Lily's engagement party.

"So, not David?"

Dahlia shook her head. "Robbie."

"*What* was she thinking? We have to work with him. We have to see him every day."

"Exactly. What could be better than going to work with your husband every morning?" Dahlia asked, mimicking the tone and words she knew her mother would use.

"How did it end?" Jina always wanted to know the ending before the beginning.

"Uh…with rejection, and little more vulnerability than I would have liked."

Jina demanded more details, and the two of them stayed up until three in the morning, sharing everything that had transpired during their time apart.

Chapter Nineteen

Women in safe spaces, connected by common beliefs and identity, are often compelled and empowered to pour forth their deepest hurts, their hidden sorrows, the things from which Jesus has healed or is healing them. By the end of the summer, that's the kind of safe space Morgan and Dahlia had cultivated among the women; they had built a place of comfort and trust where confession and need made themselves known. They had finished their reading and discussion through the book of Colossians, and had decided for the last evening that Ms. Cynthia would share with them, whatever was on her heart.

After plenty of snacking, they piled into the family room, all of them taking the same seats they had claimed over the past several weeks, Ms. Cynthia in Alan's comfy reading chair. Dahlia was so glad Jina was home so she could come this time; they sat beside each other on the floor, their backs propped against one of the sofas.

Ms. Cynthia began by saying, "All of you are much younger than me, young enough to be my daughters and granddaughters, and I just wanted to first say thank you for inviting this old woman to spend her summer with you. A few of you are married, but most of you are not, and I wanted to talk about something that is applicable to all of us, but especially to the single women—who I know, after having conversations with them, all desire to be married at some point in the future. I was married for forty-three years until my husband passed away three years ago. It wasn't always a good marriage. I don't think we got a good start, and it took a lot of work to achieve stability and happiness and any form of godliness. For me, in my generation, there wasn't a lot of waiting to get married—I was married at nineteen. I know it hasn't been like that for any of you. You have had to wait. So, let me first ask a question. What kind of advice or encouragement do you receive from others in your community about being single and desiring marriage in this season of waiting?"

It was quiet for a moment until Lily dared to speak first. "Guard your heart," she said. Her eyes cut to Dahlia, though nobody saw, because that was what her older sister had told her repeatedly when she was a teenager.

Erica said, "It will happen when you least expect it or when you stop looking."

"Or when you learn to be content with your singleness," Dahlia added.

Sera nodded in agreement. "Or when you've worked on yourself enough to become the kind of wife somebody would want."

"Be like the persistent widow at the judge's door," Jina said. "Keep praying for a husband."

Ms. Cynthia nodded her head, listening to the women. "Is any of this bad advice?" she asked.

They hesitated to respond, unsure if it was a trick question. So Morgan said, "Some of it is. And the parts that aren't bad, aren't necessarily encouraging." She had heard, and been exhausted by, many of those same comments for years.

Ms. Cynthia nodded, and then said, "Let's take a look at some of the advice given to the young woman in the Song of Solomon." There was a rustling of paper as all the women opened their Bibles to the right page. Lily used the table of contents; she was no longer as familiar with the order of scripture as she had once been. "Chapter eight, verse nine. I'll read the verse before and after."

Ms. Cynthia waited for them to find the verse, took a sip of tea, and then began reading, "OTHERS: We have a little sister, and she has no breasts. What shall we do for our sister on the day she is spoken for? If she is a wall, we will build on her a battlement of silver, but if she is a door, we will enclose her with boards of cedar. SHE: I was a wall, and my breasts were like towers; then I was in his eyes as one who finds peace.

"Most commentaries I've seen believe the OTHERS in this section are the young woman's brothers. They give two scenarios—either their sister will be a wall or she'll be a door. What are your thoughts on this? Could this metaphor be used to describe women today? What do you think you are, if you had to choose?"

Lily was quick to say, "Well, Dahlia's definitely a wall," and Erica was just as quick to agree with her.

Dahlia was too pleased Lily had attended the study all summer that she couldn't even be bothered.

Instead she shrugged her shoulders and said, "Well, that means you're both doors then."

Jina thought for a moment before asking, "Hmm…could we be somewhere in the middle, like a window?"

Ms. Cynthia chuckled. "Well, maybe. Is this window just slightly cracked to let in a breeze? Or is it wide open with a rope ladder hanging out of it?"

Morgan chimed in, "But the idea of this scripture, at least from these brothers' perspectives, and probably society's perspective, is that it's best if we are walls, right? They say if she's a wall, she gets a crown of silver. If she's a door, if she allows herself to be too open to the advances of men, they will board her up."

During the conversation, Sera was debating whether or not she wanted to share, whether it would be beneficial not just for her, but also for the hearers, whether it would bring glory to God. In the end, her tears revealed the answer. She had to tell her story, if for no other reason than to testify to the freedom Jesus gives. When Morgan saw a few tears rolling down Sera's cheeks, she handed her some tissue and tried to discreetly ask if she was okay, but the others had already noticed, expressing their concern as well.

"Are you okay?" Ms. Cynthia asked. "Did we say anything to upset you?"

She dried her eyes, and then her voice came out strong and clear. "No, no. I'm just thinking about this concept, about being a wall or a door, and I'm mourning the fact that we would ever be expected to be one or the other. I love that the bride in these scriptures can confidently say she was a wall. How many of us can do that? It's not a reality for most of us. When I was young, I was molested by an old man who lived next door, a man my mother trusted to watch me while she went to work. She thought he was like a grandpa to me, and I never said a word to her about it, until a few years ago. Once we moved away and the abuse stopped, perhaps I did build a wall around myself for a while—I never wanted anyone to touch me affectionately.

"But when I got to high school, I began seeking attention from guys, because that's what all my friends were doing. I had a crush on one of the soccer players, and one day I found myself alone with him in a hallway. We were at a house party, and he pulled me into an empty bedroom. We were kissing—and that was all I wanted to do, but his hands went other places, and I told him to stop. The music was so loud, nobody could have heard me. I tried to push him away. But he pinned me to the bed, and he didn't stop until he was finished. He told me I wanted it. Neither my words nor my physical resistance were enough of a no. And for a long time, I asked myself, had I been too flirty, too open? In this case, too much of a door? What had I done to make him think he could do that to me?

"It brought back all the childhood memories I had buried. I fell into a deep depression, and I built an unhealthy wall around me again. And I stayed that way for a few years until my college roommate began to break down the wall, sharing her faith with me, mostly through her actions, sometimes through her words. And I came to know God and who He created me to be, and now I often pray a verse from Zechariah 2 that says, 'And I will be to her a wall of fire all around, declares the LORD, and I will be the glory in her midst.' He is the wall around me; it's not something I need to build myself.

"I know so many of us have been touched in ways we should never have been touched, that our bodies have been used in ways they should never have been used. I know that we're always, each of us, vulnerable when we go out into the world, vulnerable to the desires of man, and what they choose to do is never our fault. We can aim to be walls. We can end up being doors or windows. We can desire to be married, and we can try to find contentment in our singleness. We can try not to awaken love until it pleases, even though the world is telling us to find our identity in love, and the church tells us to find a husband, to be fruitful and multiply. We can learn, in preparation, how to be good wives and mothers, should that ever be part of our stories. We can work to guard our hearts—and our bodies—by the power of the Holy Spirit. And we can still sin and be sinned against. It can still not happen for us, still not work out as we hope and pray.

"Ms. Cynthia, I appreciate this discussion and your wisdom very much. I appreciate what the scriptures give to us. But this striving…this need to somehow find the right balance of not being too closed off, too much of a wall, but not being too open, too much like a door…it's too much sometimes. These *Others*, these brothers, who want to crown their sister if she protects her purity, but if she doesn't, they want to lock her away…Sometimes the weight of it is too much." She paused for a moment before concluding, "I'm so thankful we're on this side of the cross, that we have Jesus to carry our burdens. I'm glad it's in *His* eyes we find our peace."

Through misty eyes, Ms. Cynthia said, "Amen." She cried because she felt every word Sera spoke. It wasn't just Sera's story; it was hers too. It was all of theirs in some way. The old woman wasn't the only one with tears in her eyes. "I think it's common among women to feel like we are too much and not enough. At least, that's been a constant throughout my life, trying to find a balance, and it can be hard to carry. It's a beautiful thing that Jesus sees us exactly as we are, and He gives us rest from these burdens."

After a quiet moment of them sitting in the truth they had both shared, Morgan asked, "Did you ever press charges against the young man?" Morgan knew what those house parties were like. As a cheerleader, she'd spent many nights at them, fending off the advances of teenage boys. Sera's experience could easily have been her own.

"No." Sera shook her head. "One of his team mates found out and beat him up. He was injured, and the team mate lost some college scholarship money because of it. But that was it."

When Sera said those words, Dahlia instantly suspected that she was the girl Andrew had written about in his email. Sera was the reason Andrew didn't trust Michael and wanted her to be careful around him. In his email, Andrew hadn't given details; he'd simply said sexual assault, which could mean many things—all of them wrong and horrific—but this needed to be called what it really was. Rape. Michael had done that to Sera. Morgan clearly didn't know the young man from Sera's story was Michael, that her brother was the one who had committed the crime, the he was the one she wanted charges brought against.

When everyone left, and Jina had gone to the bathroom, Dahlia said to Morgan, "Michael told me he suffered a knee injury his senior year of high school. Do you know much about how that happened?"

"Honestly, no. I was married to my first husband at the time, losing myself in drugs and alcohol. I didn't talk to my family much at all, and by the time I did come back around, he had already recovered from surgery and finished physical therapy. We never really talked about it. All I know is it happened during soccer practice. Why do you ask?"

Dahlia hesitated. Sera hadn't shared any names, and it seemed like she was also unaware that Morgan was Michael's sister. Was it her place to tell the sister that her brother was the one who assaulted Sera? What if she was wrong? What if it had been another boy? What if she was just connecting the wrong dots? Dahlia shook her head and smiled. "No reason. I was just curious how it happened."

But Dahlia's question raised Morgan's suspicions, and she determined to call her mother in the morning and find out more about Michael's senior year.

On the drive home, Jina was still contemplating the wall and door debate. "Do you think I'm a wall or door?" Jina asked her best friend.

"I think Sera was right…We don't have to define ourselves that way."

"But, if you had to say one for me…?" Jina preferred definitions.

"Like you said, you're probably more of a window, with some very pretty curtains dancing in the breeze."

Jina laughed. "You're not taking it seriously."

"I guess not," Dahlia admitted. She was still overwhelmed by the things Sera had revealed. Those were the things she took seriously. "To be honest, I was a little disappointed that was the topic Ms. Cynthia chose to talk about. I avoided the marriage Bible study at church, and Morgan and I focused on a book of scripture with only two verses devoted to husbands and wives…on purpose. *But,* maybe it was supposed to happen so that Sera could open up."

"I agree. I'm glad she felt comfortable to share. Her words were powerful."

Jina had always recognized a seed of bitterness and distrust in Dahlia in regard to marriage, and she believed it was planted when her parents divorced—maybe even before then when she witnessed so much conflict between them. She knew it would take someone with patience and gentle persistence to break through Dahlia's wall. After a couple minutes of thoughtful silence, she told her friend, "Dahlia, you can't avoid marriage, or the topic of marriage, forever. Don't be *such* a wall that you won't let anybody in."

Part Three: Fall

Chapter Twenty

It was a couple weeks into the new school year when Dahlia decided to visit Ms. Anna and Chris one Friday evening. She often took a little too much pride in not forgetting the orphan and the widow, but she had neglected them for the entire summer and felt no amount of apologies was acceptable for her actions. She had called Ms. Anna and apologized profusely anyway, but Ms. Anna brushed it off with all her kind words and invited her to dinner.

When she pulled up out front, the sun had not yet set, and the sky was painted like cotton candy. Even in September it was still a summer evening in north Georgia, just a hint of fall in the air. Dahlia could see light and movement through the kitchen window, and she knew as she approached the porch, she would smell something delicious through the screen door. When she entered the foyer, the rear screen door was also open, and she could hear Chris talking to someone; she hadn't noticed any other vehicles outside. Ms. Anna wiped her hands on a rag before she greeted Dahlia with a hug and a kiss on the cheek. Dahlia melted into the strong embrace of the grandmother.

After a few pleasantries, she asked with curiosity, "Who's Chris talking to out there?"

"Oh! We have a guest for dinner—other than you, of course." She smiled. "Andrew's here."

"Did you invite him?" Dahlia was suddenly on edge, unsure how to see him after so long, after not replying to his e-mail.

"He's been coming by all summer, usually every week or two, helps with the lawn, spends time with Chris," Ms. Anna explained. He had, without prompting, cared for the family she'd neglected; Dahlia's eyes became watery with internal gratitude. Ms. Anna continued, "We really enjoy his company. His mother died when he was young also, so he's able to relate to Chris on a whole 'nother level than most people."

"His mother died when he was young?"

"Haven't you ever asked him about his family?" Ms. Anna sounded like she was gently chiding her.

"I mean…" she hesitated. "I've learned things through conversation and meeting his cousins, but no…I have never asked directly."

Ms. Anna took a deep breath as she stirred the beans on the stove. Dahlia took the spoon from her and instructed her to sit down—she'd done enough and needed a rest. "Yes, his mother died in a car accident when he was four," Ms. Anna went ahead and explained.

Dahlia took it in. So, both Andrew and Daniel had lost their mothers at different times in different circumstances. It was no surprise the cousins had grown so close. "I had no idea."

"Well, how could you?"

"Exactly. It's not like he talks much."

Ms. Anna frowned at Dahlia's words. "That ain't what I meant. Even if he did talk much, is that the kind of information you just offer up? You have to ask questions, Dahlia, if you expect to know someone."

Dahlia had never expected to know Andrew. She had never even tried. She'd only been quick to pass judgment of him. These were the thoughts running through her mind when she heard the screen door open and then slam shut. In those few seconds before he appeared, Dahlia became so nervous, almost embarrassed to see him after their last moments together. She wondered if he felt the same way about seeing her, if he was aware of her being there. She also wondered if he had told Ms. Anna about their last encounter, but then immediately she somehow knew he would never have done that. He wouldn't have exposed her in that way. She realized then that she trusted him.

Regardless of how he felt, she knew she was alone in her shame—he had nothing to be ashamed of. Just like at church, she now wanted to flee the room, to avoid him completely—not because of him this time, but because of herself. But it was too late, and there was nowhere to hide. And she needed to be humble and face all the ways she'd been wrong about him.

When he turned the corner and their gazes met, she was struck by the green of his eyes for the first time. That's a lie. She had noticed them before, but they had never made her stomach flutter or her heart beat faster. He nodded, smiled, and said hello, but quickly turned away from her as he went to the sink to wash his hands. He was sweaty from playing basketball with Chris, and he could smell himself, the stench of outside on his skin. Dahlia was the last person he had planned to see that evening, and Ms. Anna had asked him to stay for dinner—and he'd agreed—before she revealed that Dahlia would be there also.

Ms. Anna wrapped her arms around Chris from behind and gave him a kiss on the cheek, not bothered by his usual teenage boy body odor. "Will you please wash up and set the table?" she asked him.

"I'll help," Andrew said, grabbing Chris by the shoulders and leading him towards the bathroom. Chris could have washed up in the kitchen, but Andrew was desperate to use whatever he could find in the bathroom to make himself smell better.

Dahlia took a silent, deep breath when they disappeared. He had smiled and been polite, but he'd avoided looking at her. She didn't want the meal to be uncomfortable. She owed him an apology, and she should have written it weeks earlier. Now, she didn't think she'd have a moment alone with him to offer it in person.

When they were seated at the table—him across from her, Chris beside her, and Ms. Anna on the end—he asked her, "How are you and your family?"

"Everyone is good. Thanks for asking."

"And your dad's wedding, it went well?"

She nodded. "For the most part." Andrew could tell from her face something had happened, and he was so curious to ask, but based on their previous conversation, he had concluded that she didn't want them to know each other, so he decided not to pry.

She was, of course, remembering the thing that happened, her interaction with Brian; for her it obscured all the good memories from the wedding. When her dad and Morgan got back from their honeymoon, she had shared it with them; they seemed genuinely concerned, and her dad had promised to spend some one-on-one time with his future son-in-law to try to "weed out his true character," as Alan had put it. They agreed it was best not to share the incident with Lily so Dahlia wouldn't be accused of starting any more issues. Dahlia had left it alone and was trusting her father to shed his passive skin and do what he said he would do.

"How are Katherine and Caleb?" she asked, turning the conversation away from her.

"They're great. Her husband is home, so I'm on my own again. It's been different, especially without Daniel around."

"He's still not home?" she asked in surprise. Jina still hadn't heard from him, but she assumed he would be back by then.

Andrew shook his head. "I can't believe he missed the bar exam. He said he'll take it in February."

"But you took it, right?" Ms. Anna asked. "When will you know if you passed?"

"Results won't be posted until late October."

"I know you passed," Ms. Anna said, just like a confident grandma. "I feel it in my spirit."

"And her spirit ain't never wrong," Chris said, his eyes wide as he gave her a sideways glance and smirk. They all laughed, and it really was the first time Dahlia had noticed the sound of Andrew's laughter. Why had she never paid attention to his details before? Pride. Indifference.

"If, I mean *when,* you pass, you'll be working for your father, right?" she asked him.

"Hmm, actually, things have changed," he admitted. "I've applied to work at an immigration law firm in Atlanta. My dad wasn't thrilled about it, but it's where I feel led to be."

"Definitely go where the Spirit leads you. Oh, that's wonderful," Ms. Anna said with enthusiasm.

"It really is," Dahlia agreed, impressed by him—and his choice.

During the course of the dinner conversation, Dahlia continued to hear her phone vibrating from her purse nearby. She ignored it for as long as she could, but after what seemed like the tenth buzz, she said, "I'm sorry. I need to check my phone, just to make sure nothing's wrong. It keeps going off." She grabbed it from the foyer and then stood in the entryway to the dining room, reading all the messages. Andrew's eyes were on her as she did, watching her face become more concerned each second.

She had missed three calls and several messages from Erica. As she was going to listen to a voicemail, the phone rang again, and she answered immediately. "Erica," she said and waited for a reply. "I can barely hear you…Where is Michael now?"

At the mention of his name, Andrew stood and walked over to her. "What's happened?" he asked. She stared into his eyes, more closely than ever before, as she strained to understand what Erica was saying, her cell reception continuing to go in and out. Suddenly the call ended.

As Dahlia attempted to call her back, she explained, "Erica is with Michael, somewhere in the middle of nowhere. All I could clearly make out were the words 'date' and 'barn.' I had no idea they were talking or dating or anything." Erica's phone went to voicemail.

"Was she asking for help?"

"Here's her text messages…" Dahlia said, scrolling through them. "She says that she thought they were going to dinner at a restaurant, but he took her some place in the country for a picnic dinner. He's making her uncomfortable, and she's trying to convince him that they should head back before it gets dark." In unison, they both looked out the window; the sun had just set.

"Is Erica okay?" Chris asked with concern. He'd developed a slight middle-school-boy crush on her. Ms. Anna observed them, not sure how to help.

"She's in danger," he said. "Let's just say it like it is."

"She *could* be in danger," Dahlia corrected. She didn't want to imagine the worst. "I'm sorry, Ms.

Anna. Please forgive me, but I have to go see if I can find her. I'm so sorry to leave like this." She was already throwing her purse over her shoulder.

Ms. Anna made her way around the table and pulled the anxious Dahlia in for a hug, while Dahlia was thinking she didn't have time for hugs—but it was exactly what she needed to calm the panic in her belly. "You be careful," Ms. Anna said firmly. "Call the police, if you need to. I'll be praying without ceasing." She kissed her on the cheek and then released her hold.

When Dahlia was down the front porch steps, Andrew grabbed her arm. "Wait, what are you going to do?" he asked.

Again, something she didn't have time for. "It was Sera, right?" she demanded. "The girl from high school, with Michael? It was Sera?"

He hesitated to answer her, his sense of respect for Sera's privacy stopping him.

"Look, she already shared her story with us. I just want to confirm they are the same accounts."

Finally, he nodded. "Yes, it was Sera."

Dahlia was in a low-key panic, which was far worse internally than anyone could tell externally. "And now Erica is alone with him, in some remote place, and feeling scared. I should have told her about Michael, but I had no idea they'd formed any kind of real relationship. I've got to go." She pulled her arm from him grasp, trying to ignore the fact that even in her stress she was so aware of his touch, of his strong hands.

"Where are you going to go?" he asked. "Where are you going to look?"

"I don't know. But I can't do nothing. I'll go to my dad's first. Maybe Morgan will know something."

He let her go, didn't ask any more questions, and waited until she drove away before jumping in his SUV and heading in the same, but different, direction. Andrew had a good idea what barn Erica was talking about, but he didn't tell Dahlia because he knew she would have insisted on coming with him, and he didn't want her to. He would find Erica though. He just didn't know if he'd find her in time, before anything could happen; at the thought, his foot pressed harder on the gas.

Dahlia was also speeding, alternating calls between Erica, Morgan, and her dad—none of them answered. An hour later when she arrived at her dad's house, the porch light was on, like always, but every window was dark. She let herself in, calling out to them, but the place was silent, the alarm had been set. She found Morgan's phone on the kitchen counter with ten missed calls from her. She sat on at the bottom of the stairs and began to pray, *ceaselessly* as Ms. Anna was doing, praying against every *what-if* situation she imagined. After thirty minutes, she was about to call the police dispatch, non-emergency line —even though to her, it *was* an emergency—when she heard the front door knob turning, and before they could make it all the way inside, Dahlia hopped up, pulling the door open. "Where have y'all been? I've been calling and calling."

"I accidentally left my phone here, and your dad's is turned off," Morgan quickly explained. "What's going on? What's wrong?"

They were nicely dressed, and Dahlia suddenly remembered they had a hospital fundraiser that evening.

"Do you know any place Michael would take a girl, some place with a barn?"

Morgan thought for a moment, her brow furrowed, then shook her head. "No, I don't. Why?"

Dahlia let herself fall back down on the stairs, feeling defeated. Alan sat beside her. "Honey, explain to us what's happened," he said gently.

Dahlia had tears in her eyes now. "Erica called me almost two hours ago, sounding scared…said she was with Michael in some barn in the country, and he was making her uncomfortable." Erica's exact words had been that he was *creeping her out*, and every woman knew what those words meant, how the reality of them felt. "Her phone must have died or she doesn't have service because I haven't been able to reach her again."

"I'm sure she'll be okay," Alan said, squeezing her shoulder. He looked to Morgan for help.

She asked, "Why are you so concerned about Erica being with Michael?" In the pit of her stomach she already knew the answer, she'd already put the clues together, but he was her brother, and she still hoped she was wrong.

Dahlia hesitated for only a moment before confessing, "He's the guy from Sera's story."

"What guy from Sera's story?" Alan asked, confused. "Who's Sera? Have I met her?" Morgan hadn't shared any personal information with him about any of the women from the bible study group.

He didn't understand what they were talking about or why Dahlia was so upset. Why *was* she so concerned about Erica being with Michael? He seemed like a decent enough guy to him.

Morgan took a moment to process. She wasn't shocked, but instead her eyes revealed a deep sorrow and disappointment. "You're sure?"

"Yes. Andrew is the teammate who got in a fight with him afterward. He confirmed it."

Morgan nodded, her face determined, but downcast, grieving the fact that she didn't have a hard time believing something like that about her brother. "Let's call dispatch and see if they can track their phones and figure out a location for either of them"

Just then, Dahlia's phone buzzed. It was a message from Erica, and it said: *I'm okay. I just got home. I'm sorry for making you worry. My phone's about to die. We'll talk tomorrow at Marie's. Love you.*

Chapter Twenty-One

Marie had traveled out of town to be with her mother while she recovered from surgery, and her best friend Julie was staying with her children. But on Saturday afternoon, Julie had a first date with a man she had met on a dating app—she was willing to cancel it, but Marie wouldn't even hear of it. She was beyond ready for Julie to meet someone new, to stop waiting on the same guy who wouldn't make up his mind, who wouldn't pursue a relationship, so she asked Dahlia if she would spend the afternoon with the kids, and Dahlia had in turn asked Erica to join her. She wanted Erica to get to know Marie's family better so that Marie could add another member to their support community, able to serve and love them and receive blessings from them in return. But there wouldn't be any time to privately discuss the events of the previous evening while watching the kids, so Dahlia texted Erica early that morning, inviting her, practically ordering her, to meet her for brunch before heading to Marie's house.

As soon as Erica stepped through the cafe door, Dahlia gave her the biggest hug, grateful to see that she was okay, or at least appeared okay. Erica wasn't used to Dahlia showing such a display of affection, so she let herself nestle into the embrace, also grateful—to be comforted. She also appreciated that Dahlia waited until after they received their food to begin grilling her with questions.

First she asked, "How are you? Are you okay?"

Erica nodded. "Yes, I'm okay now. I really am sorry for worrying you the way I did. I didn't know who else to contact."

"Well, I'm glad you got home safely. How long have you been dating Michael? Why didn't you tell me anything about it?" Dahlia went into mother mode.

"We haven't been *dating*. We just hung out a couple of times. He asked for my number at Lily's engagement party, but he didn't really start texting me until after your birthday party. He asked me not to tell anyone because he thought it would be weird for you."

Dahlia shook her head and rolled her eyes, irritated that he had sworn Erica to secrecy. "I could have warned you about him if you had told me. Why did you agree to go out with him?"

"Really, Dahlia. He's attractive, charming, and funny. It's not like we have a lot of other options, and I thought it would be fun. I'm sorry I'm not better at reading people, like you are," she replied defensively.

Dahlia sighed. "I didn't mean to sound accusatory. I'm sorry. This isn't your fault, at all. I'm not better at reading people. I misjudged Michael in the beginning as well. As Morgan's brother, I wanted to trust him and get along with him, but then Andrew told me the truth about him, and I probably should have shared it with you."

"Yeah, we both misjudged Andrew too."

"What do you mean?" Dahlia asked. She agreed with the statement, knew it was true, but she didn't understand why or how Erica knew it too. The surprised look on her face encouraged her friend to continue.

"He's the one who found us last night, the one who saved me."

"How did he know where you were?" she asked. He hadn't said anything to her at Ms. Anna's house

—not that she had given him much opportunity to speak.

"It was a place Michael used to throw parties and take girls back in high school, so Andrew knew about it. Michael sure was shocked to see him. I was too, of course."

"What happened?" Dahlia leaned forward, elbows on the table, very interested.

Erica laughed. "Well, I had finally convinced Michael to take me home. We were in the car—"

"Had he been drinking?" Dahlia interrupted.

"We each only had one beer. He was fine to drive. Anyway, we were in the car—I was so ready to go—but he tried to kiss me again, and I tried to shove him away, but I had nowhere to go, strapped into the seat. The windows were down, and somehow Andrew snuck up on the driver's side. He reached inside and grabbed the keys out of the ignition, and at the same time, I punched Michael as hard as I could in the stomach."

"Really?" Dahlia's face beamed with pride. "Good for you."

"I'm sure it wasn't that hard." Erica brushed it off. "But then Andrew threw open the door and dragged Michael out of the car. Michael was so angry, especially when he recognized Andrew—it was hard to tell who it was at first in the dark. He leaned against the car, clutching his stomach—as if I really hurt him—and cussing both of us. Andrew dangled his keys in the air and then turned and chucked them as far as he could into the field, into waist high grass!" She laughed. "I wouldn't be surprised if he's still searching for them."

Dahlia smiled softly, imagining Michael on his hands and knees, looking for his keys in the dark field. "Then what happened?" she prompted Erica to continue.

"Well, Michael tried to throw a few punches, but Andrew dodged them, and then we took off running to his vehicle. Michael didn't chase after us, thankfully. Then Andrew drove me home, after making sure I was okay and nothing had happened, that he didn't need to take me to the hospital or the police department to press charges. He was adamant that I contact you to let you know I was all right. Apparently, he still doesn't have your number? Why have y'all never exchanged numbers?"

Dahlia shrugged. "There was just never a reason."

"Last night was a good reason."

"Yeah, well he didn't tell me he was going to look for you…But I'm so glad he did."

"Me too. I'm just sorry Michael has to be a part of your family now."

"Yeah, I'm not sure what Morgan is going to do with him. She was just as concerned about you last night as I was. I know she loves her brother—he's her brother—but I don't know if she'll invite him around much anymore."

"That's hard, I'm sure," Erica acknowledged. "But I definitely don't want to be anywhere he is. Did Lily invite him to her wedding?" She tried to hide it, but Dahlia could hear the slight fear in her voice.

"If she did, I'll rescind the invitation. No worries. He won't be there." She squeezed Erica's hand in assurance.

—

While driving home that evening, Erica couldn't help replaying the previous night's events in her mind. She had made light of everything when she shared with Dahlia, but she had truly never been more scared in her life. During one of her many rejections—the moment when she knew it was serious—Michael asked, "Has Sera been talking about me or something? Why are you being like this?"

"Sera?" she asked, confused why he would mention her.

"Yeah, from your Bible study. I know she's been attending. I heard Morgan mention her name."

He told me I wanted it, she heard Sera's words in her head. "You know Sera?" she asked, trying to keep her voice from shaking, trying to keep him talking. If he was talking, maybe he wouldn't have his hands on her. She watched too many true crime shows; she knew how the night could end, especially now that she had figured out there was a connection between Sera and Michael, now that she knew what he had done to her, what he was capable of.

"We went to high school together."

"Oh." She nodded. "I didn't know you two knew each other." That seemed to satisfy him, removing any suspicions that Sera had been talking about him. "But, I really do need to get home, so can we leave now?" He'd sighed in frustration, but finally moved away so she could stand, and she had wasted no time exiting the barn. If Andrew hadn't shown up, she wondered if she would have been able to persuade him to take her home a second time, or if she would have had to run into the dark field and hide until he finally left—she considered that option many times.

When she pulled up to her house, she had to park in the street because the driveway was full. She had forgotten about the family gathering; all she really wanted to do was sneak away to her garage apartment, cover herself in blankets and disappear, at least for a little while. But there was no hiding with so many people around. Her grandfather and his brothers were sitting on the porch, and much to her shock, David was standing on the steps talking to them. She had already told him after the bouquet of flowers that he was only a friend, if that word even accurately described how she felt toward him. She had no desire to be unkind, but anger was rising in her chest: why was he hanging out with her family? She had not seen or spoken to him in weeks. That was about to change; she had plenty to say to him now.

"Erica," her abuelo called to her, "David stopped by to see you." He gave her a look that begged *give him a chance*. She tried her best not to glare.

She greeted her abuelo and tíos and then asked David if she could speak privately with him, leading him down the porch steps and around the corner of the house. She began, "I don't want to be rude, but I don't understand why you're here. I already explained—we are just friends. You can't come by my house unannounced. You're giving my grandfather the wrong idea."

He moved closer to her. She backed away. "I'm giving him the right idea, and he agrees with it. I just don't think you know your own feelings."

"And you do?" Everything inside of her wanted to go off on him in Spanish, but she took a deep breath instead.

"Your hormones make you emotional. You can't help it. That's why you can't follow your feelings; you have to follow what you know to be true, and I know it's true that what women really want in a man is financial stability. And I can offer that. So, I'll keep pursuing you until you see me as more than a friend."

She was disgusted by nearly everything he had said. He didn't trust the Spirit in her, but only in himself. The string of cuss words Michael had yelled at her the night before wrestled at the back of her throat, ready to make their way to the tip of her tongue. She never used that kind of language, even in Spanish when no one could understand—because

Jesus still understood—but if there had ever been a person who inspired those words to run through her mind, it was David in that moment. Her little cousins raced by with a soccer ball, headed to the backyard, their laughter quenching her anger just in time.

"No," she said firmly. "You're wrong. The only thing you said that was correct is that we can't act on how we *feel*, but rather on what we *know* to be true. And what I know is that you are not who the Lord has for me. And the truth is, I will never consider you more than an *acquaintance*." She put him in the proper category. He was not her friend. "Do not pursue me anymore." He seemed like he was going to reply, but she cut him off. "It's time for you to leave."

She followed him to his car, making sure he didn't stop to talk with any of her family members. She silently thanked God that he wasn't blocked in by any of their vehicles. Before he drove away, he rolled down his window, and said with confidence, "You'll change your mind. The Lord will change your mind." In a different life, one where she wasn't submitted to the authority of Christ, she would have picked up a rock and thrown it at his car when he pulled away. *Thank you, Lord, for self-control,* she prayed as she turned around and entered the side door to the kitchen, avoiding the men on the porch.

She hugged her abuela from behind, kissing her cheek, donned an apron, and then sat down at the table to help her aunt and cousin form the tamales. "I had a video chat with your mom last night," her abuela told her.

"Really?" Erica asked, not masking the disappointment in her voice. While she was being forcefully groped by Michael, she'd missed her mother's call. They usually could only call when they were in the city at an internet cafe; otherwise service was too spotty. "How are they?"

"They are almost done building the new medical clinic. They are so excited. By the new year, they'll start looking for medical workers to staff the place, doctors and *nurses* who speak Spanish."

Erica wasn't sure if she had imagined the emphasis her abuela placed on the word *nurses* or the looks her aunt and cousin passed between them before glancing at her. Were they implying that she should go to Mexico? Were they offering her a different option than the one the men on the porch constantly presented to her? The women surrounding her had all done it that way—married young and started having babies. She was almost positive none of them would change that aspect of their lives, but she felt their unspoken encouragement that she didn't have to do it that way. She could do it whichever way the Lord directed.

After how Michael had acted, after hearing about Julie's horrible date and Marie's husband who was planning to file for divorce, and after her conversation with David, Erica felt completely drained, done, finished. She had finally come to a point where she didn't want anything to do with dating and had, at least temporarily, lost any desire for marriage. The Spirit kept reminding her that there was time, and He was slowly revealing a new plan for her future, unfolding it bit by bit until she could resist it no longer.

Chapter Twenty-Two

When Jina texted her mother one Wednesday morning in late September, saying she wouldn't be at Bible study that evening because she was sick and running a fever, Mrs. Yoon showed up at lunch time with a cooler full of food. She dished up some soup for her daughter and then began cleaning the apartment, to rid it of general clutter and germs. Jina lounged on the couch, allowing herself to be taken care of. She hated missing school, hated having a substitute cover her classes, knowing her students would just play around and fall behind.

In the middle of fluffing a pillow, Mrs. Yoon said, "I met a new woman at church on Sunday who wants you to meet her grandson."

Now was her chance to be completely honest. "But umma…I love someone already." They had never officially said they loved each other, but that's how she felt. And she thought he had too.

"Love?" Mrs. Yoon nearly scoffed at the idea, but realized her daughter was serious. "Who do you love?"

"Remember the guy who was at my door the night we had dinner with Steve?"

"Dahlia's boyfriend?"

"He isn't her boyfriend. He was my…almost boyfriend."

"Almost boyfriend? What does that mean? Why didn't you tell me? Why didn't you introduce him? Where is this man now?" The questions flew out of her mouth, no time to answer in between.

Jina stared at her mother for a moment. "Wait, umma, you don't care that he's not Korean?"

"Is that really what you think of me, Jina?"

"What am I supposed to think? You've only ever talked about nice Korean boys, and you've only ever set me up with them."

"As long as he is a man of God who respects Korean culture, I don't care what he is. Sometimes it's easier if you share the same culture, but easy is not the most important thing."

"What about appa? Would he care?"

Her mother shook her head. "No. We only want you to have a good love and marriage like us. You say you love this man, so where is he?"

Jina frowned and pulled the blanket over her head, hating to admit the truth. "I haven't seen or heard from him in months, and I have no idea where he is."

Mrs. Yoon didn't say anything for a long moment, and Jina pulled the blanket back so she could see her mother's face. She seemed to be trying to choose her words carefully, to be sensitive to Jina's feelings, but it was in her nature to be direct. "Well, you may love him, but he left you. Did he make you any promises, any commitments?"

"No."

"Then there's no reason not to meet this lady's grandson. I'll pick you up on Saturday for lunch."

—

Jina had spent any free-thinking time that summer wondering about Daniel, where he was, how he was, if he still felt about her the way she felt about him. It was as if he had vanished from the face of the earth, as if he had never been real. Except for the fact that Dahlia could corroborate his existence, she might have thought she'd daydreamed it all.

That night, as soon as Steve, his aunt, and her mother had left her apartment, she sent Daniel a string of messages, explaining, apologizing, considering it too late to call him. But when he didn't respond by evening the next day, when he wasn't in attendance at church, she called him, many times—it always went straight to voicemail, and she only left one of those, too proud to let him hear the sound of desperation in her voice or the sound of her heart breaking. They had grown so close, so quickly, and then it was over. She knew it was her fault for not being one hundred percent honest, but she never would have considered he was someone who would cut all communication and disappear. She'd been *ghosted,* as Erica liked to say.

When she went to camp, so certain she would see him there, she was crushed a second time. And she heard so many stories about him from fellow camp employees who had worked with him year after year, all of them surprised and disappointed he wasn't there. She never told any of them that she knew him, never brought his name up in conversation, but her ears perked up whenever they mentioned him, and she listened to their stories, learning more about him, smiling and laughing when appropriate. A couple of the female counselors gushed about how he had been their summer crush and talked about how they missed his presence at camp—Jina didn't smile during that conversation. He was like a legend at the camp, like he was everywhere and nowhere. Her days with the kids were pure joy—the evenings by herself or with the counselors, not so much. She was certain she missed him more than they ever could.

When Dahlia told her that he had been in contact with Andrew by email, it should have been a comfort to know that he was okay, but it only made her angry. Wherever he was, he was able to communicate, but he was choosing not to be in touch with her. Even if he sent one line saying he wanted nothing more to do with her, she would have been satisfied. At least then there would be a clear ending. Instead, he was just gone, and she was doing her best to be okay with that, making sure not to talk about him too much with Dahlia, and instead just talking about him constantly with the Lord. Because He was their only connection now, the only One who knew them fully, the only One whose Spirit lived inside both of them.

—

Her mother was early to pick her up, preferring they arrive at the restaurant first. She had called her daughter the night before to make sure Jina was feeling better, and she was thrilled to hear she was so that she didn't have to cancel the meeting. Mrs. Yoon didn't tell Jina where they were going, but when her daughter saw the direction they were heading, she guessed, "Are we going to Big Joy?" It had been Jina's father's, her family's, favorite restaurant. If there was ever any occasion to celebrate, her father would tell them to hop in the car, and they would always end up there.

Her mother hesitated. "Yes. Is that okay? I know we haven't been there since appa died, but it's the restaurant they requested." They hadn't been there because Jina didn't think her mother could emotionally handle it.

Jina nodded. "It's fine with me."

She didn't tell her mom that she had actually been there since her father passed away. She had taken Daniel there the day after they stayed up late on the phone, talking about their experiences of losing a parent. She wanted to share a piece of her father with him. Now she questioned: had it mattered to him at all? She felt a fresh wave of anger

—at him for not caring, and at herself for being so vulnerable with him. *Maybe I am a door*, she thought, still trying to define herself.

When they entered the restaurant, the employees greeted them like family, and they chose their usual table in the back corner, waiting to order their food until the whole party arrived. Jina hadn't given much thought to what this man would be like; she hoped he would be half as kind as Steve when she rejected him. Or perhaps he would reject her. She didn't know how to fake emotion, and she was in no mood to pretend to be happy, so maybe she'd make a bad impression on him. She wondered if he was Korean American or Korean Korean; she hadn't asked her mother for the details. She didn't have to wait long to find out.

They both watched through the window as a blue car pulled into a parking space. The young man got out and went around to the passenger side to help an old woman, his grandma, out of the vehicle. Jina was frozen in place, and she heard her mother gasp in surprise. Mrs. Yoon recognized the old woman whom she had met at church, but she also had seen the young man before, outside Jina's apartment, the one Jina said she loved. Daniel held his grandmother's arm as he led her through the door, grateful for something to hold on to, for a task to focus on, so his nerves couldn't take over. He knew they were sitting in the back corner, the same table they had sat at when Jina brought him there. He took a deep breath before turning his head to look at them and smile with fake confidence.

Jina observed that his skin was darker, his freckles more pronounced, his hair lighter, the blue of his eyes more intense; wherever he'd been, he'd been in the sun. When he smiled, she finally remembered to exhale, not realizing she'd been holding her breath.

"Is this a trick?" her mother whispered to her. Jina glanced at her and shrugged. He was the last person either of them had expected to see that day. Jina had honestly prepared herself to never see him again. She had fully anticipated to one day check his Facebook page and see that he had posted a new profile picture, one with a beautiful woman, and his status would be changed to *in a relationship*—or worse, *engaged*. And because of their privacy settings, she wouldn't have been able to stalk the happy couple. That's what she had prepared herself for—not this, not him showing up with his grandmother on his arm. Jina and Mrs. Yoon stood as they approached the table.

Daniel's grandmother, Mrs. Sommer, introduced her grandson and he bowed slightly. Mrs. Yoon wasn't sure if she was supposed to pretend like she didn't know who he was, so it was a relief when the Mrs. Sommer said, "I know you all have met before. This is just a formal, official introduction." The old woman had heard so much about Jina, every detail Daniel could share, so she felt like she already knew the young woman.

Daniel went to order the food while the three women became more acquainted with each other. Jina was fascinated with Daniel's grandmother, had always wanted to meet her since first hearing her story. The interactions didn't feel awkward like she thought they would, but she avoided eye contact with Daniel when he joined them, taking the empty seat across from Jina's mother, beside his grandmother. Jina only glanced at him once, and then looked away, and though he continued to try and meet her eyes, he could tell she intentionally wouldn't allow herself to look at him.

After they ate most of the food and spent a lot of time on the usual getting-to-know-you conversation

—where did you grow up, where did you go to school, where do you work, do you have any siblings —Mrs. Yoon wanted to ask a serious question. She knew better than to mention anything about Jina's profession of love for this man, but she had to know where he had been, why he had not spoken to her daughter in months, only to surprise them now. "Daniel," she began, "Jina told me she hasn't seen or spoken to you in months. What happened? Where have you been?"

The question caught him off guard. For the first time, Jina dared to look at him and their eyes met; she couldn't read the emotion in his, but she wanted the floor to open up and swallow her. She wanted to know the answer, but she was mortified that her mother had asked the question. Mrs. Sommer responded instead of him, "He was in Korea with me all summer. I was visiting family, and he joined me and his grandfather. He spent all of his time studying the language and culture, in hopes that his efforts would make him worthy in your eyes, that you would approve of him as a match for Jina."

It was Daniel's turn to be mortified. It wasn't that anything his grandmother said was untrue, but it sounded stupid to him when it was said so succinctly, almost like it diminished the purpose and intentions behind his actions, almost like it had all been futile. But he maintained eye contact with Mrs. Yoon, internally preparing himself for rejection. But instead she said, "As I told Jina, as long as the man loves God and loves Jina and respects our culture, I have no objections. If he is the one *she* chooses." His eyes met Jina's again for a split second before she turned her face away, and he was filled with doubts—would she choose him? She seemed distant, almost cold. Had she met someone else?

But before he could dwell in that space, Mrs. Yoon began talking to him in Korean, curious to see how well he spoke, how much he had learned in such a short time. They were all speaking in Korean by the time they were ready to leave, and Daniel was good-naturedly struggling to keep up, while they laughed and kindly corrected his mistakes. Mrs. Yoon was impressed, even though she wouldn't admit it until she knew how her daughter felt; she didn't want to encourage Daniel if Jina was no longer sure about him.

Daniel had backed into his parking space beside Mrs. Yoon's car, so that both passenger side doors met. Jina waited beside her mother's car, unable to open her door, while Daniel helped his grandmother into her seat. When he shut the door and turned around, he was so close to her. "After I take my grandma home, can I pick you up?" he asked quietly, discreetly grabbing her hand and giving it a squeeze. "We can go somewhere and talk." She didn't say anything, couldn't clear the lump in her throat in order to form words, but she nodded. He opened the car door for her and she slipped inside.

During the ride home, Mrs. Yoon observed her daughter in silence for several minutes. Jina had just been biting her lip and staring out the window. Her mother asked, "Are you not happy? I thought you would be smiling."

"I am happy," Jina said, giving her mom the smile she'd been waiting for. "I think I'm just a little shocked that anyone would put forth so much effort for me."

"You are worth the effort, and more. Do you not know that?"

"I do…and I don't, all at the same time. It's strange to know that you are worth something great and also to feel unworthy of it at the same time."

"Hmm." Mrs. Yoon knew that sentiment well; she felt that way with Jina's father. She felt that way with

Jesus. She began to sing one of her favorite worship songs. "Two wonders here that I confess: my worth and my unworthiness. My value fixed, my ransom paid, at the cross." Jina pulled the song up on her phone, and they sang together in perfect harmony until her mother dropped her off.

As soon as Jina entered her apartment, finally a moment alone to process, she sent Dahlia a long text about what had just happened. Dahlia was helping Lily and her mother with some last minute wedding preparations, so Jina predicted she wouldn't get a response, but she had to tell *someone*. Daniel had spent the entire summer devoting himself to learning the culture, history and language of Korea, so he could become worthy in her mother's eyes, so he could earn her approval to pursue a relationship with her daughter.

Dahlia responded with a heart eye emoji, and "Can't wait to hear more."

Jina fixed her hair and makeup and threw on a new cardigan, and then she sat in the chair in front of the window, watching and waiting, both excited and anxious for Daniel to show up. She didn't wait for him to come to the door, but met him outside, and instead of driving anywhere, they began walking to a nearby park. Jina's guard was still up, her hands in her sweater pockets, not wanting to risk anymore hand holding or squeezing—not yet. He took his cues from her and tucked his inside his jacket pockets too.

They were silent for a few minutes until Daniel said, "You told your mother about me."

"Only just recently," she said quickly. "When she told me about today's lunch meeting."

"Oh?"

"I was explaining to her why I didn't want to meet anyone new."

He smiled softly. "Because of me?"

She rolled her eyes. "Because of you." Then she changed the subject. "Your Korean is very good for just a few months of study."

"You're being kind. It needs a lot of work."

"You did fine communicating with my mother." *But not with me*, she thought.

He could sense she was tense, and there was a coolness in her tone. "Forgive me if I'm wrong, but you seem a little…mad at me?"

It was a few seconds before she admitted, "I am, a little."

"Why? Should I not have set up the meeting with your mother? Did you not want that? Was she upset with you?" He was panicking, worried he'd done the wrong thing.

She stopped walking and looked at him, her eyes confused as to why he didn't get it.

"You left me," she said firmly, directly. "You just disappeared and never said a word."

Now Daniel appeared confused. "No, I didn't. I sent you a message. A long message, just before I got on the plane, explaining my plan to you, asking you to wait for me. I wasn't planning to be in contact with anyone while I was in Korea; I wanted to focus and make the most of my time—you being my motivation. And the fact that my phone got crushed one day into the trip, solidified that plan."

"You emailed with Andrew…"

"Yeah…I wrote a couple times just to check on Katherine and the baby."

"Well, I never received a message from you." All she had known was silence.

She opened her phone messages from him, the ones she had never deleted, and showed him to prove there wasn't a long, explanatory text.

His face dropped. "So, this whole time you thought…"

"That you were done with me," she finished his sentence, blinking back tears.

He shook his head and wrapped his arms around her, holding her tightly. "Never. I'm so sorry you thought that."

She looked up at him. "You went to Korea all summer. You had me apply to camp, and then you didn't show up."

"I'm sorry," he repeated earnestly. "I never intended for you to feel abandoned. I wanted you to feel fought for."

His words made her pause. That's what he had been doing, fighting for her, in his own way. But she hadn't done the same for him. Frowning, she said, "I'm sorry I hid you from my mother, and that I didn't tell you about the dinner with Steve."

"Oh, is *that* his name?" he joked. After a pause, he added, "We weren't exclusive. You didn't *have* to tell me about him."

"I still should have said something."

He nodded. "I won't argue with that."

"So you don't have your phone with the message?"

He shook his head. "I dropped it in the street and a taxi ran over it, right when I was arriving at the hotel. I just got a new one." He pulled it from his pocket to show her. "But, I *promise* I did send that message. I couldn't risk you dating someone else, so I definitely sent the message asking you to wait for me."

"I believe you. I just wanted to read your last words to me."

He laughed. "They weren't my last words. You won't hear any last words from me until my dying day."

She buried her face in his jacket and breathed him in, still reveling in the fact that he was there. He had not left her—he had chosen her. And she chose him. She thought, *I am my beloved's, and my beloved is mine.*

Chapter Twenty-Three

"Babe, why is Michael not invited to the wedding?" Brian asked Lily one afternoon the week of their wedding, as he lounged on the couch, his eyes glued to his phone. "I just texted him that he should come to the rehearsal, 'cause you know those things are boring as hell, and he will bring the party with him. But he said he's not even invited to the wedding."

"I just don't want him there," Lily said, thinking that would be reason enough.

"But why?" he pressed. "It's at his sister's house. He's family now."

"It's at my *dad's* house, and he is not my family."

"Well, he's my friend, and I want him there. I'm about to tell him he is invited."

"Don't," she said firmly, in the most serious tone she'd ever used with him.

He put his phone down, sat up, and looked at her. "What's the deal? What's going on? You cheat on me with him or something?"

"*Really*? That's your first guess as to why I wouldn't want someone at my wedding?"

"*Our* wedding," he corrected her. "So, what do you have against him then? You've always had fun when we've hung out with him. *You* invited him to our engagement party when you had just met him."

She nodded. "Exactly. That was before I knew what he is really like."

Brian rolled his eyes and asked in a mocking tone, "And what is he *really* like?"

She debated how much to tell him and decided to say, "He doesn't treat women the way he should, and I don't want him around my friends at the wedding."

"You're kidding?" he scoffed at her, his eyes full of derision.

She shook her head. "No…He sexually assaulted Sera in high school, and he recently kept pressuring Erica even when she said no, repeatedly." She admitted her specific reasons to him, against her judgment, hoping he would understand.

He didn't. After he paused to assess her words, he said, "Whatever happened with him and Sera was probably just a misunderstanding. And Erica is always throwing herself at guys. You really think she said *no*? And, have you seen Michael? He's a good-looking guy. He doesn't need to force himself on a woman; he can get any girl he wants. I've seen him with women at the bar. They love him."

She stared at him in silence, in disbelief, blinking back tears. With as much authority as she could muster, with the need to protect her friends fueling her, she said, "If he shows up at the rehearsal or the wedding, he will be escorted out. So invite him if you want a scene. Because I'll make one."

She went to their bedroom, shutting and locking the door behind her. Then, she let herself cry.

—

Dahlia could not have been happier for Jina and Daniel, but when she thought about the approaching wedding of Lily and Brian, her stomach twisted into knots—she couldn't muster any joy for their union. And she didn't know what to do about it, *if* she was *allowed* to do anything, if she wanted to risk creating more distance in her relationship with Lily. She hadn't paid enough attention to realize that her younger sister now had ears to hear her. Even though it had not yet been seen outwardly by most, in the quiet recesses of her heart and mind, Lily had been changing that summer, or rather the Spirit of God had been changing her.

Lily would never admit it—at least, not any time soon—but ever since Dahlia had asked those questions about Brian's faith, ever since she had taken offense and told Brian about them, she had actually begun questioning everything too. Dahlia said she didn't like the way Brian had treated Lily at the bridal shop, but to Lily his treatment had been completely normal, what she was accustomed to, and what she thought was healthy. What she would eventually learn about herself over the next few months was that she accepted that treatment because of fear—the fear of being alone, the fear of being like Dahlia, thirty and still unmarried, the fear of being like her mother, almost sixty and having to use dating apps.

When Dahlia invited her to join their summer Bible study, her first instinct was to reply with something snarky, to refuse anything to do with Dahlia, or Morgan for that matter, to run away from any opportunity for them to call out her sin or throw Jesus in her face. But that's exactly where He wanted to be with her, face-to-face; he was searching for her and refused to let her flee. So, she somehow found herself parked in her father's driveway every Thursday evening, showing up to the meetings, opening the scriptures more than she had in years, and hearing wisdom and testimony from faithful women. They had taught her about her own worth in Christ simply by displaying their own, and without even discussing the details of her relationship, they had helped her recognize all the ways Brian didn't value her.

After the final gathering, after Sera had shared so vulnerably, Lily reached out to her, and they had continued meeting one-on-one—that's how Lily had learned about Michael. A week after that Dahlia called her, sharing about what happened with Erica and requesting Michael not be invited to the wedding. Lily had already crossed him off the list. She was appalled that Brian would ever doubt the truth of her friends' experiences, especially when he hardly knew Michael. They were drinking buddies who joked around and never discussed anything of substance.

There was tension the rest of their wedding week, even through to the rehearsal dinner. Well, Lily was tense, and Brian seemed—or acted—oblivious to it.

In the end, he didn't invite Michael, nor did he ask Michael about the "accusations" against him. Even if Brian had invited him, he wouldn't have come—Morgan had already endured a hard and heartbreaking conversation with her brother, laying down new and strict boundaries.

On the afternoon of the wedding day, Lily was in her teenage bedroom with her mom and two sisters, as they helped her into her gown, hair and makeup already done. None of them could stop gushing about what a beautiful dress she had picked out—a cream lace, tea length, 1950s silhouette with a sweetheart neckline and full-length lace sleeves, that complimented her hourglass shape perfectly.

"It just screams October wedding," Dahlia said with a big smile as she fluffed the skirt.

Violet sat in the corner chair, her belly too big and her ankles too swollen for fluffing skirts, but she smiled softly with pride as she stared at Lily's reflection in the mirror. Her long, strawberry blond hair fell in gentle waves, and her bright pink lipstick popped. The makeup artist had done a good job of *not* making the freckles across her cheeks disappear; she looked sun-kissed and radiant. Unlike Dahlia, Violet *had* been observant of the changes in Lily, though she would never have attributed them to her becoming more like Jesus. In her estimate, her youngest sister was becoming more like their middle sister. Lily was still sharp, still quick-witted, but she was somehow softer around the edges, less critical, kinder with her words.

On that day though, she also seemed sadder. Violet could tell that Lily was enjoying the way she looked—she couldn't take her eyes off herself—basking in the admiration of their mother, but there was something in her demeanor that seemed unsure, unsettled. If Violet had been paying attention to Dahlia, she would have seen the same things in her, though Dahlia was doing her best to mask it, trying to put on a supportive smile, when she knew viscerally that this was all wrong. Well, not *all* of it. Just the groom was wrong, of that she was certain. Yet she didn't open her mouth.

But Violet did. "Lily, are you feeling okay?"

"What do you mean?" Elaine demanded. "Of course she's feeling okay. It's her wedding day!"

"Let her answer, please," Violet said firmly, no qualms about upsetting her mother in that moment. "How are you feeling, Lily?"

Lily stopped looking at herself and turned around, her eyes meeting Violet's and then Dahlia's, finding in them both exactly what she needed—courage. She found her voice and asked, "Actually, would all of you wait for me downstairs and send dad up, please?"

"What do you need your father for?" Elaine asked, clearly annoyed. This was her time with the bride.

"I just need to speak with him, please." Lily echoed the same firm tone Violet had used.

Dahlia grabbed Violet's arms and helped her stand, and then began ushering Elaine out the door. Their mother didn't like it, but she acquiesced. "Just make it quick," she warned Lily. "It's almost time for the ceremony to start."

When Elaine and Violet were down the hallway, Dahlia stuck her head back in and said, "Take as much time as you need. I'll send dad up." The whole way down the stairs, Dahlia was praying for the wedding to be canceled. Elaine was hoping everything would go off without a hitch.

There was a soft knock on the door, and Alan said, "Honey?"

"Come in." She was pacing back and forth in front of the window.

As soon as he saw her, his eyes became misty. "You're one of the prettiest things I've ever seen."

Lily smirked at his word choice. He always said *one of* because he had three daughters and couldn't ever be accused of picking favorites.

"You ready to go down?" he asked. "What did you need to talk to me about?"

After a long pause, she blurted out, "I don't want to marry Brian." It was the first time she'd uttered the words, and they sounded and tasted like freedom. She almost hated herself for not saying them sooner.

Alan grabbed her shoulders, smiled and shook his head. "Honey, I don't want you to marry him either."

"Really?"

"Really."

"Why didn't you say anything?" she asked.

"I trusted you to make your own decision."

She shook her head. "Please don't do that. My flesh is weak, and my heart is deceitful, and I need my loved ones to speak wisdom and offer protection."

He leaned back and examined her with skepticism. "Why do you sound like Dahlia?"

"Just promise you'll say something next time?" she asked seriously.

He nodded. "I promise."

After a pause, she sat on the bed and said, "Mom will be upset."

"She'll understand once you explain things to her." Those were the most generous words he'd said about his ex-wife in years, and he knew they were true because he knew Elaine would never want any of their daughters to end up in bad marriages, like theirs.

"Brian's going to be furious."

"Me and your uncles will stand right outside the room while you tell him. If you need help, you just call for us."

"You think I'll need help?" she asked, curious why he said or thought that.

"Well, I just know he has a short temper, and can get a little handsy, like he did with Dahlia at our wedding reception." The moment he mentioned Dahlia he remembered he wasn't supposed to.

"Wait. What?" she demanded. "Nobody told me about that."

"I thought it best not to cause anymore issues with him."

"Please, *cause issues,*" she begged. "Cause issues. Even if I'm a brat about it. I need to know the true character of the person I'm planning to marry. I need to see how he responds during conflict or difficulty. So, get involved and cause issues next time. Okay, dad?"

He nodded again. "Okay. I will."

Alan had attempted to get involved after Dahlia shared about the wedding incident. He truly was concerned, and he had intended to keep his promise to his middle daughter about getting to know Brian better. But every time he had tried to reach out to his future son-in-law, to set up a time for them to spend together, Brian evaded it with good excuses. And before Alan knew it, the wedding day had arrived. It seemed too late to do anything.

Lily pulled the yellow lace curtain back slightly to peek out the window at the ceremony spot. Brian was already standing at the altar with his childhood pastor, waiting for the bride to appear. While she had zero desire to walk down that aisle, Brian didn't seem nervous at all, laughing and joking with the wedding guests.

Elaine knocked on the door, announced who she was, and slipped inside without waiting for a response. They would get a late start if they didn't get a move on. She gave Alan a disgruntled look, and then ignored him. "Lily, you look absolutely stunning. That dress really does accentuate all your best features. Do want me to help place your veil now?"

"Actually, mom, would you ask the wedding assistant to tell Brian to come up here so I can speak with him?"

"Oh, you can't let him see you before the ceremony! I'll bring him a message for you."

Lily glanced at her father for boldness before saying, "I'm sorry, mom, but there isn't going to be a ceremony. And I need to tell him that."

Shock and distress crossed Elaine's face. She turned to Alan, and with an accusatory tone asked, "Did you know about this?"

"Only just," he replied calmly. "And she's making a wise decision."

"A wise decision! I'm a wedding florist, and this has only happened once in my career, and you want to know the horrible things the guests were saying about the bride as they took back their gifts and piled into their cars?" She began fanning herself.

"Mom, calm down," Lily said, knowing those were always the wrong words to say to her mother. "If any of the guests want to say bad things, I don't care. Let them talk. This isn't their marriage." She had never before felt so confident and sure that she didn't care about the opinions of others. She could only attribute it to the Lord, and after years of not attributing anything to Him, it was a relief to feel His presence again, to sense when He was at work.

She shooed her parents out of the room, sat on the end of the bed, and waited patiently for Brian to appear. Her anxiety was gone, and peace encompassed her. When Brian opened the door, she spotted her dad and uncles in the hallway, just like Alan had said they would be, and it gave her an extra ounce of comfort knowing they were nearby.

He quickly shut the door and then examined her. "Aw, babe, that dress," he said, shaking his head, his nose crinkled in disgust. "You should not have been trusted to pick a dress on your own. Weren't we going for a more modern look? What is wrong with those sleeves?"

"What is wrong with *you*?" she countered, angry at herself for having ever let him criticize to her like that.

"What? I know I'm supposed to say you're the most beautiful bride I've ever seen, and *you* are, but that dress, no. I can't lie. Man, our kids are going to laugh at our wedding photos."

She almost felt sick at the thought of having children with him—something she had once daydreamed about with joy. "I think this dress is perfect," she finally said, taking another peek at herself in the mirror. "And I'm going to keep it for when I get married one day."

He was perplexed; she could see it in his eyes from his reflection in the mirror. "What do you mean?" he asked, coming to stand in front of her, taking her hands in his. "You mean, you'll wear it *again* for our vow renewal in twenty years? If it still fits you."

The thought of spending twenty years with him felt like an eternity. The thought of spending even twenty more minutes with him seemed like too much. How had she lived with him for eight months?

"The wedding is off," she said. "We're not getting married."

He was silent for a long moment. "Do you mean we're not getting married today or we're not getting married *ever*?"

Pulling her hands away from him, she began to remove her engagement ring. "I'm sure we'll both get married one day—just not to each other." She placed the ring in his palm and closed his fingers around it.

"Why are you doing this?" he asked, almost sounding sad, but mostly accusatory.

"We're just not right for each other."

"You're gonna need to be more specific. We sure have seemed right for each other for over a year now."

"Who I am now is no longer right for you."

"And who are you now? 'Cause I still see the same old Lily."

"That's because you don't really see me. I'm being made new."

Those words triggered him. He'd spent enough time in church to know that scripture. With disdain, he asked, "Is this about God? Did Dahlia really get to you?"

"No, she didn't…Jesus did."

He coughed, pretending to suppress his laughter. "You're not serious, are you?"

She remained calm and nodded, unfazed by his mockery.

He glared down at her, his face almost becoming redder by the second. "Don't come begging to get back with me when you can't find anyone better than me. We're done." She understood he wanted to be the one to end things. His pride wouldn't let it be any other way, and she allowed it so she wouldn't provoke his anger any further. With his hand on the door knob, preparing to leave, he looked back at her and said, "I'm still going on the honeymoon. Maybe I'll take Michael, and we can get with all the ladies. Move your stuff out of the apartment before I get back."

He had hoped to incite jealousy or anger in her, but she just felt sorry for how lame he sounded, and she tried not to smile at the thought of those two men sharing a honeymoon suite. When he slammed the door behind him, she let out a sigh of relief—mostly because she had just narrowly avoided the biggest mistake of her life. She fell back on the bed, feeling light, liberated, and grateful for Jesus.

Chapter Twenty-Four

"We've been talking about getting married in the spring," Jina said with a sweet smile on her face, and then took another bite of food. Because it was a Tuesday evening, the restaurant was relatively quiet, and they were the only ones dining in.

"Really?" Dahlia asked, blowing on her steaming soup. "Is he planning to propose soon, then?"

It was already dark and cold outside, but the fluorescent lights cast a warmth over the two friends.

Jina nodded and chuckled. "He's been asking me about my ideal ring."

"I'm sure he could choose the perfect ring on his own." Daniel had been so intentional in getting to know Jina that Dahlia sometimes thought he might already know her friend better than she did.

"That's what I told him!" Jina agreed. "Besides, I don't really have any preferences. I'll cherish any ring, even the ugliest of rings, if it means he wants me to be his wife."

Dahlia had observed Jina and Daniel closely since their reunion. It was if they had never been apart, although Jina would occasionally tease him about leaving her, and then he would, again, promise to always stay by her side. In those moments, Dahlia would try not to feel like a discontent third wheel.

"I know you and Andrew aren't fond of each other, but would you mind walking down the aisle together, as maid of honor and best man?" Jina asked. "I mean, I guess we can just have the bridesmaids walk down alone, if that makes you both more comfortable."

Dahlia got stuck on the first part of her sentence. "Has he said he's not fond of me?" she asked, trying not to sound hurt, feeling she deserved it if he wasn't.

"Well, not exactly," Jina said. "He just always makes excuses when we invite him to join us if he knows you'll be there too. I mean, it could just be a coincidence—his excuses always sound legitimate, but Daniel has wondered if there's something else to it." When Dahlia remained silent, Jina pressed, "*Is* there something else to it?"

Dahlia shrugged. "How should I know what he's thinking? He's probably just busy at the law firm." But in her mind, remembering his words from the day she'd rejected him, she answered herself: *He's thinking he'd rather not be around me. He's thinking he's no longer grateful to have met me nor did he enjoy knowing me nor would he ever want to go on a date with me.*

But Jina wasn't satisfied; she was suspicious. "*Is* he fond of you? Are *you* fond of him? Is that why he's staying away?"

"What kind of sense would that make?" Dahlia asked, trying to act nonchalant, but Jina could read her.

"Perfect sense. You know that quote from that movie. The one about how people don't do the things they want to do because they don't want people to know that they want to do them. He doesn't come when we invite him so that we won't know that he wants to see you."

Dahlia shook her head. "I'm sure he doesn't want to see me."

She hadn't seen him since the night at Ms. Anna's. She thought about their final moments, how he had grabbed her arm, how his touch had been firm and gentle at the same time, how it was the first time she'd recognized her attraction to him. She hadn't shared any of these details with Jina, had mentioned very little about her interactions with him over the summer.

And Jina could tell. "What happened between you two?" she pressed for more.

It seemed silly to Dahlia for her to talk about it because in the end *nothing* had happened, but she sighed and then gave Jina a basic summary. When she finished, she wanted to make Jina promise not to tell Daniel, but that seemed completely futile, so instead she said, "I'm sure you can't contain yourself. I'm sure you can't wait to talk to Daniel about it. But please, neither of you make it more awkward between Andrew and me. Especially if you want us to walk down the aisle at your wedding."

"At *my* wedding? Forget *my* wedding." Jina laughed. "At *y'all's* wedding."

She couldn't quit grinning and giving Dahlia insinuating looks.

"Stop it," Dahlia ordered. "This is why I didn't tell you to begin with."

"Not-uh. You didn't tell me 'cause you were protecting my feelings."

"That too."

After a pause, Jina leaned forward, elbows on the table, grin still on her face, and softly asked, "So…are you fond of him?"

Dahlia glanced at her cell phone. "Look at that." She showed Jina the screen. "Time to go." She stood. "Can't be late for class. Thanks for dinner." She disappeared out the door, running to her car to avoid the cold—and Jina's questions.

—

The entire semester Dahlia had been teaching English language classes at the local learning center on Tuesday and Thursday evenings. Two of the clients from Andrew's immigration law firm, a middle-aged married couple, were her students, though she was unaware of the connection, and once a week Andrew would give them a ride home after class. He had seen Dahlia several times from the safety of his vehicle as she walked across the parking lot to her car, and he would listen proudly as the husband and wife told him about what a good teacher she was, never revealing that he knew her. Because, like she had said that day at church, he didn't *really* know her—but he still wanted to.

One November evening, a week after Jina's dinner interrogation, Andrew watched as Dahlia rushed to her car; she exited the building before her students, which was unusual. She stopped short of getting in and pulled a note—one Andrew hadn't noticed—from her windshield, and then she walked around her car, examining the tires. He only faltered for a moment before he took the key out of the ignition, hopped out, and headed toward her.

"Andrew," she said, surprised when she looked up and saw him. "What are you doing here?"

"I'm just picking up a couple people. Is something wrong with your car?"

"Just this completely flat tire," she said, squatting down to touch it. "There's a nail in it."

Just then the married couple came up behind them.

"Everything okay, Ms. Marshall, Mr. Sommer?" the husband asked.

"You know Juan and Gloria?" Dahlia asked Andrew.

"He gives us a ride home on Thursdays," Juan answered. "You know each other?" Juan softly backhanded Andrew on the chest. "You never told us you knew Ms. Marshall."

Even though it was dark, with just a soft glow from the parking lot lights, it seemed to Dahlia that Andrew may have blushed, embarrassed. Jina was right. It wasn't a coincidence that he never joined them when they got together. He had been avoiding her.

"Do you have a spare?" Andrew asked, changing the subject, ready to roll up his sleeves and get to work.

Dahlia shook her head. "No. It can just stay here for tonight. Jina can give me a ride to work in the morning, and we will deal with this tomorrow after school—in daylight."

"Okay…well, can I give you a ride home then?"

Dahlia hesitated. She had planned to call Jina. "… I actually need a ride to the hospital."

"Hospital?" Gloria asked with concern, her English not yet as good as her husband's. "You okay?"

"Yes, yes." Dahlia nodded. "My sister is having a baby."

"Su hermana va a tener un bebé," Juan translated out of habit, even though Gloria had understood.

"A baby!" Gloria clapped her hands with excitement.

"Violet's in labor?" Andrew asked.

"She has been all day. She had to be induced," Dahlia explained. "Adam texted all of us ten minutes ago to say she's about to start pushing."

"Well, let's go," he said with a sense of urgency, ushering all of them toward his SUV. "I'll drop you off first," he said to Dahlia. Before she could protest, he added, "It's on the way." He opened the passenger door for her while Juan and Gloria climbed into the backseat, Juan supporting his wife's elbow.

During the ride, Dahlia didn't say much, feeling like an inconvenience, like Andrew felt obligated to help her even though he clearly didn't want to be around her. He hadn't even admitted to Juan and Gloria that he knew her.

Juan asked, "How did you two meet?"

"At church," Andrew answered when Dahlia didn't.

"Oh, that's where we met too," Juan said, and then he launched into the story of how he'd fallen in love with Gloria. Andrew had heard it before, but he was grateful to Juan for filling the silence. There was plenty Andrew wanted to say to Dahlia, but not in that moment, not with an audience.

When they pulled up to the hospital, Dahlia said, "Thanks for the ride. I really appreciate it." Before closing the door, she waved to Juan and Gloria. "See you next week!" It wasn't until she was through the sliding glass doors that she felt like she could breathe again.

When Dahlia reached the labor and delivery waiting room, she found her mother sulking, and occasionally complaining to Lily. "Why couldn't they let me stay? It's my first grandchild," she whined to both of them.

"I'm sure they just want a peaceful, stress-free environment," Dahlia said. "With less people in the room," she quickly added when Lily gave her a look.

"Are you saying I don't bring peace to an environment?" Elaine demanded.

Lily and Dahlia glanced and each other and then stared at their mother, pressing their lips together in an attempt to hide their laughter. Elaine glared at them until she couldn't stop herself from laughing too; peaceful had never been used to describe her, and she knew it.

Elaine had been there since Violet checked in early that morning. She almost convinced her oldest daughter to change her mind and let her stay in the room during the birth, but Violet and Adam had always been a private couple, and they planned for their birth experience to be private as well. They wouldn't even tell their families the sex of the baby; they enjoyed the secret and surprise of it all. Violet had welcomed her mother for most of the labor process, but the nurses ordered her out before delivery began. Lily had only been there for a couple of hours, and their father stayed away—no way he could be around Elaine for that long—but he promised to visit in the morning before he began seeing his patients. Adam's family also planned to visit the next day.

So it was just the three women waiting for the baby's arrival. It was another hour until the received a text from Adam—the baby had been born at 10:43PM, seven pounds, three ounces. Still, he didn't say if it was a girl or boy. "They're moving them to another room, then we can visit for just a few minutes," Elaine explained out loud, as if they all hadn't received the same message.

As soon as Adam sent them the room number, Elaine was power walking down the hall, Dahlia and Lily trailing her. Elaine tapped on the door and waited for a response before entering. Violet was reclining in bed, holding the baby. "Meet your new granddaughter," Violet said to Elaine, offering the baby to her. "Poppy Rose St. Clair." Instantly, all the women teared up.

"She's the most beautiful baby I've ever seen," Elaine said, softly brushing Poppy's cheek with one finger.

"Hey, what about us?" Lily asked, teasingly.

"All of you were pretty. But, Poppy wins," the new grandmother declared. None of them could argue with her because they agreed. At least for that moment, they all agreed on one thing.

Dahlia held her next and couldn't stop staring at her perfect face. "Welcome to the world, Poppy Rose," she whispered. "I'm going to be your favorite aunt." If there was ever something she felt competitive about, this was it.

Lily made a face and rolled her eyes. "Good luck with that," she said, ready for the challenge. "Now let me hold her."

After a few minutes of baby cuddling turned into half an hour, Lily offered to give Dahlia a ride home, and the new aunts promised to come back the next day. Dahlia hated that she would have to get her car fixed after work before she could return to her sweet niece.

During the drive, Lily apologized to her sister. "I know I haven't said this before, but I'm sorry for how I treated you, and I'm even more sorry for how Brian acted toward you—You should have told me about that. I'm really thankful you asked those questions, even though it took me a long time to process them and stop living in denial."

"I forgive you. I'm sure I could have said things better than I did. I'm just relieved you didn't go through with the marriage."

"Me too. It would have been a miserable one." She frowned, imagining what her life would have been like.

After a moment, Dahlia asked, "Did he really go to the Bahamas with Michael?"

Lily laughed a little. "Yes, but they had to leave early because of the hurricane."

"Good." Dahlia wasn't sure what she would say to Michael the next time she saw him. She knew at some point she would see him at her father's house or some family event. For the time being, she was determined to avoid him, and Morgan would give her a heads up if he was going to be around.

When she got home Jina's apartment was already dark. She couldn't figure out if she was disappointed or relieved. Part of her wanted to share the events of the evening, mainly to analyze the details pertaining to Andrew, but most of her didn't want to be cross-examined.

—

When Jina entered Dahlia's classroom the next afternoon, Dahlia asked unenthusiastically, "You ready to get this tire fixed?" One thing she hated was automotive maintenance and repairs.

Robbie walked past her classroom at that exact moment. He came back and popped his head in. "Y'all need some help?" He had pulled back from engaging with Dahlia since the school year had begun. He had even mentioned at lunch that he'd been on a few dates with a woman he'd met at the gym.

So Dahlia felt comfortable that they were just friends, and she was tempted to accept his offer, but Jina said, "No. We're good, thanks." When he disappeared, she turned to Dahlia. "I guess you haven't checked your phone. Daniel and Andrew already changed the tire this morning. It's good to go. I just have to drive you over there."

"Why did they do that? How much did it cost? I need to pay them back."

"Pretty sure they're not gonna accept any money from you. And why do you *think* they did it? It certainly wasn't Daniel's idea—not that he wouldn't have helped—but Andrew was the one insisting they get it done."

Dahlia didn't say anything else about it on the way to her car, except she did respond to Daniel's text and ask him how much she owed. He simply replied, "Nada," which frustrated her even more.

Jina didn't ask Dahlia anymore about her feelings toward Andrew—she just talked about it with Daniel. She knew her best friend well enough, and she knew that Dahlia wasn't even yet aware of how deep her feelings for him were. Because Dahlia was trying to protect herself from getting hurt—even if she wasn't aware of that yet either.

—

The following Thursday, neither Juan nor Gloria were in class, and Dahlia was disappointed that she wouldn't have an opportunity to see Andrew. She told herself she just wanted to see him so she could thank him for helping with her car, but beneath it all, she realized she just wanted to see him. Period. To know him, as he had said he wanted to know her.

There was a ballroom dance studio in the same shopping center, next door to the English school, and Dahlia sometimes enjoyed standing outside and watching the dancers through the windows. That's what she planned to do that evening when she heard the music start up at the end of her class. But when she stepped out into the cool night air, she found Andrew sitting on the stairs that led to the dance studio. He stood when she approached.

"Juan and Gloria weren't in class," she told him, feeling shy, her hands in her coat pockets.

He nodded. "I know. One of their kids had a school play this evening."

"Oh."

"I came to see you. I hope that's okay."

"Sure." Her voice was calm, but her insides were full of jitters. "I was going to watch the dance class up here." She began walking up the stairs, and he followed. They leaned against the railing, side-by-side, the light from the studio just barely illuminating their faces. The couples inside were dancing a waltz, the music slow and soothing.

They watched for a minute and then broke the silence at the same time. "Thanks for changing my tire," she said as he said, "Congratulations on your niece."

They chuckled. "I was happy to help," he said.

"I'm happy to pay you back."

He shook his head. "No. It's fine."

She took a deep breath before saying, "I'm really sorry for being so rude and unkind to you this summer. Please forgive me. My best friend is going to marry your cousin, so I don't want things to be weird between us. You don't have to avoid me."

"If I wanted to avoid you I wouldn't be here right now." He inched a little closer so their arms brushed against each other. She turned her head to the left, trying to hide a nervous smile from him.

"Well, Jina said you always had an excuse not to join us…"

He grinned. "I think Jina's been saying a lot of things. I hope some of them are true. I heard some things that gave me cause to hope that maybe your feelings toward me have changed." He shifted his body to face her. "But if you're still not interested, please tell me directly, and I will respectfully leave it alone. Things don't have to be weird between us. But my interest has not wavered, and I still want to know you more."

"What things did you hear?" she asked, already guessing the answer.

"Jina thinks you're smitten with me," he teased.

She smirked and rolled her eyes. "*Smitten?* Who uses a word like that except Jina?"

"I think that was actually Daniel's word choice."

"Oh, well then they really *are* made for each other."

They both laughed softly, their breath visible in the air. Andrew inhaled deeply, and then dared to say, "Maybe we could be too. Made for each other."

It was a long, excruciating wait for Andrew, but Dahlia finally lifted her chin and looked directly in his eyes. She took his hand, intending to lead him to the restaurant down the strip, and with a gentle smile, she said, "Let's find out."

austenshepherd.com
@austenwrites

CPSIA information can be obtained
at www.ICGtesting.com
Printed in the USA
LVHW090145191220
674215LV00006BA/417

9 780578 801001